Y040001

D1333141

SKELTON'S GUIDE TO SUITCASE MURDERS

By David Stafford

Skelton's Guide to Domestic Poisons
Skelton's Guide to Suitcase Murders

SKELTON'S GUIDE TO SUITCASE MURDERS

David Stafford

Allison & Busby Limited
11 Wardour Mews
London W1F 8AN
allisonandbusby.com

First published in Great Britain by Allison & Busby in 2021.

A CIP catalogue record for this book is available from
the British Library.

First Edition

ISBN 978-0-7490-2688-2

Typeset in 12/16 pt Adobe Garamond Pro by
Allison & Busby Ltd.

The paper used for this Allison & Busby publication
has been produced from trees that have been legally sourced
from well-managed and credibly certified forests.

Printed and bound by
CPI Group (UK) Ltd, Croydon, CR0 4YY

To Ted and Ev

PROLOGUE

Saturday 2nd November 1929

Andy, Spud and Reg had been coming down the gravel pit since they were eight or nine. You weren't supposed to. A kid had died there once. The story they'd heard was that the ground just opened up and ate him. They could believe it. Sometimes you saw it. The gravel would start sliding about for no reason and make holes easily big enough to eat somebody.

So, after the kid had died, some blokes came and fenced it all in and put signs up saying it was dangerous. Andy, Spud and Reg took no notice. They just climbed over the fence and carried on as normal. It was good for playing war. There were lots of places to hide and the sandy bits were like trenches. But they'd grown out of war. Andy and Spud were fourteen now, and Reg thirteen, so mostly they sat in the shed up at the end and played cards and smoked and talked about girls.

None of them had ever had a girlfriend. This was a shame because the shed would be the perfect place to bring a girl. Much better than the back row of the Regal, or the waste ground behind the rope works which was where Andy's big brother used to take his girl.

Andy got the cards out and they went inside the shed for a game. Usually they played three- or five-card brag for matchsticks, or pebbles when they'd run out of matchsticks. They'd like to have played for money, but they didn't have any. Andy had tried to teach them cribbage once, but Spud said it was as bad as sums at school and he'd rather stick with brag. Or nap. Sometimes they played nap.

After a bit they got fed up of cards, so they just lay down and smoked Spud's fags. He'd nicked a packet of Rhodian off his mum.

It'd been drizzly earlier on but now it brightened up, and they could see the sun was a good bit lower than they'd thought. Usually their bellies told them when it was time to get home for tea, but Mr Ingram had been chucking out three-day-old breadcakes earlier and they'd filled up on them. All the same, Reg said he had chips for tea on a Saturday and his brothers and sisters'd nick them all if he was late, so they headed for the gap in the fence.

They skirted the big puddle they called 'the lake'. Andy spotted something in the water.

'Wasn't there before,' Spud said.

One of the great things about the gravel pit was, just like it had ate the kid who died, sometimes it sicked stuff up.

'It's a box,' Andy said.

They could have done with a stick to help pull it out but there was never a stick to be had in the gravel pit, so Andy had to put one foot in the water, testing the ground very carefully before putting any weight on it.

Closer, he saw that the box had reinforced corners.

He managed to pull it far enough over for Spud and Reg to grab hold, and between the three of them they pulled it onto dry land.

It was a suitcase. A big one. Not metal or leather, made of fibre stuff. One side had gone soft in the wet. The catch wouldn't give so Reg gave it a bash with a stone. A couple more bashes and it fell away.

They opened it.

CHAPTER ONE

Thursday 28th November 1929

The rain that had been falling heavily all day held off for a few minutes as Arthur Skelton emerged from court. There was a bounce to him. He had won his case. The press photographers, sheltering under the portico, spotted him immediately. It wasn't difficult. A skinny six foot three, he loomed over any crowd, his pebble-lensed glasses twinkling. The press mob pushed their cameras into his face, and he smiled obligingly until they saw the meatier prey of his client, Addison Lyle, the BBC announcer.

Some weeks earlier, Lyle, while announcing a talk entitled 'What is Right?' given by the eminent philosopher, Sir Harold Overton, had mispronounced 'Overton' as 'Overdone'. It's doubtful whether one in a thousand listeners noticed the mistake, but it put Overton off his stride. His talk was fraught with stumbles. The phrase 'fundamental 'principle' came right only after several attempts and an entire paragraph about the contribution made in the field of ethics by the seventeenth-century German philosopher Samuel von Pufendorf caused so much trouble he abandoned it entirely.

After it was all over, the microphone turned off and the studio door opened for ventilation, Hilton Scott, another announcer, and Margery Desmarais, the mezzo-soprano, chatting in a hospitality room a little way down the corridor, heard angry words being exchanged between Lyle and Overton, then sounds of a scuffle. They went to investigate and found Overton lying unconscious on the ground with a telephone in his hand. Lyle was poised above him, brandishing a Marconi-Reisz carbon granule microphone with table-stand.

A doctor was summoned.

When he regained consciousness, Sir Harold claimed that Lyle, as appearances had suggested, had struck him with the microphone. Furthermore, he claimed that Lyle had mispronounced 'Overton' because he was falling-down drunk; and indeed, had, upon arrival at the studio, actually fallen down. After the broadcast, the two men had had words, and Lyle, inflamed with drunken rage, had attacked him.

The police took Lyle into custody.

He was the first BBC announcer ever to be arrested for a crime committed during the course of his duties. For the newspapers, leery of the effect that wireless was having on their circulations, it was Christmas and birthday all in one. They called the BBC the 'Bish Bash Corporation' and suggested that the entire organisation was a 'coven of dipsomaniacs and mountebanks'.

The BBC, worried that their reputation as a God-fearing bastion of moral rectitude might be in the balance, put the matter in the hands of their own solicitors, who instructed Arthur Skelton, the Yorkshire barrister who had recently found fame for winning a couple of apparently hopeless cases.

Skelton did try to point out that, in this case, the evidence weighed so heavily in the plaintiff's favour that it was not so much apparently hopeless as plain hopeless.

Sir Harold was seventy-two years old. His voice was a measured rumble that hypnotised the listener with its seashore cadences. He was Master of St Luke's College Oxford, adviser to the League of Nations and a Nobel laureate. During the war he had spoken in favour of pacifism but never with the vehemence required to merit an arrest. He had played tennis with Gandhi.

Addison Lyle, on the other hand, was a BBC announcer with all that that implies.

Lyle claimed that he had acted in self-defence. Overton, he said, irrationally enraged by the harmless slip of the tongue ('I once introduced Vita Sackville-West as Rita and she didn't seem to mind') had started it. The Master of St Luke's had bludgeoned him several times with the telephone, leaving him no option but to strike back with the first thing that came to hand, which was the microphone.

Skelton pictured the scene in court. Sir Harold looking the picture of innocence, his rheumy eyes blinking behind his horn-rims, would sit upright and dignified, his white hair peeping through the bandage he still felt compelled to wear despite several weeks having passed since the assault. Sir Thomas Peebles KC, leading the prosecution, would point at him and, in a voice oozing sceptical contempt, say, 'And *this* is the man you accuse of striking – nay, "bludgeoning" you – unprovoked – with a telephone?'

The jury would snigger, Lyle would stammer and that would be the end of that.

The first gleam of hope came when Skelton saw the list of character witnesses Peebles intended to produce. There were seven of them, eminent academics, peers of the realm, distinguished clergymen.

The best Addison Lyle had been able to rustle up was the leader of a jazz orchestra, a lithography teacher from the Chelsea School of Art, and Joseph Mitchell, the manufacturer of Mitchell's Hygienic Spray. But that, Skelton thought, wasn't the point.

Wasn't it surprising, when Overton's reputation and integrity had never been brought into question, that Peebles thought it necessary to call even one character witness, never mind seven?

Did it suggest that there was more to Overton than met the eye; a dirty secret, perhaps, that needed, in the event that it should crop up, an army of witnesses to deny?

It could only be a matter for conjecture. Finding somebody to spill the beans would mean first of all knowing what the beans might be, and Skelton couldn't even be sure there were any beans in the first place.

On the way into court, he spotted Lord Esterbank, one of the character witnesses, getting out of his Rolls-Royce assisted by his liveried chauffeur.

Esterbank was reaching the end of a distinguished career in public service. He had served every Conservative Prime Minister since Balfour in one capacity or another and now offered clamorous opposition to the Labour government in the Lords. His appearance was not, however, imposing. He was a tiny man, with jaundiced skin and a gargoyle face. His clothes were stained and rumpled in the way that bespeaks great rank and privilege. On his way out of the car he handed the chauffeur an umbrella, a newspaper, a book, a parcel wrapped in brown paper and a cup. Barely noticing that the cup had emptied its contents down the chauffeur's front, Esterbank waited until the umbrella had been raised, then, under its shelter, took the few steps from the car to the portico, dismissed the chauffeur and surrendered himself to the attentions of a court usher.

The chauffeur put the clutter back in the car and looked down helplessly as the contents of the cup, an unctuous, pale fluid, dripped from his jacket and waistcoat. He reached into first one trouser pocket then another, looking for a hanky.

Skelton pulled out his own and offered it.

'Thank you very much, sir, that's very kind.'

The chauffeur dabbed.

'What is it?' Skelton asked.

'Horlicks. His Lordship likes it, hot or cold.'

'Very messy,' Skelton said. 'Milk-based, and the malt would make it stickier.'

They both nodded knowingly, the way men do when a technical assessment is made.

'It's gonna stain, all right,' the chauffeur said, 'Mr Lightfoot's gonna have my guts for garters.'

'Who's Mr Lightfoot?'

'His Lordship's valet. Good with stains and the like, but short-tempered. Little drop of oil and he goes through the

15

roof at me. As if you can do a job like this without getting a drop of oil on your clothes now and then.'

'Or a cupful of Horlicks.'

The chauffeur laughed.

'Tell you what,' Skelton said. 'There's a haberdasher just around the corner run by a very nice lady called Violet, who can work miracles on stains with fuller's earth and oil of camphor and suchlike. It's up a side street, a bit difficult to find. I could show you, though. Won't take a minute.'

'That's very generous. Streep's the name.'

'Skelton.'

They shook hands.

'I thought it was you,' Streep said. 'I've seen your picture in the paper. And, of course, the voice gives it away. You're from up north.'

'Leeds. Yorkshire.'

'One of the maids is from up that way somewhere. Says "bath" instead of "barth". Do they all talk like that up there?'

'Yes. And you'll never believe this but in Leeds they'd think it was funny to hear somebody say "barth".'

The chauffeur threw his head back and said, 'Chhh! Takes all sorts, dunnit?'

They walked on. 'And you're doing the thing in the court, are you? The one His Lordship's come for?'

'I am,' Skelton said.

'Sir Harold bloody Overton.'

'That's right.'

'Nasty piece of work.'

'Is he?' Skelton asked.

'He set about me with a starting handle for taking him from Marston Moretaine to Aylesbury via Woburn.'

'Which way did he want you to go?'

'He wanted me to go via Dunstable.'

'Dunstable?'

'And Princes Risborough. I said it'd add twenty miles at least to the journey. He said I should know better than to take him anywhere near Woburn Abbey because of the Duke of Bedford.'

'What's he got against the Duke of Bedford?'

'No idea. He made me stop the car just by Sheep Lane and he started shouting at me and swearing, and then he got the starter handle and hit me with it. Four times. He did the same with Billy Fleming.'

'Who's he?'

'Footman,' Streep said.

'With the starter handle?'

'With a billiard cue. In the billiard room. Billy was just standing there with a tray of brandy waiting for him to finish a shot. His Lordship misses the shot and takes it out on Billy with the thick end of the cue, swinging it round his head. Nearly broke Billy's nose. Half an inch higher and he could have gone blind. I mean, he was sorry afterwards. Gave Billy ten bob.'

'Did you get ten bob?'

'Fifteen. Difference between a chauffeur and a footman, I suppose,' Streep said.

Violet did a marvellous job on the chauffeur's jacket and waistcoat. There wasn't even a smell afterwards.

In court, Esterbank was second up. When he'd finished telling Peebles that Overton was the finest human being ever to have drawn breath, Skelton had his turn and asked, 'Did Sir Harold once assault your chauffeur, Mr

Streep, with the starter handle of a motor car?'

Esterbank was under oath. He looked sheepishly at Overton and Peebles, but had no option other than to say, 'Yes.'

'And was this assault prompted by a slight difference of opinion about the best route to take from Marston Moretaine to Aylesbury?'

'I'm afraid I don't know the exact details.'

'So, you didn't witness the assault?'

'No.'

'But you did witness another assault when Sir Harold hit your footman with a billiard cue, almost breaking his nose.'

'I thought it *was* broken,' Esterbank said. 'It's never looked the same since anyway.'

After that everything fell into place nicely.

Next up was a bishop who, in response to, 'Have *you* ever witnessed an assault similar to the attacks on Lord Esterbank's chauffeur and footman?', told garish tales of Overton attacking a curate with a leather-bound copy of Richard de Courcy's sermons and a nun with his bare fists.

Peebles stopped calling witnesses after that.

Skelton's only witness was Addison Lyle himself, who told his story and, despite being a BBC announcer, was believed.

Edgar Hobbes, Skelton's clerk, a precise, barrel-chested man with tiny feet, joined his chief under the portico.

'You look like a man who deserves cake,' he said.

'Ooh,' Skelton said.

They set off towards Kembles, a tea room they favoured at the Aldwych end of Drury Lane.

It was famous for its uncompromisingly modern decor.

Black and silver arranged in arrow motifs dominated. The cloakroom had a screen made of beige celluloid. Mirrors were positioned so that wherever you sat you could see the back of your own head, and the lights, which hung from the ceiling on thick chromium rods, had shades in the shape of beehives.

Skelton was unmoved by celluloid cloakrooms and the back of his own head, but the cakes at Kembles were good, the buns fresh and the tea excellent.

The cafe attracted a theatrical clientele. Sometimes Ivor Novello could be seen dipping his perfect profile into an egg rissole or a Dresden cream, and once, Edgar had heard, just as the cafe was closing, Noël Coward had swept in with a retinue but swept out again when he discovered that Veuve Clicquot could not be obtained.

Norman, the cafe's proprietor, was proud of his celebrity clientele and counted Skelton, who had had his picture in the paper a few times, among them. It had its advantages. If extra gravy was required, there was no mucking about. It was there on the table almost before you'd finished asking for it.

As they sat down, Edgar, a keen theatregoer, scanned the room to see who was 'in'.

'Don't look now, but that's Cathleen Nesbitt. Doesn't look a day over twenty-five, but she must be at least forty.'

Skelton didn't know who Cathleen Nesbitt was and probably wouldn't have cared if he did.

They ordered the sandwich assortment along with some mocha fingers, coconut kisses and a pot of tea.

Edgar glanced at *The Evening News* he'd bought on his way over from court and sighed.

'What is it?' Skelton asked.

Edgar showed him the headline: WAKEFIELD SUITCASE MURDER, DENTIST SOUGHT. 'It's preposterous,' he said.

The 'Wakefield Suitcase Murder Mystery' had been in the papers for the past three weeks. Some boys had found a suitcase containing the mutilated and partly decomposed body of a woman in a quarry on the outskirts of Wakefield. The police were having difficulty establishing the identity of the corpse and were hoping a dentist somewhere would be able to recognise the woman's false teeth.

Edgar's principal grievance had nothing to do with the horror of the murder. Skelton knew this because he'd mentioned it several times before. It was luggage-related.

'The Bournemouth one was the Bournemouth Trunk Murder. The Widnes one was the Widnes Trunk Murder. So why are they calling this one the Wakefield *Suitcase* Murder?'

Skelton took out his pipe and slowly filled it. This, he knew, could take some time.

'I have three suitcases,' Edgar said. 'Nice leather ones. I bought them two years ago at the Army & Navy in a sale. Small, medium and large. I'd say the large one's as big as a suitcase can get before you'd call it a cabin trunk.'

Skelton lit his pipe and, between puffs, said, 'I'm not really sure of the precise differences between a suitcase and a trunk.'

'It's a matter of handles,' Edgar said. 'A suitcase has one, a cabin trunk many.'

Skelton nodded. 'So presumably, the container they found the mutilated body in only had one handle, so they're calling it a suitcase murder rather than a trunk murder.'

'You're missing my point.'

'Sorry . . . go on.'

'As I say, my large suitcase is as big as a suitcase can get without it needing more handles and becoming a cabin trunk. And yet, even with careful packing, I can't see how you could get a complete corpse in there. Arms, legs and possibly torso, but you'd need a separate Gladstone bag for the head.'

Their attention was distracted by a small party, visible in the mirrors along with the backs of their own heads, who came in shaking umbrellas and delivering soaked mackintoshes to the chap behind the celluloid screen. Edgar registered that none of them was famous and lost interest.

'You could get a corpse in my suitcase,' Skelton said.

'Which one?'

'The big one.'

'The Revelation?'

'What?'

'Your big suitcase. It's a Revelation. Revelation is a brand of suitcase.'

'Is it? I didn't realise you'd ever seen my big suitcase.'

'Of course I have. I even carried it briefly when we were at the Gloucester assizes.'

'For the indecent assault?'

'Exactly. And you're mistaken.'

'Am I?'

'Yes, it's big. It's a big suitcase. Nobody could deny that. But it's nowhere near big enough to contain a whole corpse with the head.'

'It expands.'

Edgar bridled. 'What?'

'It's got sort of ratchets so that you can make it deeper.'

'A lot deeper?'

'Perhaps double the original depth.'

'Deep enough for a head?'

'Possibly.'

'Well, there's food for thought,' Edgar said. 'I take it all back.'

Outside the rain had got worse. They sheltered in the doorway of Kembles, hoping it might slacken off enough to avoid a soaking.

'Did you hear that?' Edgar said.

'What?'

'When Norman asked the waiter to get my coat and hat.'

'What?'

'Norman went over to the cloakroom and asked the chap to get my coat and hat. But he didn't realise that I had followed him, and I was standing right behind him.'

'Yes?'

'And he said to the chap, "Can you get Mr Hobbes' coat and hat?", and the chap said, "Which one is Mr Hobbes?", and Norman said, "The portly gentleman."'

'Are you sure?'

'I heard him say it. I'm portly.'

'You're not,' Skelton said.

'I'm a portly gentleman.'

'Do you want to stop coming here, then?' Skelton asked.

'Why?'

'Well, if Norman was rude to you—'

'He wasn't rude to me. He was merely stating the truth. I'm fat.'

'You're not fat.'

Edgar stood to one side to let a customer, trying to get into the restaurant, pass. It wasn't exactly a squeeze, but it was close.

'There,' Edgar said. 'You see?'

CHAPTER TWO

On the Saturday evening, Skelton let himself into his house as quietly as he could and took his shoes and socks off in the hall. He was wet through.

He hated having to go to town at the weekend, but it would have been churlish to have missed Evan Leslie's retirement do. Leslie had given him a great deal of help and useful advice when he was first starting out. But attending had meant changing into evening clothes at his chambers in Foxton Row, then back again before getting the train home. The first soaking had come while he was trying to get a cab on the Strand. The second came when the Bentley, which he'd left parked at Lambourn Station, had refused to start. He'd had no choice other than to walk home. The rain was falling sideways by this time, so his umbrella provided no protection whatsoever.

A light had been left on in the dining room. Mila was in there, hunched over the table, absorbed by something in front of her.

Skelton hovered in the doorway, unwilling to startle her, knowing a suspected intruder would come off worse in any encounter with his wife.

'Are you making puddles on the parquet?' Mila asked, without looking up.

'I didn't think anybody'd still be up,' Skelton said. 'I'll go and towel off.'

He went upstairs, hung his suit, shirt and waistcoat from the window ledge in the bathroom so that they could drip in safety, dried himself off and put on his pyjamas and dressing gown. Downstairs he packed his shoes with newspaper and placed them by the embers of the kitchen fire to warm. This, he knew, was the right thing to do with wet shoes, but he had no idea why.

He put some milk on to boil and went back into the dining room.

'I'm making cocoa. Do you want some?'

'Yes, please. Did you enjoy your evening?'

'Not really. A pigeon got into the Great Hall.'

'Did it go away again?'

'Grantby asked somebody to get him a 12-bore, but then Montague pointed out that the timbers date back to 1490 and the stained-glass windows are among the few to have survived the Reformation. So, a member of staff who keeps pigeons fetched a ladder and, rather deftly I thought, covered the bird with a cloth, brought it down and released it outside. Why are you doing a jigsaw?'

'It's *The Laughing Cavalier*.'

'I didn't know you liked jigsaws.'

'I don't.'

Skelton ran back to the kitchen and caught the milk just before it boiled over. By the time he returned with the cocoa, Mila had completed a decent sized bit of lace collar.

'You're doing well,' Skelton said. He picked up a piece and tried to fit it.

'Please don't mess with the pieces,' Mila said. 'They're organised according to a system.'

He pulled a chair from under the table and sat down. 'You're in a mood,' he said.

'Lawrence was supposed to go boating on the river with John and Susan Turner and their parents.'

Lawrence was their elder child – the ten-year-old. Elizabeth, the younger, was a whimsical eight.

'But it was cancelled because of the rain,' Mila continued, 'so he took out his disappointment on me.'

'What did he do?'

'He played the gramophone.'

'"I Lift up My Finger and I Say Tweet-Tweet"?'

'Over and over again.'

'They break very easily.'

'Children or gramophone records?'

'Sometimes if you ask him nicely—'

'I did ask him nicely and he obliged by playing the other one.'

'Which other one?' Skelton asked.

'"You're the Cream in my Coffee, You're the Salt in my Stew".'

'I am *so* sorry.'

'So, I got the jigsaw out to distract him. But after half an hour he said it was too hard.'

'So, he went away, and—'

'Played the gramophone again,' Mila said.

'And you had to finish the—'

'Of course.'

Skelton examined the picture on the box. 'There is ever such a lot of brown.'

'If you look closely, some of the brown is more greyish.'

'What time did you start?'

'At around four o'clock.'

'So, you've been at it for' – Skelton looked at the clock on the mantelpiece. It was twenty-five to one – 'eight and a half hours. Is this a bit of moustache?'

Mila spoke with the mournful regret of a Chekhov heroine asking about the meaning of life. 'How many times have I picked up that piece thinking it was moustache?'

'It looks like moustache,' Skelton said.

'They design these things deliberately to undermine your sanity.'

'I'd stop if I were you.'

'I can't.'

The note of desperation in her voice caused Skelton to put his cocoa down and gently take her hand. She allowed it to be taken and turned to look at him. Were her eyes glistening with tears?

'The wallpaper is coming off the walls,' she said.

Skelton looked up at the corner of the room, above the window. A corner of the paper had folded back on itself revealing something black, green and living beneath it. He'd been meaning to get up there with some glue and stick it back again but wasn't sure it was wise to do so without knowing what the living stuff was first.

'I'll get somebody to look at it,' he said.

'Also the kitchen range is smoking,' she said, 'Lawrence uses the gramophone as an instrument of torture, Elizabeth informed me today that her ballet teacher told her that fairies are caused by God sneezing, Mrs Bartram won't talk to Dorothy because she left the lid off the biscuit tin at teatime and the ginger nuts have gone soft . . .' Mrs Bartram was their daily and cook, Dorothy the nanny, '. . . and then this arrived.'

She picked up a newspaper from the pile strewn across the other side of the table. Mila read a lot of newspapers but had recently cut her consumption to just four a day. The paper was already folded to the right page. She thrust it towards her husband, clearly irked.

Between ARRIVALS AT THE ZOO – GIANT FROG AND SILVER FOX and MR THOMAS ON THE COAL SITUATION was a headline: MRS PEMBERTON LANDS SAFELY IN CAPE TOWN.

Mrs Pemberton, Skelton read, was an aviatrix who, accompanied by her flying instructor, had piloted an aeroplane from Casablanca to Cape Town, making her the first woman to have flown the African continent from north to south.

It took him a moment to realise why Mila found the story so irksome.

Mrs Pemberton, née Cissy Thornbury, had been at school with Mila. They were rarely on speaking terms. When Mila became captain of hockey, Cissy became captain of lacrosse. When Mila had taken up archery and became county champion, Cissy had taken up tennis and, if it hadn't been for one unlucky serve and a disputed net call, might have beaten Suzanne Lenglen at Wimbledon.

Cissy had married Franklin J. Pemberton, an American millionaire and amateur artist who had spent several years living *la vie bohème* in Paris before settling in an eighteenth-century pile with parkland in Leicestershire. Here he showed off the fine collection of increasingly fashionable impressionist and post-impressionist paintings he'd acquired, for the most part, from the artists themselves, bathed naked in the lake and shot anything feathery or furry that moved. Then he'd had the decency to get killed in France while doing something intrepid, leaving Cissy magnificently wealthy and with the freedom to become the first woman to fly to South Africa.

Mila, meanwhile, had married Arthur Skelton from Leeds and was on her way to becoming the first woman in Lambourn to complete a jigsaw puzzle of *The Laughing Cavalier* in less than twenty-four hours.

She heard news of Cissy Pemberton, either from the newspapers or from other school friends, perhaps twice a year. Each time it brought her to the brink of despair.

'I didn't realise old Cissy could fly an aeroplane,' Skelton said, trying to sound jolly.

'She can't.'

'Well it says—'

'It *says* she had her instructor with her. Like Amelia Earhart.'

'I thought—'

'No, she didn't. Amelia Earhart sat in a passenger seat all the way across the Atlantic like a sack of potatoes while men piloted the aircraft.'

Skelton was reading to the end of the story. 'It said she landed the thing herself at Khartoum in a sandstorm.'

'And then in Cape Town,' Mila said, quoting the newspaper verbatim and speaking a little more loudly than was consistent with the children being in bed, '"She was greeted by a military band. And Mr J. H. C. Farley, President of the Cape Town Aviation Society, presented her with a baby lion." I am thirty-four years old, and what have I done?'

This could have been a rhetorical question, but the subsequent pause and raised eyebrows suggested an answer was invited. Skelton knew that the fate of his marriage and the fragile balance of his domestic tranquillity could depend on what he said next.

'Well, you have two fine children,' he said.

'A girl who believes in fairies and a boy who listens all day to "I Lift up My Finger and I Say Tweet-Tweet". They are ninnies!'

'Lawrence would have gone boating if it hadn't been for the rain.'

'A motor yacht on the Thames is not "boating". When I was his age, I rowed across Djurgårdsbrunnsviken in a tempest.'

Mila's grandfather was Swedish. She had spent many childhood holidays in Stockholm or at the family's summer house on Vaxholm.

'What else?' she asked.

'Pardon?'

'What else have I done?'

'You've got your . . . causes . . . and your discussion group in Maidenhead. There's your teaching work at the Lambourn Academy.'

Mila took a Saturday morning archery class at the local girls' school.

30

'Miss Gladwell has made it clear that under her headship physical education will always take second place to domestic science, needlework and the madrigal group,' she said. 'I am wasting my life. By the time she was my age Gertrude Bell had been around the world twice and had had an alpine peak named after her. Mary Kingsley had travelled by canoe up Ogooué River and braved the ferocity of the Fang people.'

'There's a very active rambler's group in Slough,' Skelton said.

'Piloting an aeroplane is no more difficult than driving a car,' Mila said. 'Easier, because apart from trees when you're going up and the ground when you're coming down, there's nothing to hit except birds. I shall form an Association of Women Pilots. We will fill the airways. Flying isn't a matter of brute strength; it's a matter of endurance. And women endure. Women endure.'

'Yes, they do. I've noticed that.'

'I shall call in at Woodley Aerodrome tomorrow. Next year I shall buy an Avro Avian and fly it to Australia.'

Skelton collected the empty cocoa cups and put them in the kitchen sink ready to be washed in the morning.

He knew he had to tread carefully. There was no doubt that Mila had the endurance required to fly an aeroplane halfway around the world, but he wasn't sure that aeroplanes did. Cars, he knew, could be very unreliable, but when a car breaks down it stays pretty much where it is. An aeroplane doesn't do that. It falls a thousand feet into a jungle or the sea, where the occupants, in the unlikely event that they survive the crash, are eaten by lions or sharks. His children would be motherless, and he prostrate with grief.

On the other hand, offering a word of discouragement

would only stiffen her determination to go through with it. For now, it would be best to stay calm, smile and go along with anything she said.

The dining-room fire was almost dead. He put the fireguard in place and cleared the hearth of anything that might catch if a spark should escape. He'd already bolted the front door.

'How long does it take to fly to Australia?' he asked.

'Last year an Australian called Bert Hinkler did it in under a month.'

'Perhaps I could sail out with the children and meet you at the other end. It'd be an adventure for us all. I'm for bed, anyway,' he said. 'Are you coming?'

'Not until I've finished.'

The cavalier's sash and brocade sleeves were coming together nicely.

CHAPTER THREE

Edgar followed the tea tray, borne by one of the lads, into Skelton's room at 8 Foxton Row some weeks later, bringing the post with him.

The two men sat, as was their custom, in the easy chairs, one either side of the small table. Edgar lit up a Gold Flake and poured the tea. Skelton filled his pipe.

'Have you ever had tea with lemon?' Edgar asked.

'Why would I want to do that?'

'Some people like it.'

'Russians, you mean?'

'I thought they had it with jam.'

'I've never actually believed that. Flies in the face of reason.'

'I read that tea with lemon instead of milk and sugar is very good if you're on a reducing diet.'

Skelton sighed. 'You're not portly.'

'I am.'

'You're not.'

'I see my full-length profile in shop windows as I pass. It's very dismaying.'

Edgar added just enough milk to make his tea opaque, then turned to the briefs. There were three of them.

'What order do you want them in? Keep the best till last?'

'Of course.'

'Right. *Rex versus Thomas Winthrop*.'

'Yes?'

'Winthrop, a lorry driver, stands accused of stealing, from a warehouse in Billiter Street, three lorryloads of ostrich feathers.'

'Of what?'

'By weight, ostrich feathers are more valuable than diamonds,' Edgar said. 'Except that while fifty thousand pounds worth of diamonds could be slipped into a coat pocket, or at least an evening bag, you'd need something around the size of Wigmore Hall to accommodate the same in feathers. They mustn't be crushed, you see, because it damages the curl.'

'Strong prosecution case?'

'Not very. There's no doubt at all that Winthrop went to the warehouse three times, presented the apparently appropriate documentation to collect the feathers, helped load the lorry and delivered them to their destination.'

'What was the problem, then?'

'The problem was that the documentation he presented was false and the warehouse he took them to, in Ealing, West London, was, when the police got there, empty.'

'So somebody had taken the precaution of removing the feathers to a third warehouse.'

'Exactly.'

'Who's the solicitor?'

'Banham.'

Banham had instructed Skelton twice before. Sound man. Knew his stuff.

'Defence?'

'Winthrop claims he was hired to do the job in good faith with no idea that the paperwork was forged or that he was in fact stealing the feathers.'

'Good character?'

'No previous convictions. Excellent references.'

'Should be all right, then. What's next?'

Edgar poured the hot water into the pot so as to brew for a second cup.

Skelton watched him, thoughtfully. 'It'd mean an awful lot of fuss,' he said.

'What would?'

'Going into Brixton gaol to see a defendant. The warders offer you a mug of tea. And you say—You couldn't do it, could you?'

'I could take my own,' Edgar said.

'A lemon and a little knife?'

'I could keep the lemon in an oilcloth tobacco pouch, like yours, to stop the juice leaking.'

'You've given the matter some thought, then.'

'I am a fat man with bad feet.'

They both looked at Edgar's feet. To the naked eye, their only remarkable feature was their size. They were disproportionately small. Skelton had often wondered whether the troubles he had with them were essentially a question of bad design. In terms of structural engineering,

Edgar was the equivalent of an upside-down Eiffel Tower. The weight would crush the little pointy thing that should have been at the top.

'Do they hurt a very great deal?' Skelton asked.

'They're agony,' Edgar said. 'The chiropodist tells me there's little hope. It's a malformation of the bones. He told me it was just one of the things that can happen when you reach a certain age.'

'You're no age at all.'

'That's easy for you to say. In your prime at—'

'Thirty-seven.'

'I'm forty-six at my next birthday. That's nearly fifty. By the time you're my age I'll be nearly sixty. And crippled with bad feet.'

Skelton had been born with a displaced hip, spent his childhood in pain and traction, still limped and suffered agonies when he was cold, wet or tired, but he knew better than to mention it when Edgar was complaining about his feet. He had once known a chemist in Slough, who, if you went in for a headache pill, would show you the scars left by two bullet holes in his head and say, 'That's what a headache looks like.' He went out of business within a year.

Edgar looked up at the top of the bookcase, as if inspecting for dust, then, after a moment, took up the second brief.

'*Rex versus Ashworth and Jeanes*. Motor bandits. Luton town centre.'

Over the previous six months or so, the newspapers had been using the phrase 'motor bandit' to describe any criminal who, during the course of his business, used a car. Headlines condemned 'the plague of motor bandits' and called motor banditry 'the scourge of our times'. One theory had it that the similarity of some of the crimes, particularly the wages snatches, suggested that there was a mastermind for whom all the 'bandits' were working. Others took the view that the car was an evil contraption, so it should come as no surprise that it would promote criminal activity. Old colonels in Petersfield and Guildford began writing letters pointing out that they never had these 'motor bandits' threatening public order when they were lads, but neglecting to mention that this could have been because they didn't have motors.

'Young woman working for a jam factory picked up the week's wages from the bank on a Friday morning,' Edgar said. 'The "motor bandits" stopped, leapt out, bashed the girl, snatched the bag with the wages and drove off.'

'Bashed the girl badly?'

'Pushed her over. Scraped a knee. No harm done.'

'Is this from Aubrey?'

Edgar nodded.

Aubrey Duncan, reputedly the best criminal solicitor in the country, had his offices in Hogg's Yard, just around the corner from Foxton Row. A trust had grown. They were practically family.

'Defence?' Skelton asked.

'The only evidence against them is that, according to inattentive witnesses who'll probably crumble as soon as you look at them, the robbers looked a bit like the defendants – Reginald Ashworth and Leonard Jeanes – inasmuch as they were two men, somewhere between the ages of fifteen and twenty-five, dark hair, slim build, grey or brown suits. Ashworth and Jeanes are eighteen and nineteen respectively and vaguely fit the description. Both have been in trouble with the police before and neither can give an adequate account of their whereabouts at the time the robbery took place.'

'Do they look like felons?'

'In photographs, yes. But Aubrey has seen them in court and says they can look like angels when they stop scowling.'

'Ask Aubrey to do the usual. New Woolworth collar and tie, sixpenny pot of brilliantine and some shoe blacking. When they come to court make sure they call everybody "sir", blush when spoken to and mention their mothers as often as possible, even if they have no mothers. And try to slip in a reference to the King. Oh, and see if Aubrey can get one of his minions to find out how many men between fifteen and twenty-five there are living in Luton, and how many blue and grey suits Burton sells in a week. It's always good to have some numbers to bandy about. Pass us the biscuits.'

Skelton took one. Edgar looked at them mournfully, restraining himself.

'D'you not think a reducing diet might make you miserable?' Skelton asked.

'Being portly makes me miserable. I shall make my way through a tunnel of deeper misery to find the light of trim happiness at the other end.'

'What's next?'

'*Rex versus Dr Ibrahim Aziz.*'

'Ah, the Wakefield Suitcase Murder. You did save the best till last, didn't you?'

The identification of the body in the suitcase had been an ongoing saga in the newspapers since the beginning of November when it was discovered. The suitcase itself offered few clues: a standard, cheap fibre one made by Tookey & Sons in Birmingham, the lining torn but nothing concealed within it, the only identifying feature being a tiny number, probably a stock number, on a gummed label inside the lid. The papers had printed pictures of the label, and the police had checked every luggage shop and department store in the West Riding of Yorkshire, but nobody had recognised it.

The breakthrough came from the victim's dentures. A dental plate, manufactured in some unorthodox way using Bakelite, stainless steel and something called 'cobalt-chromium' was found rammed halfway down the woman's throat. Details had been published in the *British Dental Journal*, and fifteen dentists who had made plates along the same or similar lines came forward. Closer examination led a Wakefield dentist, a Mr Broadley, to recognise the plate as his own work and identify the wearer as Mrs Edna Aziz, the wife of Ibrahim Aziz, a respected local doctor.

Everything fell into place after that. The quarry where the suitcase was found was less than half a mile from Dr Aziz's house. A search revealed a bloodstained rug bundled in the doctor's coal shed for which he had no credible explanation. Neighbours reported they'd heard arguments and even screams not long before the murder was presumed to have taken place.

Aziz had admitted that he and his wife had had arguments. After one of them, he said, his wife had left and gone to stay with a sick aunt in Whitley Bay, Northumberland, to whom she had paid frequent visits over the course of the previous year. He believed that the corpse had been misidentified and his wife was still alive. As proof, he produced a postcard from her, sent just a few days earlier, saying she was well.

Police enquiries, however, had revealed that the aunt in Whitley Bay had died some months earlier.

Aziz's solicitor, a Wakefield man who mostly dealt with petty offences and matters of contract and property, was sensible enough to recognise that he might not be the right man for this particular job and had advised Aziz to go to Aubrey Duncan in London. Almost inevitably, the brief had now found its way to Skelton's desk.

'It doesn't make sense, does it?' Skelton said, when he'd read it through.

'What doesn't?'

'This thing's been in all the papers for a month. Aziz is an educated man, a respected doctor. We've every reason to assume that he's careful, methodical. So why would he make such a botch job of killing his wife? Why would he dump the body in a quarry just up the road? He's had weeks to think up a credible explanation of his wife's disappearance and he must have known the neighbours would have heard their screaming matches, but all the same, the best he can come up with is "She's gone to Whitley Bay to visit an aunt." Why not "She's gone to China to be with her lover the Emperor" – that'd be a good bit more difficult to disprove, wouldn't it? Or, even better, "We had terrible rows because she told me she had fallen in love with a man she called 'Bonesaw Harry' and, deaf to my pleadings and warnings, she ran off with him."'

'I take your point,' Edgar said.

'If you'd killed your wife and wanted to appear innocent, you'd report her missing to the police, wouldn't you? The whole thing's shot to pieces. Who'd keep a bloodstained rug in his coal shed all this time? Why didn't he burn it? Or wrap the body in it and dispose of the lot down – I don't know – a disused mine shaft in Cornwall, or weight it with pig iron and chuck it off a cliff somewhere? None of it makes sense.'

'Perhaps that's your defence. Unsound mind. Only a madman would make such a mess of it all.'

'Or for some reason he *wants* to get caught.'

'That's good, too. The act of a madman.'

'Or he's so ridiculously overconfident he thought he'd never get caught.'

'Again, insane behaviour.'

'Or, most likely as far as I can see . . . he *didn't do it.*'

That gave them both pause for thought.

'Not much of a defence, though, is it?' Edgar said. 'He must be innocent because there's too much evidence proving his guilt. And a clever man like him would have been more careful. And that's beside the fact that the jury will find him guilty before they've heard a scrap of evidence and probably before they even clap eyes on him.'

'Why's that?'

'He's Egyptian.'

Skelton saw the point. Foreigners, unless they conformed to one of the acceptable stereotypes, rarely played well with juries. Aziz was Egyptian – which might possibly have been excusable if his name had been Old King Tut, but he was neither a pharaoh nor made of gold. He was just a doctor from Wakefield. Worse still, his photograph, which had been in the morning papers, suggested that he had olive skin.

To a certain – frighteningly large – section of the British public, this alone would be enough to hang him.

Some years before, Sir Edward Marshall Hall, often described as the greatest advocate England has ever known, had played hard on the jury's bigotry in his defence of Marguerite Fahmy, a Frenchwoman who had shot and killed her Egyptian husband, Prince Fahmy Bey, suggesting that the gun was the only defence a decent European woman would have against the vile sexual habits of a more exotic foreigner. It worked. Despite the weight of evidence against her, the jury acquitted and she walked free.

If a white woman could kill an Egyptian and get away with it, an Egyptian who killed a white woman would not stand a chance. Skelton imagined counsel for the prosecution suggesting, if not overtly stating, that foreigners who marry Englishwomen only do so in order to make it easier to cut them up and put them into suitcases.

It wasn't just the man on the Clapham omnibus that harboured these prejudices either. Luminaries like H. G. Wells, George Bernard Shaw and Bertrand Russell had all spoken out in favour of the science of 'eugenics', advocating it as a possible solution to mankind's problems. They all believed in 'selective breeding' of the human race and more particularly the British race. Some suggested a 'procreation licence' so that only those judged to be mentally and physically tip-top would be allowed to breed at all. Others favoured compulsory sterilisation of the weak and feeble in body or mind. Still others – although none of the beliefs were mutually exclusive – sought to forbid marriage between British men and women, and people of other races.

Skelton wondered what they'd make of him, born with a defective hip and married to a woman who was one-quarter Swedish. He couldn't see the sense in any of it. 'Selective breeding' never worked. A ratty old mongrel, for instance, is nearly always tougher and lives longer that a pure-bred King Charles Spaniel – or even a British Bulldog.

'They'll convict him as soon as they look at him,' Edgar said.

'Was it Duxford who used to say that the presumption of innocence is the bedrock of English common law,' Skelton said, 'which is why it doesn't apply to foreigners? And a foreigner accused of killing an Englishwoman—'

'She's not actually English.'

'No?'

'Scottish. And, I suppose, technically, she's Egyptian.'

This was true. A British woman who married a foreigner automatically renounced her citizenship and adopted that of her husband.

'When are we free to go to Wakefield?' Skelton asked.

Edgar was already browsing through Skelton's appointments book.

'We could go at the beginning of next week if I manage to rearrange one or two things. And anyway, he's not in Wakefield. They've taken him to Armley Gaol in Leeds.'

Skelton knew Armley. His parents still lived in Hunslet, over the other side of Leeds, but one of the specialists he'd been taken to with his hip when he was a child had had a surgery on Hall Lane in Armley. You could see the prison from there, and once he'd seen a hand appear between the bars and grasp a tiny fragment of outside.

CHAPTER FOUR

That Sunday, Skelton went to Leeds to see his parents.

It was a blustery day. From the tram, down the side streets, he could see the washing stretched across the road from house to house, billowing like the sails of a galleon. They didn't hang their washing out across the street in Berkshire, not in Lambourn, anyway, and as far as he could remember Skelton had never seen it in London either. London didn't have the open feeling of Leeds, that sense of being so close to endless miles of moorland. The food was different, the clothes were different, the faces were different, the talk was different.

He hadn't been home – if he could still call it that – for six or seven months. He missed it, but he was never sure whether it was the city of Leeds he was missing or just the person he'd been when he lived there; raw, awkward, funny, at odds with himself but at peace with his surroundings.

In Lambourn and London they saw him as a Yorkshireman. Round here, though, he was a toff, these days, a southerner. And even though he didn't feel like one, it was no good him pretending he was anything else.

The key was still on his key ring, but he knocked so that his dad could pull his braces up and his mum dab her hair before they saw him. They'd want to look their best even though it was only him.

There was no fuss. There never was any fuss. Just 'All right, our Arthur' and 'I expect you want a cuppa'.

His dad was in his slippers with no collar on his shirt, sitting by the fire. Skelton was shocked by how much older he looked. This was a man who'd always been full of life, incapable of sitting still for a moment.

Skelton took the other chair and offered his dad a fill from his tobacco pouch. Dad had always smoked cheap stuff called Matheson's Reserve, which Skelton had only ever seen at Hodgson's, the newsagent's on Dewsbury Road. It was rumoured to be made from dog-ends picked up at the Crescent Picture House and bits of old privet. Dad usually made a joke about Skelton's Balkan Sobranie being a lot of money for a bit of crackling (it did crackle as it burned).

But today, he didn't make the joke. He just helped himself, nodded a silent thanks, filled his bowl and put a spill to the fire to light it.

'You're keeping well, are you, then?' Skelton asked.

'Same as ever,' Dad said.

Mum came in with the tea and when Dad went out to the lav, Skelton said, 'Is he all right?'

'If you mean "Is he getting on my nerves?", you wouldn't

45

be wrong,' Mum said. 'Is he getting on your nerves?'

'Has he been to the doctor?'

'There's nothing wrong with him. It's just idle-itis.'

'I thought he was looking forward to retiring.'

'He was. Now I'm worried that this was what he was looking forward to. Sitting by the fire looking miserable all day. And getting under my feet every time I want to put them anywhere. Have you seen my glasses?'

'Have you got glasses?'

'No, I mean, that's what he says hundred times a day, "Have you seen my glasses?" Every time they're either on top of his head or on the box where he left them.'

Dad had a box next to his chair where he kept his things; pipe, baccy, matches, penknife, glasses, tin of Germolene for his sore ear and Zubes for his throat.

'I tell you,' Mum said, 'the way he's going on, if I bumped into John Gilbert at the Co-op bacon counter and he said, "Come with me to exotic shores," I'd be off like a shot.'

John Gilbert, who'd been in *Flesh and the Devil* with Greta Garbo, was a surprising choice for Mum. Skelton had always had her pinned as a Douglas Fairbanks type.

Dad came back, went straight to his chair and stared at the fire.

Skelton had had his dinner on the train, and it wasn't time for tea, but all the same Mum had put some cake and biscuits out just in case.

She asked after Mila and the children. Skelton didn't tell her about his wife's plan to fly to Australia. She'd only worry.

Dad ate some cake, blew on his tea and drank, but said nothing.

'I wouldn't mind a walk,' Skelton said, after a bit. 'It's

years since I've been down Middleton Park. D'you fancy a walk, Dad? It's windy out but it's not too cold.'

'It'll be dark in ten minutes,' Dad said.

'Just up the Moor then.'

Hunslet Moor was a rather more modest park a short walk away.

'Look at the crumbs you've made,' Mum said. 'Get out a bit so I can sweep up.'

She went out to the kitchen, came back with the broom to show she meant it and stood there waiting for him to move.

'I haven't got a collar on,' Dad said.

'You'll be wearing a scarf, nobody'll see.'

Skelton limped along at his usual sprightly pace. Dad followed, walking like an invalid, slow and unsure.

They'd barely set foot on the grass before he said, 'It's cold. Can we go home?'

Amy, Skelton's sister, came round later with Jean, her eldest. Skelton resisted the temptation to say 'My, you've shot up' when he saw Jean, but she had. The last time he'd seen her she was a little girl. Now she was a young woman with a job at Woolworth. She blushed when her mum referred to somebody called 'Where-You-Goin'-Owen' as her boyfriend.

'Honest, Uncle Arthur, I don't know what she's going on about. He's just a fella I went to the pictures with. The once, that's all.'

Skelton said he'd been to the Moor with Dad. Amy said she was walking that way the other night after she'd done a late shift. It was a bit foggy, and she saw this weird white shape floating in front of her. She was too petrified even to scream or move. It came closer and closer until she thought she was going to pass out she was so scared. Then, instead of going 'whoo-whoo' like a ghost would, it neighed. It was Benny, the milkman's horse, that was always running away.

This led to a lot more stories about Benny and how Brian Biggs found it once up their ginnel and thought he could keep it because it was their ginnel it was up. He got ever so upset when his mum said it wasn't his to keep and, even if it was, where were they going to keep a horse? Brian Biggs said it could live in the back kitchen.

'What about when I have to cook the dinner?' his mum had said. And Brian had said he could train it to stand in the area every dinner time.

They laughed.

Dad didn't laugh. Dad didn't speak. He sat in his chair, smoking his pipe and staring at the fire.

Skelton slept in his old room, in the double bed he'd shared with his brother Eric. Stanley, the eldest, had had the single bed under the window.

He was woken just after one o'clock by a terrible noise like thunder in the earth. It took him a moment to gather his wits, then he realised that the nightshift at the nail mill were 'turning the rows'. He had no idea what this entailed, except that it involved a lot of banging, possibly from mechanical hammers. Sometimes it had woken him as a child, but never for long. You got used to it, like you got used to the rushes of flame from the steelworks and the taste and smell of sulphur from his dad's chemical factory. It got in your food, that did, and on your clothes. They said it was good for you, that it kept the TB away. At school you could tell whether a boy was from round your way by the smell of him. Boys from his bit of Hunslet smelt of sulphur. Like the devil.

In the half-light he could see the damp patches on the ceiling that had been there for at least thirty years.

He'd thought often about how it would feel when his mum or his dad died, but he now realised he'd never entertained the thought as a serious proposition. It was something he thought about to scare himself, like Amy might scare herself remembering her encounter with Benny the milkman's horse. But the change that had happened to his dad had rattled him.

There were – he could count five – there were five people walking around alive because he had saved them from the hangman. Admittedly there were about the same number he'd failed to save, but all the same, in the courtroom he felt he had the power to stop people dying. He had control. It was what he did for a living.

By three in the morning, he had decided to buy his parents a house by the Thames. They could move down there. The air would be cleaner and the winters milder. His dad could have a garden with a huge rhubarb patch covered in buckets. He'd heard of some very good doctors in Maidenhead, and there were all kinds of specialists in Reading and Oxford and God knows how many in London. They could do things these days with X-rays and so on. He'd pop over to visit as often as possible with Lawrence and Elizabeth. That way he'd keep them alive for a long, long time.

CHAPTER FIVE

The train from King's Cross to Leeds had not been kind to Edgar.

'My eggs were hard and my bacon soft. Then a mother and son got on and sat opposite, and the child stared at me relentlessly. I thought of having a word with the mother, but she seemed very sad, as if she'd recently suffered a bereavement, and I didn't want to intrude on her grief. Although later it occurred to me that probably anyone with such an impertinent son would live in a state of constant sorrow. Then, worst of all, a gent in a grey bowler hat got on, and, as he was putting his bags on the luggage rack, trod heavily on my foot.'

'Oh dear. How are they?'

'Well, I told you the chiropodist said there's little hope and now, after the gent in the bowler, I suspect there's even less.'

There was a taxi to be had outside the station, but Edgar, who was sometimes sick in cars, wondered whether a tram might be more convenient, so they caught a number 14 down the Armley Road.

'There's a smell of sulphur,' Edgar said, looking suspiciously at Skelton's overcoat.

'That's what normal smells like,' Skelton said.

Dr Aziz was in solitary confinement. The prison authorities had decided that, because he was a foreigner, it wouldn't be safe for him to be in the company of other prisoners.

His cell wasn't too bad, though. Skelton had stayed in commercial hotels that weren't much better appointed.

Aziz was a scholarly-looking man, slight of build, with round spectacles almost identical to Skelton's. Despite his situation and surroundings, his collar was spotless, his suit looked newly pressed, there was a shine on his shoes, his hair was brushed, and his fingernails trimmed and clean.

As a remand prisoner, he was allowed books, magazines and writing things. Skelton noted that the books were mostly medical texts and the magazines professional journals in both English and Arabic. They were arranged very precisely on the table and on the little shelf where he kept his toilet items.

They shook hands. Aziz sat at his 'desk', Skelton and Edgar perched on the rickety chairs that the warder had brought in.

'Now, what can I do for you gentlemen?' Aziz asked. He was a doctor beginning a consultation with a couple of none-too-bright patients. Introductory chit-chat, Skelton decided, about the weather or the prison food, would not be welcomed. He nodded at Edgar, who passed him a couple of sheets of paper from the file he carried.

Skelton examined them for a moment and said, 'We've just got a few questions – a few small matters to clear up.'

'Excellent,' Aziz said, 'and I have some questions for you.' He opened a quarto-sized notebook and turned to a page covered in very small, very neat handwriting. His margins did not waiver. There were no crossings out.

'Do they have any evidence of the identity of this poor woman other than the dental plate,' Aziz asked, 'and if not, why are they still insisting it is my wife?'

'I think they're taking the dental plate to be fairly conclusive evidence.'

'This is Broadley's testimony, is it?'

Broadley was the Wakefield dentist who had identified the plate.

'I know this man,' Aziz continued. 'He is a good enough dentist, otherwise I would not have sent my wife to be treated by him, but he is young and ambitious. He has his own practice in Wakefield but has his eyes on Harley Street. I am not saying he would tell a deliberate lie, but the opportunity to glean a little publicity might make him less likely to admit to any doubt. They have not let me see any photographs of the body, but I gather from general comments that it is badly decomposed.'

Skelton nodded. He had seen photographs. They were less distressing than he had feared, but only because the parts were barely recognisable as human flesh.

'Who conducted the autopsy?'

Edgar found the reference in the file. 'After examination by the police surgeon in Wakefield,' he said, 'the remains were transferred to Leeds General Infirmary. A Doctor Moffat made the initial examination and then Sir Bernard Spilsbury, the Home Office Pathologist, was called in. He requested that the remains be transferred to Bart's Hospital in London where they have facilities for further investigations.'

'Was the woman wearing a wedding ring?'

'The assumption is,' Edgar said, 'that the ring would have been removed to further disguise the identity.'

'Was there a mark or indentation where the ring would have been?'

'I fear that the deterioration—'

'Edna has quite a large mole in the middle of her back and a brown birthmark on her shoulder just here.' He gestured to his left shoulder 'Traces of the mole might still be visible even after advanced decomposition.'

'I'll make sure the pathologists are aware of that,' Skelton said, but, having seen those pictures, he knew that the chances of there being anything among that mess that could be identified as a birthmark or mole were negligible.

'Good.' Aziz looked down at his list of questions. 'Two things puzzle me. The first – and I'm sure it must have occurred to you – if I was the killer, why would I go to all this trouble to disguise the identity of the cadaver then dump it in the nearest available quarry and fail to destroy the bloodstained rug?'

'That thought had indeed occurred to me,' Skelton said. 'As a basis for a defence however I fear that the criminal's failure to do the crime well rarely carries much weight.'

Aziz nodded. The point was clear. 'The second,' he said, 'was that they estimate the death to have taken place six to eight weeks before the boys found the suitcase. That would be in the middle of September last, yes?'

'Between the 7th and the 21st,' Edgar said. 'That is assuming that the remains were in the quarry the whole time. If it was transported from somewhere else, then their estimate could be out by three or four weeks.'

'Since the beginning of October, I have received three postcards from Edna, sent from Whitley Bay, all saying that she is well. Why do the police not accept these as evidence that she is alive?'

'They have made enquiries and established, as you know, that the aunt she claimed to have been visiting died almost a year ago and no trace of Edna has since been seen in Whitley Bay or the surrounding area.'

'What does that mean, "No trace has been seen"? How can you prove the absence of something? She could have been lying to me about the aunt. She could be in disguise.'

Aziz's measured voice and professional demeanour was unchanged, but his hand, though resting on the table, had begun to tremor, rattling his pen against a cup. He reached into his pocket and pulled out a packet of Player's. Skelton was vaguely disappointed that they weren't some exotic Egyptian brand, perfumed perhaps, or the kind he'd seen at his tobacconists that were flattened into an oval shape. He'd always wanted to try an Egyptian cigarette but had never dared risk the swank of actually buying a packet.

Aziz offered them and produced, from the far side of the table, an ashtray on a wooden stand of a kind you often saw in doctors' waiting rooms. It was clearly not prison issue and seemed an odd luxury to request, but was quite in keeping, Skelton supposed, with the pressed trousers and the precisely arranged magazines.

Edgar accepted a cigarette. Skelton took out his pipe and tobacco pouch, and looked around.

'Stone walls do not a prison make,' he said, 'nor iron bars a cage.'

'Minds innocent and quiet take,' Aziz said continuing the poem, 'that for an hermitage.'

'John Bunyan, is it?' Skelton said. 'In the prison at Bedford?'

'Richard Lovelace,' Aziz said. 'And while Bunyan might have found his freedom in God, Lovelace had his mind on more carnal matters.'

'And where do you find your freedom?'

Aziz smiled. 'It is like being a student again. I am a doctor without patients, which means I have time at my disposal to catch up on the studying I should have done twenty years ago. And *my* mind is "innocent and quiet".'

Skelton lit his pipe and listened to the crackling of his Balkan Sobranie.

'You were a student at Edinburgh,' he said.

'I was. And you were at Cambridge.'

'I was. And your wife's from that part of the world.'

'She is from Fort Blaine.'

'I'm afraid I don't know it at all,' Skelton said.

'It's a small town, thirty miles or so from Edinburgh.'

'And you met your wife in Edinburgh?'

'She was at the university, too, reading mathematics.'

'How did you meet?'

Aziz's face clouded for a moment. He wasn't used to being asked personal questions and wondered whether it was an acceptable part of the procedure or just impertinence.

'When you're conducting a defence in court,' Skelton explained, 'sometimes the tiniest details can make the difference between acquittal and conviction.'

Aziz pushed loose shreds of tobacco into the end of his cigarette with his thumb and decided to answer.

'While I was up at Edinburgh, I preferred to study at the Central Library rather than in any of the university buildings, which were distressingly full of students. There is a certain kind of boorishness I like to avoid. Edna is also very shy and she, too, found the upstairs reference library to her taste. For a month or so we studiously avoided looking at each other. Then, for another month, we would sometimes nod before looking away. Then the nod might be accompanied by a smile. She spoke first. She said, "I wonder would you have a ruler I could borrow? I seem to have come without mine," and two years later we were married.'

'Very romantic. And during the war?'

'I served with Royal Army Military Corps, stationed here in Leeds.'

'Out at Beckett Park?' Skelton asked.

'Of course. You're a native of Leeds.'

'I was with my mum and dad last night. They're in Hunslet.'

Aziz nodded vaguely. He had barely ventured outside the grounds at Beckett Park for the three years he was there. Hunslet could have been in China as far as he knew.

'Would you say yours was a happy marriage?'

'Edna is highly strung. Troubled.'

Aziz leant forward, lit a fresh cigarette and stubbed out the old.

'Over the course of our marriage, I have been obliged to take on the role of doctor as well as husband. As the years have passed, I'm afraid that the doctor has too often taken precedence. Circumstances have greatly exacerbated her condition. Eighteen months ago, her father died.'

'He was still in Scotland?'

'Yes. Her mother was ill and needed constant nursing. I said she should bring her to Wakefield, and I could supervise her care and perhaps engage a nurse. But her mother had already decided on a nursing home in Edinburgh. She was there for just a few weeks before she died as well. And then her mother's sister, Edna's Aunt Hilda, fell ill, too. Cancer. A nice lady. She had been married to a marine engineer of some sort. I believed they lived in Aberdeen for a while, then the husband took some official post in Northumberland and they moved to Whitley Bay. She stayed there after her husband died. Do you know the place?'

'I'm afraid not.'

'It is a seaside resort.'

'So I gather.'

'So, Edna would travel once a month and stay for three or four days.'

'Did you ever go with her?'

'Before Aunt Hilda fell ill, Edna and I spent a short holiday with her there, but over the past year I have been dealing with a flu epidemic. I have perhaps fifty patients with chronic problems that need attending to once a week and perhaps another eighty who suffer intermittently. I know from my appointments book that I have not had more than a few hours' respite since May 1928. If you need proof of this, you can look at my appointments book yourself or at the patients' notes which are meticulously kept, or ask Miss Devereux, my receptionist.'

'Did your wife feel you were neglecting her?'

'Of course. What wife wouldn't? She found these trips to her aunt's emotionally draining,' he said. 'Afterwards she would be irritable. She would take offence at the slightest provocation.'

'You say you took on the role of doctor? Did you prescribe pills of any sort?'

'Why do you ask?'

'I'm trying to get a sense of the overall picture.'

Aziz smiled. 'You were wondering whether the swarthy foreign devil was drugging the white lady for his own perverse gratification.'

'I assure you—'

'I am joking, Mr Skelton. One gets used to people making these sorts of assumptions. They run deep within us all.'

Skelton wondered whether they ran deep within him. It would be the mark of a civilised man if they didn't, and the mark of a well-mannered man not to show them even if they did. He knew he wasn't entirely civilised – not in a London way – but his mum had always laid great stress on good manners.

'I try to prescribe as little as possible,' Aziz said. 'A little chloral hydrate now and then to help her sleep. Sometimes a proprietary nerve tonic that I hope will have some placebo effect, even though it is little more than coloured water.'

'Tell me what happened on the day she left.'

'She had bought a new dress and been to the hairdresser. She had had a gentle wave put in her hair by some new process. It suited her. The dress was perhaps a little daring for a doctor's wife, but I had no objection to her wearing it. I told her she looked very glamorous. She took this as a criticism. I tried to assure her that it was not intended as such, but she grew very excited. She shouted and screamed.

At one point she insisted that I had called her a prostitute, which was not true. I tried to calm her, but this made her angrier still. She went upstairs. She had already packed her bag to go to her aunt's. She left saying she might return when I had learnt to treat her with some respect.'

'What time of day was this?'

'In the middle of the afternoon. I think I believed that she would cool off in an hour or so and return. I also had a waiting room filled with patients who needed my attention.'

'Had they heard the argument?'

'They had. They were most concerned. I assured them that Edna was under a great deal of stress because of her poor aunt.'

'And when she didn't come back?'

'I assumed she had gone to Whitley Bay.'

'I'm sorry for having to bring this matter up, Dr Aziz, but did it ever occur to you that your wife had taken a lover?'

'Of course. I tried to tell the police this, but they seemed criminally disinterested. It explains everything. My theory is that while she was caring for her aunt, she met someone. When the aunt died, she wished to carry on seeing this person, so continued the pretence that the aunt was still alive in order to maintain the visits. This would also account for the new dress, the glamorous new hairstyle and the increase in her irritability. Every second spent away from her lover was torture and I was her torturer. She is probably in Whitley Bay now with him. I received the first postcard from her just a few days after she left, assuring me that she was in good health but would stay a little longer. Since then, I have received one a month proving she is alive and well and has – I don't know – dyed her hair a different colour or some such. A disguise of some sort.'

Skelton's pipe had gone out. He relit it and looked down at his notes.

'Tell me about the rug,' he said.

'This is all in my statement to the police.'

'Tell me again.'

'Late one night there was a knock at the door. A man had cut his hand and wrist very badly. Two friends had brought him in a car. They said he had had an accident while cutting wood for a fire. I guessed that he'd been in a fight, but the demeanour of the two friends discouraged questions. They didn't want to come into the surgery, so I treated him in the hall. He bled all over the rug. I disinfected the wound and stitched it. I warned them that tendons had been severed and he might lose the use of his fingers. After they had left, I threw the rug in the coal shed meaning to put it out for the dustmen.'

'And the man gave you no name?'

'They said his name was Joe Soap, which clearly—'

'So, the police had no way of checking the story?'

'Exactly.'

'The story of your wife's supposed murder has been front-page news in all the newspapers. Your wife must be aware that you've been arrested. All she'd have to do is walk into a police station and tell them her name and all this would be over.'

'That has worried me. But who can tell what kind of man her lover might be? He could be preventing her. He could be hiding the news from her. They might be living some lovers' idyll in a house by the sea with no newspapers, no telephone, no wireless set to interrupt their bliss. Were there any other questions?'

'Do you have any particular enemies, Dr Aziz?'

'I am too busy to have either friends or enemies.'

'No aggrieved patients?'

'Grievance against a doctor is a luxury few of my patients can afford. I assume what you're asking is whether I can think of anybody who may have wanted to manufacture false evidence in order to "frame" me for the murder. And my answer is no, I cannot.'

'Your wife's lover, perhaps?'

'That would be to assume that my wife has or had a lover and that it is indeed my wife's remains in the suitcase. If one were prepared to stretch conjecture so far then there is of course a possibility that someone is trying to "frame" me for the crime. Of more pressing concern for the moment are the two matters – I have mentioned them to Mr Duncan, the solicitor – two matters that need to be attended to urgently, before my trial date which is, I believe, the thirteenth of February. Less than two months away. The first, of course, is to find my wife. The second is to find out who that unfortunate woman in the suitcase really is and figure out who killed her before – if you will excuse the lapse into melodrama – he kills again.'

'It'd be daft to think it was all a chain of coincidences, wouldn't it?' Skelton asked, on the train back to London.

'What?'

'A body turns up that bears a slight resemblance to his wife, with a dental plate that's like one his wife wore, and the arguments and the rug . . . all just a chain of unfortunate coincidences.'

'I've been piecing together a hypothesis,' Edgar said.

'Go on.'

'Edna and her lover want to fake her death so that she can begin a new life, and they also want to get Aziz completely out of the picture. So, they kill another woman who bears a resemblance to Edna, put Edna's dental plate into her mouth to help things along and dump her in the quarry.'

'What about the bloodstained rug?'

'Aziz is telling the truth about that. It was this Joe Soap.'

'What about the postcards from Whitley Bay?'

'That might take a little more thought.'

Edgar stared out at the darkness.

'And who's the lover?' Skelton asked.

Edgar stared some more.

'And who's the woman in the suitcase?'

CHAPTER SIX

Among the post that Wednesday was a letter from Skelton's cousin Alan, which was always a welcome event.

Alan was the son of Skelton's Auntie Mildred, who had married Uncle Gilbert, a Welshman. Gilbert worked at the Pavilion Theatre in Rhyl, doing all the backstage and front of house business. Mildred and Gilbert had had twins. Alan and Norah, just a bit younger than Skelton.

For a time, Alan had had a decent job as a clerk in the offices of E. B. Jones, the grocery chain on Water Street, but he'd been bothered from an early age by visitations from angels, who kept calling him to higher things. He did a bit of preaching on the beach – or rather a combination of preaching, joke-telling and singing jolly songs to the accompaniment of his banjo. It was well received. Over the weeks he built up quite a crowd and his sister, Norah, joined him, playing her piano accordion. So, after the war, when he came out of the army, Alan had bought an ex-army Rover Sunbeam ambulance. He and Norah, with help from their mum and dad, had kitted it out as a caravan and painted 'The Joy of Jesus Mission' on the side. They took to the road, singing and preaching wherever they went, and spreading their message that even in the depths of despair hope can be found because 'God loves those who laugh'.

Their journeys were guided by need. Wherever there was trouble – a pit disaster, a flood, a fire, a sudden or unexpected death – that, they decided, was where they should go. They saw themselves as great bringers of comfort.

Sometimes their cousin Arthur, the barrister, was able to help them find places where the need was greatest. Earlier in 1929, for instance, they had spent time in Collingford, near Birmingham, where a dreadful poisoning had taken place, and were able to bring solace and, they hoped, a little joy, into the lives of the bereaved and the horrified.

As they went about their calling, they were often able to send nuggets of information to Arthur, too, which helped bring the truth to light. For they, quite rightly, believed that they and their cousin – even though Skelton was avowedly agnostic – served the same God: the Lord of truth, the Lord of justice, the Lord of hope and joy for the innocent.

In return for their nuggets of information, Skelton made regular and sometimes very generous contributions to their mission. When their Rover Sunbeam had been burnt during their stay in Collingford, Skelton had supplied funds to buy a replacement. Now they were the proud owners of a five-year-old Morris Oxford saloon and a four-year-old Eccles De Luxe four-berth caravan – both with 'The Joy of Jesus Mission' painted on the side.

Rhyl, Monday 16th December, 1929

My dear cousin Arthur,

Has it been raining a lot down your way? My goodness, we have had sheets of it up here. Usually, if you mention that it is raining in North Wales, you get funny looks because that is the normal way of things. It is like saying 'I am breathing' or 'Grass is green'. But these last few days people have been talking about it without restraint. 'Look at this rain,' they say. That is how heavy it has been.

As you can see from the above address, we are at home with Mum and Dad in Rhyl, and very nice it is, too, apart from the rain.

We are a little worried, though, and would very much appreciate a spot of advice from a legal man such as yourself.

Here is the long and short of it.

Last week, as you may remember from my previous letters, we were in Carlisle in Cumberland where we got to know a very nice lady by the name of Iris Whittington, who was a district nurse. It was she who arranged for us to hold our meetings at the Working Men's Institute and also obtained permission for us to park the Morris and the Eccles in the yard around the back of the building.

Anyway, Iris, as well as working at her district nursing, does a lot for charities, particularly those devoted to the care of sick and needy children. Recently she has been writing letters to the local newspapers urging the council to build a children's hospital for Carlisle, along the lines of the ones they have in London and Liverpool. To the end of raising money for such a hospital, she decided to organise a Christmas raffle with a first prize of £50 and a grand draw this Saturday just gone. She asked us if we would sell tickets – at threepence a go – as we went about our ministry, knocking on doors and speaking to people. This we gladly did. We sold them at our meetings as well.

When the Saturday came, we were proud to have sold no less than four hundred and twelve tickets and delivered all the threepenny bits and pennies and ha'pennies and farthings that we had collected, along with the ticket stubs, to Iris in the little office at the Working Men's Institute. To this, Iris added her little pile – she had sold two hundred and seventy-three – and asked us to count up the money because she did not have much of a head for figures. Norah, who is an arithmetic wizard, told her that six hundred and eighty-five tickets at threepence each should come to £8 11s 3d and wondered when the other ticket sellers would be arriving.

'No, that's it,' Iris said. 'Just both of you and me.'

Norah pointed out that we only had £8 11s 3d, and people were already assembling in the hall expecting a fifty-pound prize.

By this time, Iris's face was white as a sheet. She asked us if we had fifty pounds, and of course we did not and neither did she.

I said that all would be well if we went out and told the simple truth. That we had got our sums wrong. There would no £50 prize after all, but if people would form an orderly queue, we would make sure that every ticket holder got a full refund.

So that is what we did.

Upon addressing the audience, however, I quickly realised that a crowd that has come expecting a £50 prize is not to be trifled with. Somebody at the back said, 'I told you it was a swindle,' and that seemed to turn the general mood ugly.

I explained again, more abjectly this time, 'I would like to extend our sincere apologies for any inconvenience this may have caused.' I also pointed out that although, if all had gone well, one person in that room would have gone away tonight £50 richer, everybody else would have gone away threepence poorer, and if they had bought four tickets, which some people had, a shilling poorer. As things stood, everybody would get their money back so nobody would go home poorer. I also tried to point out that it was all for a good cause anyway.

This turned them very ugly. 'Cheats!' they shouted. 'Swindlers!' 'Thieves!'

Somebody threw something, and a couple of big chaps left their seats and started advancing on the stage. Others followed.

Iris seemed incapable of speech or movement, so Norah and I grabbed her, one either side, and hurried her off the stage and out of the back door. We slammed it behind us and threw beer crates against it to try and keep it secure.

Thankfully we had left the Eccles hitched to the Morris and I had driven it enough to know exactly how much choke to give it so that it would start first time. We shoved Iris into the car. Norah opened the back gates of the yard and leapt into the passenger seat as I drove out. There was a great clattering of crockery from the Eccles as we hit the first bump in the road and we realised we had not put the tea things away, but we did not want to stop. We were lost for a moment in a maze of streets before we found a main road. This took us south. We did not care in what direction we went as long as we could shake the dust of Carlisle from our tyres as quickly as possible.

After forty-five minutes or so, Iris seemed to come to her senses. She said she had friends that lived in Penrith who would be able to put her up for a few days. So, we stopped there. The friends were very welcoming, gave us tea and assured us that they would look after Iris. They also reckoned that the anger in Carlisle would abate in a day or two and it would be safe for her to go back.

We left her there and drove on to Rhyl.

My questions are as follows:

Was the raffle legal in the first place? Should Iris have secured a licence or some such before selling any tickets?

If it was illegal, would we, as accessories, be liable for prosecution?

Could we be prosecuted for fraud or some similar offence? In our hurry to leave, the £8 11s 3d was left on the stage in a shoe box, so it should be stressed that neither Iris, Norah nor I gained a penny from the enterprise.

I gave our address in Rhyl to Iris before we left

her in Penrith saying she should get in touch if she needed any help dealing with the repercussions of the debacle. If the police question her, I am sure she would give them this information. Should we expect the Carlisle police, or perhaps officers from Rhyl acting on information passed on to them by the Carlisle force, to come knocking at Mum and Dad's door?

As I am sure you will understand, we would not want police knocking on Mum and Dad's door. There would be neighbours to consider apart from anything else. I have no idea how serious a crime it is to be involved in an unlicensed or fraudulent raffle. I know that illegal bookmakers, which is possibly a similar crime, often go to prison. Can you imagine how terrible it would be for Mum and Dad if we were led away in handcuffs?

The only thing that brings me a crumb of comfort in this sorry business is the thought that, if we were to be arrested and the case came to court, we would have you at our backs.

We have given some considerable thought as to where next – providing we do not end up in gaol – it would be best to direct our steps.

Carlisle was the furthest north we had ever been and all the while we were there, Scotland, virgin territory for our mission, seemed to beckon. I have never been to Scotland and have met precious few Scottish people, so it would be an adventure and, since we have heard – possibly erroneously – that Scottish Presbyterians are not much inclined to joy, something of a challenge for our mission.

Then we read in the newspaper that you had been

given the responsibility of defending Dr Aziz in the dreadful business of his poor wife's murder, and we saw in the same newspaper that Mrs Aziz was from Fort Blaine, which, we saw from our maps, is not long over the border, up towards Edinburgh. There will be distressed people there as there always are when a shocking tragedy like this one visits a community; people in need of the joy of Jesus. A coincidence like this – the conjunction of our predisposition to pay a visit 'over the border' and your connection with Fort Blaine – can only be seen as a 'calling'. It is not to be ignored.

Accordingly, we have resolved to stay in Rhyl for Christmas and set off for the great adventure of Scotland early in the new year – weather, of course, permitting.

If I do not get a chance to write again, let me take this opportunity of wishing you a peaceful, blessed and above all JOYOUS Christmas.

I am ever yours faithfully in the joy of Jesus,
Alan

CHAPTER SEVEN

Christmas was never an easy time in the Skelton household. Mila had strong views about spoiling the children. Under her rules, they were allowed three presents each: one frivolous, one active and one educational. This year Lawrence's list was a Hornby train set, roller skates and a book about the Vikings; Elizabeth's was a doll with eyes that close, roller skates – same as Lawrence – and an arithmetic primer that pretended to be a story called *Dora Goes Shopping*.

Mila had intended to come up to town on the Friday before Christmas to do the shopping, but on the Wednesday, Dorothy, the children's nanny, had phoned to say that she had a cold. Then, on the Thursday, Mrs Bartram, the housekeeper, came down with it, too. So, Mila was having to take the children to and from school, cook them nourishing meals and try to clear at least the top layer of toys, soot and crumbs from the carpets and floors.

Skelton, therefore, had been given a list. As well as the children's presents there were things to be bought for Dorothy and for Mrs Bartram.

He had given a great deal of thought to Mila's present. The difficulty was that he was an idealist about such things. To his mind, the perfect present would be something that Mila didn't even know she wanted until she unwrapped it; and with the unwrapping would come the realisation that she had wanted it all her life, with a need so deep that now she had to weep with gratitude and acknowledge that her husband knew her better than she knew herself.

If she carried out the plan of flying to Australia and came to grief, this might also be the last gift he would ever give her. The undesirability of this brought another element into play. As well as fulfilling the 'weep with gratitude' criterion, he also, more cunningly, wanted the present to be something that might, very subtly, discourage her from that Australia venture altogether – and by 'subtly' he meant so subtly that it would almost seem like encouragement.

When Lawrence was a baby they'd stayed for a week in a cottage near Keswick. On the second day, from the back garden of the cottage, Mila had watched a man, a pinprick in the distance, climb a cliff all by himself with ropes. And she had said that she would like to do the same thing. Skelton had assumed it was one of those things you say, like, 'I wouldn't mind having a go at the trombone', or 'I'd like to live on wine gums for a week'. But later Mila found a cafe where the people who do that sort of thing had their tea and fell into earnest conversation with them. Afterwards Skelton had spent a long time trying to persuade her that climbing up cliffs was not a sensible activity for someone with a baby son and no experience. And the more persuasive he became, the more determined she had been to do it.

It wasn't stubbornness. He knew that now, although didn't realise it at the time. Stubbornness would imply a sort of childish defiance. It would suggest that he had some sort of power or control over her that she was resisting. That had never been the case. The defiance, if that is what it could be called, was of herself. Her grandfather, the noble Swede, had taught her that self-doubt is the enemy of life.

Of course, she doubted herself at every turn, everybody does. But there was the cliff. There was a man climbing it. Could she do that? Having spoken to the men in the cafe, she might have realised that, with the right equipment and the right training, she could have done it easily and that would have been that. She wouldn't have bothered. But when her husband gave voice to the doubts in her own head, they had to be conquered.

One of the men from the cafe agreed to take her on some easier climbs. She was, of course, a natural. At the end of the week, she did the big cliff just as she'd said she would, with ropes and clanking metal around her waist. Skelton stood at the bottom with three of the climbing men who shouted advice and encouragement while he clutched little Lawrence tight enough to hurt both of them. She endured.

He found the children's books in a shop on Bedford Street which saved him the trek over to Foyles. Then a bus to Oxford Circus where he gritted his teeth and entered the sixth circle of hell that was Peter Robinson. After two small altercations with other customers involving elbows and the sharp corners of boxes, he managed to get the scarves for Dorothy and Mrs Bartram parcelled up and paid for.

Then came the real challenge. He'd been told by many people that, if you value your health and sanity, you should never venture into a toyshop at Christmas time. Climb the Matterhorn by all means, take the waters in Moscow during a cholera epidemic, but stay away from toyshops.

In Hamleys, he saw people in a frenzied thrall to the demons of Christmas. All trace of civilisation had fled. They shouted, pushed, grabbed, jostled. They thrust money at the girls working the tills and, even as they left, loaded with packages and parcels, their purchase-lust seemed unabated.

Skelton looked at the toys on offer and sighed. On Santa's sleigh, in his cloud cuckoo land version of Christmas, the toys were sturdy, bright and mostly made of wood. All he could see here was gimcrack, Brummagem ware. Children have an innate understanding of good engineering, of sturdy manufacture. Every day they see stoves and motor cars and letterboxes. So why did manufacturers think that they could be fobbed off with tinplate and varnish?

He examined a cricket set, far too small for Lawrence, suitable, perhaps, for a six-year-old and snorted with contempt. When he was six, he'd handled a real cricket bat. He knew the heft and the smell. How could any child, receiving this pale, odourless imitation, fail to be disappointed?

Eventually he located the Hornby train set for Lawrence. It was made not of iron and glory like a real train, but of bits of tin. Then the doll with eyes that close for Elizabeth. The face was garish. Children in fever wards have better colour.

It was dark when he finally escaped the store. A fog was beginning to thicken. The faces that emerged from the gloom had a grim determination that reminded him of photographs he'd seen of Captain Scott's last expedition to the Antarctic. And thoughts of Scott led to other thoughts, and all at once he knew what the special present for Mila was.

'Did you get the tinsel?' Mila asked when he arrived home.

'What?'

She was in the kitchen, making something with grey meat.

'Did you get the tinsel?'

'It wasn't on the list.'

'I asked you to put it on the list. With the wrapping paper and the string.'

'I'll go to Maidenhead on Monday.'

'Mrs Bartram is going to her brother and sister-in-law's for Christmas lunch. She hopes she'll be well enough to come here on Christmas morning to help prepare our lunch, but she won't be able to do any shopping, so she's drawn up another list.'

She gave him a sheet of notepaper. Two dense columns of items that needed buying.

'And it's no good thinking you'll get any of those things at Caxton's in the village. They've run out of nearly everything there and aren't expecting any deliveries until the new year.'

Skelton did the washing-up, fetched coal and sorted out the fires. In the drawing room, he picked up various toys, books, newspapers and items of clothing but didn't know what to do with them, so put them in a pile on the table where at least he wouldn't fall over them. Mila, meanwhile, hustled the children to bed and tried to make sense of the bathroom. She came down just long enough to make a glass of warm milk, then went to bed herself.

Skelton smoked a last pipe and banked up the fire for the night.

It had barely stopped raining since the start of December. Occasionally you'd get a dry day when you'd think it'd turned for the better, but then it would start again. Around the middle of the month it had been torrential. The Thames had burst its banks. The floods in London weren't as bad as they'd been the year before, but Maidenhead and Oxford both turned into Venice, with water two or three feet deep in some places.

The council in Maidenhead thoughtfully provided wooden walkways on stilts so that the braver and better balanced could still go about their business. But it was more fun to commandeer punts and other craft. 'Ahoy!' became the accepted mode of address and 'Aye Aye!' a substitute for 'Yes'.

The floods subsided a week or so before Christmas but left a fearful lot of mess behind. As he parked the Bentley, Skelton noticed great piles of silt had been shovelled and swept ready for removal.

Mrs Bartram's list was comprehensive and varied. Skelton wasn't too familiar with the Maidenhead shops, so planned to walk from one end of the street to the other, taking mental note of where the butcher, baker, grocer, greengrocer and dairy were located, then working his way methodically back again. The sheer quantity of goods to be obtained would possibly demand two trips. Up and down the street, put the bags in the car, then up and down a second time.

He'd been worrying about the Hornby train set. It had one engine, a tender, two goods carriages, a circle of track and a key to wind up the clockwork. Lawrence would assemble the track, wind up the engine, watch it go round and round until the clockwork wound down, perhaps do it again, then get bored. He might put soldiers in the goods carriages and watch them go round a couple of times, but there would be no real interest in the toy until he could get more track, points, signals, stations and another engine so that the two might crash. After Christmas, the shops wouldn't be open until Friday at the earliest. Lawrence would be bored on Christmas Day and kicking his heels on Boxing Day.

Same with the doll. Elizabeth would put it to bed, close its eyes, wake it up, open its eyes, then go back to playing with one of her prettier dolls.

By teatime both of them would have decided that their presents were junk. They wouldn't say anything because Dorothy had taught them good manners. But a father sees these things.

On his first up and down, he popped into Woolworth, the department store, looking for ways he might assuage the children's disappointment, but it was almost as hellish as Hamleys, so he left.

On the second up and down, just at the top of Queen Street he noticed that Greshams, the hardware store, had started selling wireless sets, valves and other bits of electrical apparatus. In the middle of the window display was a kit for building a crystal set. The picture on the box showed a boy and his father. Both seemed utterly absorbed and utterly delighted. The father didn't look much like Skelton, but the boy could have been a bad drawing of Lawrence. It said the set was suitable for 'Boys 11 yrs of age and older'. Lawrence was ten, but a bright and capable ten. He'd be flattered with a gift that he wasn't supposed to have for another year. There would be a need perhaps to prove himself equal to it. To be responsible. Capable. And it would keep him absorbed all Christmas afternoon and probably Boxing Day, too. Then he could spend hours with his earphones on, tuning into wireless stations in Hilversum, Athlone, Paris and Berlin. Listening to French and German might possibly give him an edge when he moved up to the grammar school.

A little further on, Skelton was intrigued by a sign in the window of a pet shop that said, in huge letters: NO MORE PARROTS IN THIS STORE! WALK IN WITHOUT FEAR.

The proprietor, in a brown coat, was feeding rabbits on display in a line of hutches outside the shop.

'Have they been pecking customers?' Skelton asked.

'The rabbits? No.'

'The parrots.'

'Eh?'

'Or were they swearing?' Skelton nodded at the sign and the proprietor cottoned on.

'No. No, it's just to say . . . you know. They've all gone. Incinerated.'

'Incinerated?'

'They actually came in a consignment from Argentina.'

'I don't quite—'

'The disease. Parrot fanciers' disease. Psittacosis.'

Skelton vaguely remembered reading something about it.

'Started in Argentina,' the proprietor continued, 'then worked its way up to America. Then over here. Woman died in Birmingham. They thought it was typhoid, but then they found out she had a parrot called Pedro and put two and two together. Next thing you know, wallop. I lost nearly twenty-pounds' worth of stock. They've had it terrible in America.'

'Have they?'

'An American admiral ordered all the sailors to throw their parrots overboard.'

'Wouldn't they just fly around and come back?'

'Doesn't make sense to me neither.'

The man took a broom from the shop's porch and began to sweep up spilt straw and seed.

His mood darkened.

'We had one,' he said.

'A parrot?'

'George. He was good company for my Lilian. We're right out at Oakley Green and I work long hours. Sometimes I'd come home and stand by the front window for a bit listening to the two of them chatting away. He used to take nuts from Lilian's lips. She was heartbroken to see him go. I gave her a guinea pig, but it's not the same. It's a child's pet, really, isn't it?'

'Is it?'

'Oh, yes. Ideal pet for a child. Very clean.'

'Are they?'

'Not like a rabbit.'

Skelton nodded and examined the rabbits. They seemed unfriendly. A box of white kittens in the window caught his eye.

'What about a cat?' he asked. 'Would a little eight-year-old girl like a cat, do you think?'

'Course she would.'

'More than a guinea pig?'

'This is a specific eight-year-old you're thinking about.'

'My daughter.'

'Has she had pets before?'

Mila had always said she admired working dogs but, since they had no work for a dog to do, it would be wrong to keep one.

'No, she hasn't,' Skelton said.

'I wouldn't start with a cat. Too much of a personality in the house. Your guinea pig really is just a step up from a stuffed toy really. And they make this noise: a squeaking noise that little girls find appealing. I'd start her off with a guinea pig and work your way up to a cat. And the other thing is if something goes wrong and a cat dies, everybody gets upset, but if it's a guinea pig . . . you know. You get another. Same difference.'

'Do you have them in stock?'

'Thirty or forty.'

'Could I see one?'

'If you'd like to come with me.'

'You bought what?'

'It's black and brown with white patches.'

Mila, slicing carrots, looked suspiciously around the kitchen.

'Where is it now?' she asked.

'It's not in here. I put it in the shed.'

'In a cage?'

'Well, obviously, I bought a cage as well.'

'We can't keep it. You'll have to tell Elizabeth that we've just borrowed it for a day or so and take it back to the shop after Christmas.'

'They're very clean.'

* * *

He gave up trying to sleep at five, went downstairs and, as silently as he could, lit the fires and laid the presents under the tree. He brought the guinea pig and cage in from the shed, fed and watered the animal according to the instructions he'd been given, tied a ribbon around the cage and hid it behind the sofa.

Elizabeth, wide-eyed and garrulous with excitement, was up at about six and Lawrence shortly afterwards.

Skelton boiled eggs and gave them toast for breakfast, insisting they eat it before opening any presents. Then he put some things on a tray and took them up to Mila. She was in a deep sleep, so he left the tray by the door and crept away.

At seven-thirty, Mrs Bartram arrived, still sniffly but insisting that she was feeling much better. She put the turkey in the oven, prepared everything else and gave instructions as to when Skelton should boil this, baste this and stir that.

Mila came down, wished everyone a merry Christmas, showered Mrs Bartram with gratitude and gave her the scarf Skelton had got from Peter Robinson. It was green cashmere. Mrs Bartram stroked it against her cheek, smelt it and seemed delighted.

Skelton got the car out and drove Mrs Bartram to her brother's house. Only five minutes each way.

When he got back, the children were allowed to open their presents.

They gave every indication of delight. Elizabeth loved the doll and said the guinea pig was the most adorable thing she'd ever seen. She wanted to take it out of the cage and stroke it, but Skelton said it would be better to leave it inside so it could get used to them and wouldn't be so frightened. Lawrence was excited about the train but didn't seem sure about the crystal set. Skelton expected he'd change his mind when they started to assemble it.

Mila gave her husband a very plain, very elegant, Omega wristwatch. His old one had been to the menders and was still playing up. He put the new one on and they both admired it.

Then he gave her his present to her.

'It's heavy,' she said, and tore off the paper. A mahogany box bound with brass. 'What is it? Duelling pistols?'

She undid the catch and for a moment still wasn't sure what she was looking at.

'It's a sextant,' Skelton said. 'You'll need it when you're navigating in your aeroplane.'

It was an impeccably engineered thing of brass and glass and steel, with bits that folded and numbers engraved on a sliding scale.

Lawrence was intrigued.

'What's it for?'

'It's for telling you where you are,' Mila said.

'How do you use it?'

'I have no idea. I'll have to learn.'

'Do you like it?' Skelton asked.

'It's the most beautiful thing I've ever owned.'

He thought he might have seen a tear in her eye and heard a catch in her voice, but he was probably fooling himself.

CHAPTER EIGHT

All over New Year, Skelton had been reading up on ostrich feathers. A smattering of technical knowledge always impresses a jury, and the grading of ostrich feathers came with a rich and wonderful vocabulary.

During the walk to court on the first Tuesday morning of the new year, he practised rolling the words around his tongue.

'Boos, blacks, drabs, floss, feminas, byocks, spadones.'

'Is it spad-own-knees, spayed-own-knees or spad-owns?' Edgar asked.

'I'm assuming it's related to the Latin, *spado*.'

'Which means?'

'Eunuch.'

'I'm sure you're right. You never went to the British Empire Exhibition in '24, did you?'

'No.'

'They had a huge display of the Prince of Wales' feathers constructed from a thousand ostrich feathers, or ten thousand, something like that, and then, just below that, they had two live ostriches, tethered. You could buy a ticket and they gave you these shears so you could cut one of their feathers off and keep it.'

'Did you do it?'

'At six pounds a go? Never. And anyway, I don't think the ostriches liked it.'

'They don't have to kill the ostriches to get the feathers, then?'

'Apparently not.'

'Just make them bald?'

'Perhaps they cut off a few and wait for them to grow back. Do you mind if we stop for a moment?' Edgar sat on a wall, looking miserable.

'Are you all right, old chap?'

'It's my feet,' he said. 'The chiropodist said I should wear plimsolls. I told him I can't possibly wear plimsolls. What would clients think?'

'Perhaps if you spent a fortune on some handmade shoes.'

Edgar's voice rose to a whine. 'These *are* handmade shoes. I had them made three months ago by Garrards of Jermyn Street. I took them a letter from the chiropodist describing the problems and suggesting a way of making the shoes to accommodate the various . . . deformities. And for a while they were perfect. Very comfortable. But now . . . I think the feet have got much worse. I can't afford to have new shoes made every three months. And besides, eventually they'd have to be built with monstrous bulges like Jerusalem artichokes.'

'What about patent leather pumps?'

'Like a dance-hall gigolo?'

Skelton sat down with him.

'We'll probably both get piles sitting here,' he said.

'One damn thing after another.'

Skelton reached for his pipe, then decided it was too cold to take off his gloves and fiddle with pouches and matches.

'I don't suppose they found that mole, did they?'

'Which mole?'

'The mole Edna Aziz was supposed to have on her back?'

'I did ask,' Edgar said, 'but they said the state of decomposition was such that concepts such as "front" and "back" were largely academic.'

Skelton nodded slowly.

Edgar raised both feet into the air, holding the railings behind for balance.

'How are they now?' Skelton asked.

'Still throbbing, but the pain is easing.'

'Tell me when you're ready.'

They watched the passers-by. An elderly woman's collar was trimmed with ostrich feathers.

'Would they be spadones?' Skelton asked.

'Look more like boos to me.'

'I thought ostrich feathers were a pre-war thing,'

'They've come back. You see them quite a lot up west of an evening. It used to be mostly hats before the war, but now it's doo-dahs and trims,' Edgar said.

'Ladies with their doo-dahs decked in boos.'

'I'd have thought boos would be more on the Soho side of Regent Street; the Mayfair side would be byocks and spadones.'

'You're an authority,' Skelton said.

'I like to keep up.'

* * *

They arrived at court.

Prosecution was led by Miles Colleton-Ward KC, thirty years older than Skelton and a dancer. Some barristers stood still as a rock to demonstrate their probity and resolution, others, like Skelton, were pacers, one hand on the lapel, walking up and down, stopping now and then to emphasise a point. Colleton-Ward executed pirouettes, made extravagant hand gestures, sometime rose *en pointe* or bent the knees in a *plié*. It kept him in excellent physical condition. The dancing reflected the devious circumvolutions of his arguments.

For the most part, all seemed to go well for Skelton and his case. He claimed that Winthrop, the lorry driver arrested for the theft of the ostrich feathers, was no more than a pawn in a greater game, an innocent dupe of some criminal mastermind. He'd been a lorry driver all his working life. There was not a stain on his character, and neither was there any indication that he had the resources or experience to plan and execute such an elaborate venture, which would have required a sophisticated understanding of the ostrich feather business and the ability to produce, or commission, technically proficient forgeries of requisitions, invoices and other documents. Though he might have had many attributes and abilities, he was most certainly not a criminal mastermind.

Colleton-Ward seemed to accept early on that he had lost his case. He was coasting, it seemed, making little attempt to prick holes in Skelton's arguments. Until, that is, Skelton called Lionel Hargreaves, a haulier who had employed Winthrop for several years and, as well as acting as a character witness, could provide expert testimony about the way the haulage business operates.

When Skelton had finished his questions, Colleton-Ward rose, his feet in first position, took three muted *pas ballonné en avant* and two *en arrière* and began a sequence of quite mundane questions about Hargreaves' acquaintanceship with Winthrop that seemed to lead nowhere. Neither Skelton nor Fenton, the judge, interrupted, but both looked puzzled.

Colleton-Ward asked Hargreaves whether he and Winthrop were interested in football. Hargreaves said that they had played together in a neighbourhood team, and when they had grown a little old for the rigours of the game, had organised a local league – or rather Winthrop had done most of the organisation.

'And what, exactly, did this involve?'

'He books the various pitches, arranges transport if it's needed and works out the fixtures required to establish each team's position in the league. He finds referees, and lately he's been involved in discussions with the local council and schools about the use of pitches in general and maintenance issues.'

'In fact,' Colleton-Ward said, with an *épaulement à droite* to bring his head around to face the jury, 'you could perhaps describe him as the "mastermind" behind the entire operation.'

'You could indeed, sir,' Hargreaves said.

'No more questions.'

The jury got the point. Two of them nodded.

They were a long time gone. Presumably one or two had realised that masterminding a football league was not the same as masterminding a sophisticated robbery, but they were outnumbered and eventually persuaded to defer to the majority view that poor Thomas Winthrop was guilty as charged. Mr Justice Fenton clearly saw the flaws in the verdict, but could not, given the nature of the offence, sentence him to less than six months.

Afterwards, Skelton agreed with Banham, the solicitor, that the sooner an appeal could be lodged, the better.

'Am I losing my touch, Edgar?' Skelton asked as they walked back to 8 Foxton Row.

'The occasional defeat brings added glory to the victories,' Edgar said.

'It was Colleton-Ward's offhand manner in the early part of the trial. Put me off my guard. I walked straight into a trap, didn't I? How are the feet?'

'Terrible.'

CHAPTER NINE

Rose Critchlow, twenty years old, lumpy ginger overcoat, long knitted scarf, stylish cloche hat, new patent shoes, had only been in London a week and already she knew more shortcuts than a taxi driver.

She was a solicitor's daughter from Birmingham. A year before, she had been doing her articles with her father's firm. Her assistance in building Skelton's defence of Mary Dutton, the so-called Collingford Poisoner, had been invaluable. Shortly after the conclusion of that case, her father had passed away. He'd been suffering heart trouble for some time. Edgar had written a condolence letter asking whether she had plans for continuing her career in the law and, if so, was there anything he could do to help. She had replied in her impeccable copperplate, saying that ever since she could remember her only goal in life had been to go into the law and asking which of the many Birmingham solicitors – Edgar, who had once worked in Birmingham, knew them all – she should approach with a view to continuing her articles. She had no money worries. Her father had left her well provided for, so, theoretically, the world was her oyster.

Edgar replied, suggesting that, if she was particularly interested in criminal law, she might be better off moving to London and would she like him to have a word with Aubrey Duncan? She had replied that she had considered a position at Aubrey Duncan's practice as more than she should ever hope for. And Edgar, who liked to think of himself as having wings as capacious as an albatross and was more than pleased to take her under one of them, moved into action.

He had had a word with Aubrey Duncan and with Mrs Westing, his landlady in Swiss Cottage. The next time Edgar wrote to Rose he was able to offer the possibility of her moving down to London to continue her articles with Duncan, the top criminal solicitor in the country; and Mrs Westing had said that she could have, at a slightly reduced rent, the good room at the back of the house that Miss Dundridge used to occupy before she fell ill and went to a nursing home in Streatham.

Rose gratefully accepted.

After a mournful Christmas spent with an aunt and uncle in Castle Bromwich, she had written detailed instructions to her late father's housekeeper and to the various solicitors and estate agents involved with her father's estate, packed a few essentials in a suitcase, caught the next train to London and presented herself at 8 Foxton Row at the start of the new year.

Edgar took her round to Aubrey Duncan's office in Hogg's Yard and introduced her. Duncan was impressed, not to say astonished, that Rose had already familiarised herself with the nature of his practice and had a detailed knowledge of his past cases.

Miss Summers, one of Duncan's secretaries, was appointed to show her round the office. She gave Rose the usual talking-to about punctuality, behaviour and modes of address, and suggested a couple of shops where Rose might be able to replace her tweed skirt, plaid stockings and brogues with clothes more suitable for a London solicitor's office.

At Bourne & Hollingsworth, she had looked at rows of frocks but had no idea what might be deemed 'suitable' and what 'unsuitable'. In the end she went for a two-piece 'costume' in an almost black navy blue and a cream imitation silk blouse with covered buttons and smocking. In other departments she bought a pair of low-heeled shoes to replace her brogues and a cloche hat to wear instead of her knitted thing. The overcoat, scarf and gloves she already had would do for now, as would the voluminous satchel in which she carried all the bits and bobs she deemed essential to everyday life.

She was back at 8 Foxton Row at six on the dot and accompanied Edgar to Swiss Cottage. There she delighted Mrs Westing by paying her eight weeks' rent in advance, complimenting her on the beauty and cleanliness of the room, and readily accepting second helpings of the fish pie when Edgar had left most of his on the side of his plate.

Edgar barely recognised her when she came down for breakfast the following morning in her new clothes.

'You look as if you're about to sit on a committee

concerned with sick animals or road safety,' he said. 'And I do intend that to be a compliment.'

Rose ate porridge, four sausages, eggs and enough toast to feed a stable of navvies.

She observed Edgar's eating habits closely, worried that her Birmingham table manners would not be up to London standards.

'Do a lot of London people put lemon in their tea?' she asked.

'No, just Lady Cunard, the Archbishop of Canterbury and myself,' Edgar said, and smiled either because he wanted Rose to know he had made a joke or because he had amused himself.

Rose tried to smile back, but dissembling was not really in her nature.

She had learnt that the quickest way of getting around London, central London anyway, was to walk. Blessed with superhuman orienteering skills, her party trick – she had never actually done it at a party and didn't get invited to many – was her ability, even in the pitch-dark, to know where north was without the aid of a compass. 'I can smell it,' she used to say. And she walked fast.

Miss Summers was at first mystified as to how Rose could hand-deliver a package to an address in, say, Bedford Square and be back at the office within the half hour, but was, all the same, delighted that, at last, she had a reliable messenger who didn't dawdle.

Sending Rose off with an envelope in her hand was also a useful way of getting her out of the office when her ingenious ideas for reorganising the stationery cupboard grew wearisome. Nobody could doubt that Rose was good at her job, that she was likeable, kind, thoughtful, generous and all the rest of it, but the hundredth time somebody jots down a telephone message in handwriting that's better than the Book of Kells or uses a date stamp in such a way that every corner of the image is as crisp as the middle, it's human nature to want to smack the top of their head with the edge of a twelve-inch ruler.

When the remains of the suitcase corpse had arrived at Bart's Hospital from Wakefield, much of the paperwork was missing. The clerks at Aubrey Duncan's had been chasing it up, and at last it had arrived. Rose was asked to take it round to the hospital.

She knew an alleyway off St Bride Street that didn't appear to have a name but took her on a straight route across Farringdon, up Fleet Lane to Old Bailey and on to Giltspur Street.

Inside the entrance to the pathology department there was a window, like the ticket window at a cinema. It was unmanned. Rose looked for a bell or some such to summon attention but couldn't find anything, so she tapped on the window, waited, then tapped again.

Going through the big double doors and into the corridor beyond seemed impertinent, and besides, who knew what horrors might lurk. There would be dead people in there. She had never seen a dead person. At her father's funeral, only once did the image of him lying inside the coffin come into her head. She banished it by practising her mental exercises – she was a keen student of Pelmanism – reciting to herself, in order, working left to right and upwards, the counties of England and Wales with their county towns. Then she started on the Kings and Queens of England.

When she was fourteen, a girl at her school had died of scarlet fever and she was among the five classmates chosen to attend the funeral. The girl was a Methodist. At the service, they had sung a hymn that went,

Ah, lovely appearance of death,
What sight upon earth is so fair?
Not all the gay pageants that breathe,
Can with a dead body compare.

Rose did not believe that a dead body could possibly be more lovely than a gay pageant, but she didn't say anything at the time because she was tolerant of other religious creeds, even though she herself was an agnostic. The 'what sight upon earth is so fair?' line struck her as particularly odd. Did Methodists really look at a dead cat floating in the canal and think, 'There's a lovely thing. I'd rather look at that than a living kitten playing with a ball of wool any day'?

She knocked a third time and called out, 'Hello!'

At a loss to know what to do next, she sat on a bench to one side of the double doors and waited. After five minutes or so a young man emerged, went over to the window of the ticket kiosk and called, 'Chas!'

When there was no reply he turned to Rose and asked, 'Is Chas not here?'

'I haven't seen anybody,' Rose said. 'I've been here ten or fifteen minutes.'

The young man looked at his wristwatch. He had bony wrists.

'Usually when he goes for his lunch, Mr Renwick stands in for him.'

'I just wanted to leave this envelope.'

'Who's it for?'

'Professor Fawcett.'

'Oh, I can take that for you.'

'I was asked to deliver it personally.'

'Of course. I think he should be in his office. I'll show you.'

He held one of the double doors open for her.

'Are you from Clover's?' he asked.

'No, I'm from Aubrey Duncan's.'

'The solicitors?'

Rose nodded.

The young man was perhaps a couple of years older than Rose and shabby, but in a neat way, which is to say that his tweed suit was darned and his soft-collared shirt faded, yet everything was nicely pressed. His shoes were polished too, although his hair, which was a chestnut colour and fell in big floppy curls, needed cutting. His glasses, horn-rimmed, were too small for his face, as if he'd had them since he was a child. *An impecunious student*, Rose thought. *Making the most of what little he has.*

'I'm doing my articles,' she said. 'Not long moved down here so I'm the lowest of the low.'

'Is that a Rangers badge?' he asked.

Rose had her little promise pin on the lapel of her overcoat. 'Yes, it is.'

He showed her the tiny brass fleur-de-lys he wore on his own lapel.

'1st Wolvertons. It's actually one of the earliest troops to have been formed. BP inspected us in 1917.'

'You've met Baden-Powell?'

'Shook hands with him. He presented me with my Tenderfoot Badge. I'm Vernon, by the way.'

He extended his left hand, the hand used by Scouts and Guides for a handshake. Rose took it, smiling.

'Rose. Rose Critchlow.'

'Vernon Goodyear.'

'Wolverton?'

'Yes. It's between Buckingham and—'

'Bedford,' Rose said. She did not need to be told. 'No, I mean, is that where you're from?'

'Born and brought up.'

'I'm from Birmingham.'

'I've been there,' Vernon said. 'A place called Yorks Wood.'

'That's just near where I live – used to live – in Yardley.'

Yorks Wood was a camping ground owned by the Birmingham Boy Scouts Association.

'Did you make dens in the bracken?' Vernon asked.

'Everybody makes dens in the bracken.'

'And play the tracking game with the bits of wool in the trees.'

'But so many people had done it before there was wool in practically every tree,' Rose said, 'and no way of knowing which was yours and which was some troop that had been there the week before.'

'Complete chaos.'

They laughed.

Vernon's teeth were very even.

'So, do you work here?' Rose asked.

'I'm a postgrad at Imperial doing forensic entomology,' Vernon said.

'I don't know what that means.'

'Forensic entomology is the study of insects in relation to crime.'

'I still don't think—'

'Hold on, Professor Fawcett should be in here.'

Vernon knocked at a door. There was no reply. He knocked again and called out, 'Professor?' Still no reply.

'He's probably in B29,' Vernon said. 'Come on, I'll show you.'

They walked a little way down the corridor and Vernon held open another door.

Rose entered and was confronted by the corpse of an elderly woman, mostly covered by a sheet, with just the face and feet showing. Part of her neck was cut away and the flesh held back with clamps.

'Oh God, I'm so sorry,' Vernon said. 'I had no idea she'd be out.'

'Don't worry,' Rose said. 'A bit of a shock, but it's all right.'

And it was all right. Rose did not faint. She did not blench. She did not even look away. She stood her ground.

This is what her dad would have looked like in his coffin. A different sex, obviously, and without the things on the neck, but dead just like that. And she was right about the Methodist hymn. Death did not have a 'lovely appearance' but neither was it anywhere near as horrific as she had imagined, perhaps because the corpse bore so little resemblance to a human being. It had, of course, all the features – the nostrils, ears and eyelids – but she was surprised how much of a person is made up simply of life. A less scientific person might have thought in terms of 'soul', 'spirit' or 'aura'. Rose preferred skin colour, breathing and the almost imperceptible but nonetheless constant movements of facial muscles in a living person.

'Have you seen . . . er . . . ?' Vernon asked.

'No, this is my first.'

'I'm impressed. A lot of medical students decide to become accountants after their first visit to the mortuary.'

Rose smiled but did not take her eyes off the woman's face. She was having an 'experience' and must drink it to the dregs.

Vernon came and stood beside her.

'She's quite famous, actually. Matricide. Her son's been arrested for strangling her. You've probably read about it in the papers. I think it's the first matricide we've had in about five years.'

Rose couldn't recognise Vernon's accent as anything specific. Certainly he wasn't posh like Aubrey Duncan. She imagined him living in a house with a bay window and a bit of front garden. School with a uniform. Helping his mum fold wet sheets to go through the mangle. Dad in his shirtsleeves training sweet peas up canes. He would have been the first person in his street, in the whole town possibly, to win a scholarship to a university.

He was inspecting the dissection of the throat.

'Remarkable work Professor Fawcett does, isn't it?' he said. 'Looks just like a diagram in a textbook.'

'Does this prove the strangulation?'

'It more likely disproves it. There was a fire in her bedroom. The son saved her from the fire, but she was dead. The local doctor reckoned she died from smoke inhalation, but then the police surgeon saw bruises round her throat which he thought might tell another story. So, the son was arrested – he'd taken out some big insurance policies or something. They say he strangled his mother for money, then set the fire himself. Spilsbury was called in. He's the—'

'The Home Office pathologist,' Rose knew these things.

'Spilsbury agreed with the police surgeon. But Professor Fawcett says the hyoid bone's intact and so's the cricoid cartilage.'

Rose looked closely. 'Which ones are those?'

'I don't know. Not my field. But Professor Fawcett says it means it's less likely she was strangled. And there were traces of soot in her trachea which meant she was still breathing after the fire broke out. So how could he have strangled her, then lit the fire? And anyway, nobody can work out how the fire started. Could have been clothes left to dry in front of a gas fire, or could have been something wrong with the electricity, or could have been spontaneous combustion in some rags that had been left in a bucket.'

Rose felt like a ballet student who had somehow found her way backstage at the Paris Opera, or a trainspotter invited into the signal box at Crewe. It was the casual tone of Vernon's voice when he said 'it means she can't have been strangled' that thrilled her most. Professor Fawcett's dissection could save a man from the gallows and yet, to Vernon, it was an everyday occurrence. Almost humdrum.

Vernon opened a thick, heavy cupboard door. Inside, Rose caught a glimpse of offal. He took out a tin box. It had frost on it. She realised that the cupboard was in fact a refrigerator.

He struggled a bit to get the top off the box and Rose braced herself to be resolute in the face of whatever it contained.

Sandwiches and an apple.

'My stuff is through here,' Vernon said, and opened a door into a side room, about the size of her own at Mrs Westing's house. There was a desk and a couple of shelves of books, but most of the space was filled with jars and tanks that appeared to contain nothing but old leaves and dirt. She looked more closely and saw maggots, beetles, spiders and flies.

She despised girls who shrieked when they saw a spider in the tent and had trained herself to accept the presence of even the hairiest moth with fearless equanimity. She had held a jam sandwich steady while two wasps explored its contents and removed a slug from a plate of bacon with her bare hands.

She looked up and smiled at Vernon to show him that if he was the sort of boy who liked to frighten girls by putting spiders down their necks, he'd picked the wrong girl.

He offered her his sandwich box.

'Do you want one? My landlady always does far more than I can manage. Egg and cress today. Ham, cheese and pickle, egg and cress. Three-day cycle. Always with an apple.'

Rose was hungry. She looked in the box. There was a lot.

'If you're sure you can spare it.'

The sandwich was very cold, and she had to remind herself that it had been in the tin all this time so could not have touched or been otherwise tainted by the offal in the refrigerator. Human offal. It tasted all right.

'So, I know entomology is the study of insects,' she said.

'Right. Forensic entomology. I give a lecture every year to first-year students telling them about it, so I've got the lecture notes off pat. Any human remains, from a bloodstain to a complete cadaver, is a source of food for thousands of different life forms, from microscopic bacteria to carnivorous birds and mammals. Determining which of these have visited or taken residence in the corpse, whether they've laid eggs, whether the eggs have hatched and so on, enables you to read the history of that corpse like a book. Different stages of putrefaction attract different flora and fauna, all of which will develop at different rates according to temperature, humidity and other factors. A close study of these enables you to pinpoint not just the time of death, but where the corpse has been since – in a house, a field, a forest, in Somerset, China, Brazil.'

Vernon went on in this vein, explaining technical points about the chemistry of putrefaction and the life cycles of various species of fly for another ten minutes or so. Rose did not interrupt. She had come to London to learn everything she could about her chosen profession from the best teachers available. Half an hour earlier she had never heard of forensic entomology. Now she was being told all about it by a man who lectured on the subject at Imperial College, University of London.

'These over here are interesting,' Vernon said, and took her to three tanks in the corner. 'Samples from the Wakefield suitcase body. You know the Edna Aziz case?'

'That's one of Mr Duncan's cases. The one I brought the papers about for Professor Fawcett,' Rose said. 'Mr Skelton's been instructed.'

'Skelton? Have you met him?'

'When I was in Birmingham, my father was the solicitor on the Collingford Poisoner case, except Dad was ill so I had to, sort of, take over.'

Vernon's eyes widened. And there was he, thinking he was talking to a promising office junior.

'I'd like very much to meet Mr Skelton,' he said.

'I'm sure it could be arranged. He's ever so approachable. Mr Skelton's clerk, Mr Hobbes, helped me get set up in London with Mr Duncan when . . . my father passed away.'

'Oh, I'm so sorry.'

'So, what have you learnt about the suitcase murder?'

'She was in a greenhouse. Probably after she was dead.'

'What?'

With tweezers he picked up a fragment of leaf and gave her a magnifying glass. Rose took it and saw tiny white insects.

'First larval stage of *trialeurodes vaporariorum*, the greenhouse whitefly. Life cycle got all messed up by coming out of the greenhouse and into the cold. Does Dr Aziz have a greenhouse in his garden?'

'I don't know. This definitely proves that she's been in one, does it?'

'Could have been on a plant in a house. Have to be somewhere warm, though.'

'That's extraordinary.'

'I'll freeze them for evidence.' He pointed at a group of tiny maggots, sucked one into a tiny pipette and held it up to the light. 'I'm keen to have a proper look at these chaps, too. Feeding them is always a problem. Flesh from the original corpse is obviously ideal, but there are ethical considerations.'

They heard a noise next door.

'That'll be Professor Fawcett back.'

Fawcett was a bald, colourless man with almost no eyebrows.

'Has Vernon been showing you his creepy-crawlies?' he asked, when Rose gave him the envelope. 'I can't go in there myself. Gives me the willies.'

He laughed.

Outside, in the courtyard, above an imposing-looking door that led to who knows where, Rose saw an inscription: 'Whatsoever thy hand findeth to do, do it with thy might'. It could, Rose thought, have been written for her, just as much as Agnes Baden-Powell's 'Be prepared and always in a state of readiness in mind and body to do your duty'.

She hoped she wouldn't get in trouble for taking so long over what should have been a straightforward delivery. Back on Giltspur Street she broke into a run. She'd never done this in low heels before and almost tripped. After a couple of paces, she got the hang of it, then began to enjoy the way it pushed your weight forwards. It made her giddy. She kept running all the way back to the office. She was inexhaustible. She had seen a dead person. She had eaten an egg sandwich taken from a refrigerator filled with human offal. She was capable of anything.

CHAPTER TEN

c/o The Cross Keys Public House, Fetterick

Monday 6th January, 1930

My dear cousin Arthur,

I trust you received our Christmas greetings. We got yours together with your generous donation to the mission, for which many thanks indeed. Thank you also for your reassuring words about our legal position vis à vis the Carlisle raffle debacle, which brought great comfort to our worried minds. Just as you predicted, we have received no visits or other communications from the police or any other authorities and, the best news of all, at the end of last week, we had a letter from Iris Whittington, who told us that she has now returned to Carlisle and has had people coming up to her in the street and telling her that the complaints about the fateful evening came only from a small group of troublemakers. Most of those present were sympathetic to her difficulties and have since made donations to the children's hospital charity. So, all is well that ends well.

I am pleased to hear that you had such an enjoyable Christmas, despite the indisposition of Dorothy and Mrs Bartram. I trust that they are all back on their feet again now. Please give our best regards to Mila and the children.

Mum and Dad had, as usual, pulled out all the stops at Christmas. They had a huge tree, endless visits from neighbours, friends and relatives, lots of singing and laughing, too much eating, and Norah, not realising a drink called Dubonnet was alcoholic, got a little bit tiddly, but neither did nor came to any harm.

It was a time when any doubts that we have about the importance of our mission were dispelled. Joy brings us closer to each other and closer to God. That is all there is to it.

We set off for Scotland last Thursday and did the trip in two days, taking a bit of a detour to avoid some of the more difficult hills. The Morris has a powerful engine and, I am sure, unfettered it could practically drive up a vertical cliff, but, with the Eccles behind it, it is touch and go. We have never failed yet, but we always take care to stop for a while at the end of a climb to let the poor old engine calm down and cool down.

It was dark and very cold by the time we arrived in Fort Blaine, with a thick frost already laying, so we just pulled onto a grass verge outside of the town for the night, planning to look for a more permanent site in the morning.

We had no sooner brewed a cup of tea than two policemen came along on their bicycles and told us we could not stay there. This is the first time in ten years that this has ever happened to us – Norah tells me I am wrong about that and that a similar thing happened once outside Cheltenham Spa, but I am fairly sure the circumstances on that occasion were a good bit more complicated. Of course, I agreed to their request but wondered, just in case we might need the information on another occasion, whether there was a particular reason we would not be allowed to stay there.

The older of the two policemen took offence at having, as he understood it, his authority questioned and told us to move on or risk spending the night in the cells. The younger of the two, however, explained that there were local ordinances forbidding tinkers and travellers from the town and a local resident had registered a complaint. This surprised me because there was no house or cottage visible, nor light from a window, nor even the smell of smoke from a fire. He – as I say – was a kindly soul, and he mentioned that a few miles or so further down the road we would find a village called Fetterick, which we might find more welcoming. So, we thanked him, packed up and moved on.

In Fetterick, the first thing we saw was a pub called

the Cross Keys, blazing with light. There was patch of grass next to it, so we parked.

The pub seemed quite a jolly place. Only twelve or fifteen people in there, but it had reached the time – it was about half past nine – when the singing usually starts.

They sing different songs in Scotland. Some of them are the Will Fyffe and Harry Lauder songs that are known all over – 'I Belong to Glasgow', 'A Wee Deoch an Doris' and 'Roamin' in the Gloamin''. But others were completely new to Norah and I, and incomprehensible too, which, from the sly smiles and salacious glances exchanged by the singers, was probably for the best. Norah and I listened for a while, then popped back to the Eccles for the banjo and accordion, both of which, when we returned, were greeted with a welcome cheer. As you know, Norah has a remarkable ear for music and can provide at least a rudimentary accompaniment for any tune after one hearing. They sang some more of their Scottish songs, and we sang some of our English and Welsh songs, too, and discovered that they are as well known here as they are in Norwich or Cardiff. By eleven o'clock, we had moved on to 'What a Friend We Have in Jesus' and 'The Old Rugged Cross'. The vigour and sentiment with which they put over these songs was, despite being somewhat exaggerated by the drink, nonetheless sincere.

During the course of the evening, I managed to have a word with the landlord of the pub, Mr Chalmers, who told us that the patch of green where we had parked the Eccles and the Morris belonged to him. He said we were welcome to stay there and to use the outside facilities of the pub, as long as they were not frozen.

When I told him about our experience with the police in Fort Blaine, he told us that we would be all right about that sort of thing in Fetterick because, unless the circumstances were exceptional, there were no police.

On the Saturday morning, we asked Mr Chalmers whether he knew of any friendly ministers who might be amenable to our preaching in their chapel or perhaps an attached hall. The phrase 'friendly ministers' puzzled him. He said he had encountered vicars on his infrequent visits to England who smiled and made jokes, but could not see such a thing catching on over his side of the border. In Scotland, he said, life is seen as a dreary waiting room for hell and ministers are there to stop you enjoying the wallpaper.

He said our best bet would be the Reverend Balfour, the minister at the Baptist chapel. He had the advantage of being old and ill, which meant it took him longer than most to build a head of self-righteous steam and, even then, there was no real edge to his venom.

I mentioned Edna Aziz, guessing that her death must have had a profound effect on the people of Fort Blaine. For a moment he did not seem to know what I was talking about. Then he said, 'Oh, the suitcase woman,' and I realised that my notion of a community in mourning might have been misplaced.

'Yes,' he said, 'she was from round here. Her dad died a couple of years ago.'

The dad, he told us, was Alistair Goldie, boss of A. W. Goldie's – you may have heard of them. They make floor coverings, I believe, linoleum and that sort of thing. We don't have much need for it in the Eccles. They lived at a place called Aldwin House, about halfway between Fetterick and Fort Blaine. After the dad's death, Mrs Aziz sold the house to a Mr Dugdale, a printer and publisher. This is another name you might know. Does your Lawrence use *Dugdale's English Grammar* at school, or *Dugdale's British History*, or *Dugdale's Latin Primer*? That is him, or rather it is the publishing firm he inherited from his father. Reverend Balfour said he had never met Mr Dugdale but had heard that he is a somewhat colourful gentlemen who, though he makes his money from these solid schoolboy texts, writes – and publishes – poetry.

I needed to go into Fort Blaine anyway, to get a new cap. I left my old one behind when we fled from Carlisle. I have brimmed hats, but feel more at home in a cap.

We saw Aldwin House just off the road into Fort Blaine and decided it was as good a place as anywhere to start our door-knocking.

It is a grand house in what I think is called the classical style. As we came up the drive, we could see something of the grounds, too: a large kitchen garden, with outbuildings, what was possibly a small orchard, then a great expanse of lawn sloping down to a lake with woodland beyond. None of it was being properly looked after. Houses and gardens are never their best at this time of year, but a lick of paint here and there never did anyone any harm. And the windows were so filthy I was tempted to get a ladder and bucket and have a go at them myself.

We rang. The door was answered by Mr Dugdale himself. He is an artistic-looking Englishman with dark red hair and horn-rimmed glasses, dressed in hairy tweed trousers, a Fair Isle jumper and dark green shirt. We introduced ourselves and outlined the nature of our mission. He seemed amused by the phrase 'the joy of Jesus' and asked if we were Panbabylonianists – I think that is what he said, anyway. This was not a term I was familiar with, so, there, on the doorstep, he delivered a lecture on the subject, spoke of the role of Enkidu the trickster god in the Mesopotamian Epic of Gilgamesh, then moved on to Rabelais and Pantagruelism. We listened in silence.

A freezing drizzle began to fall, so Mr Dugdale, happy to have found such apparently attentive listeners, invited us in.

We were ushered into a large hallway where a gaunt young woman dressed in mauve velvet took our coats and hats. Mr Dugdale introduced her as Sophronia, without making it clear whether she was his daughter, wife or maid. We gave her a hearty hello. She gave us a withering glance. Mr Dugdale led the way into his study.

One glance was enough to get the measure of the man. The bookcases were filled with great tomes

110

bound in leather and vellum, many of them with titles in Latin or German. Below them, I saw more modern works. I did not have a chance to read the titles but the mystic symbols and pentagrams on the spines were enough to tell me they were by the likes of Aleister Crowley, A. E. Waite and their cohorts. Above the fireplace was a painting of a naked woman with the head of a bird eating another naked woman.

Mr Dugdale is an occultist or something very like it.

Norah and I have a great deal of time for all faiths and creeds, even esoteric religions, but we do draw the line at devil worship and table rapping. Mr Dugdale belongs to the breed who claim an understanding of the world that goes beyond everyday learning. They live with superior smiles on their faces because they are convinced that they know something that you do not know, when all they actually know is some ancient and long-discredited mumbo-jumbo. They are dangerous because they attract gullible followers and, with their own madness, can drive the followers into a madness that is darker still.

Mr Dugdale spoke of the Aeon of Horus and Hermes Trismegistus. After ten minutes, another woman, this one looking like Tennyson's Lady of Shallot 'All raimented in snowy white', brought tea. Mr Dugdale paused his monologue just long enough to introduce her as Ottoline. She gave us a half-smile and slipped out of the room.

Surprisingly, the tea looked and smelt like ordinary tea and came with milk and sugar. You always have to watch out in these circumstances for tea made of camomile or linden flowers into which any number of drugs and poisons can be slipped.

He talked some more, referring to 'that old fraud Darwin', 'that idiot Hegel' and 'Freud and Einstein, the Austrian Laurel and Hardy', then moved on to a diatribe about the nature of knowledge and faith, and how, ultimately, nobody could *know* anything.

Norah interrupted. 'Alan does,' she said.

'What do you mean?' Mr Dugdale asked.

'Alan knows things.'

'In what way?'

'He knows what the angels say to him.'

I do not like people talking about the angels, because it does often lead them to assume I am touched in the head and have delusions. But I know that they are real. Mr Dugdale did not scoff or laugh, but seemed intensely interested. I answered his questions as best I could.

His telephone rang, and after a brief conversation he said that urgent business called him reluctantly away, but he hoped very much to see us again.

'Why don't you come along to one of my regular Wednesday meetings? It's essentially a discussion group for men and women with an interest in esoteric matters. I'm sure they'd be fascinated to hear more about your angels. How much do you know about involution?'

Luckily, I did not get a chance to answer this question because Sophronia arrived with our coats and hats.

Norah and I were on the road again before either of

us spoke. Then she said, 'Who d'you think those young women were?' And I said, 'It does not bear thinking about.'

We got the cap. Scotch tweed. No end of wear I'll get out of that. The man in the shop had a very loud voice. He saw 'The Joy of Jesus Mission' written on the side of the Morris parked outside and struck up a conversation about the Bible. He was particularly interested in the plagues of Egypt and, more particularly still, the plague of frogs. I have never met a man who knew more about frogs than he did. An absolute mine of information, the imparting of which took most of the afternoon.

This morning we sought out the Baptist chapel that Mr Chalmers had spoken of and found it in a dreadful place called Abbotsbank. The village of Fetterick seems to have two distinct ends. There is Luggateside, where the houses are, for the most part, cottagey or decent-looking terraces; and there is Abbotsbank. Most of the houses there look unoccupied and some derelict. A rank-smelling stream runs in a ditch at the side of the street, the kind that Mum would call a 'fever beck' because you could catch terrible diseases just from standing by it. We saw no sign at all of anybody living there. Nobody on the street, no children playing, but this perhaps was not so surprising seeing as how cold it was. The wind would have had your ears off if you had not had the sense to keep them covered.

The chapel, when we found it, could barely be called a building at all. Sheets of corrugated iron seem to have been leant against each other, much like a house of cards, with more corrugated iron laid on the top for a roof.

Reverend Balfour lives nearby in a house a bit bigger but no more handsome than those of his neighbours. We knocked on the door and it was answered by a woman with tiny eyes like little black dots either side of her nose and a squeaky voice. We introduced ourselves and learnt that she is May Balfour, the minister's sister, who keeps house for him. The Reverend Balfour himself, she told us, was too sick to receive visitors. We asked about using the chapel for our meetings. She said that, owing to the minister's poor health, the chapel had not been used for several months, and she was sure that her brother would be only too pleased to see it open once again for worship, providing we could assure her that we were not Roman Catholic. Any other religion, it seemed, Methodist, Russian Orthodox, Muslim or Hindoo, would have been acceptable, but not Popery. We promised there would be no incense, statues, saints or sacerdotalism, and she gave us the keys.

It was dark by this time, but we decided to have a look inside the chapel anyway. The door was stiff and had grown an accretion of frozen mud at its base, which had to be kicked away as it opened.

An oil lamp had been put ready on the table by the side of the door. We got it lit and held it up to see what we had.

It was an ice palace, with crystalline walls and icicles hanging from the ceiling, glistening in the light of the lamp, quite beautiful in a forbidding way. Some of the icicles were eighteen inches or two feet long and perhaps three inches wide at the base, coming to a lethal-looking point. We stood there for a while entranced, holding the lamp this way and that. It was like standing in a cave filled with diamonds.

Then more practical matters came to bear. There was a moment of despair when we wondered whether the place had been left so long empty that it could never be restored to a usable condition. There were two decent-sized stoves in there, one either side of the room. We have resolved to go back there first thing tomorrow morning, find some coal, get them going and see if we can thaw the place out.

If I have not said it before – and even if I have there will be no harm in repeating it – may I wish you a blessed and joyous New Year.

I am ever yours faithfully in the joy of Jesus,
Alan

CHAPTER ELEVEN

Charlie 'Bottomless' Pitt had forged a career in crime that was lucrative without being artful. By the time he was twenty-five he'd seen the inside of five different prisons and was on first-name terms with all the coppers in H Division.

Skelton had defended him on three occasions, twice successfully. Then in 1925, Bottomless did over a jeweller's shop in Ponders End. The prosecution case was unassailable and Summerson, the merciless judge, sentenced him to 'five and a bashing' – five years and eighteen strokes of the cat. In prison, the TB that had bothered him in childhood returned and saw him off, leaving a wife, Phyllis, and a fourteen-year-old son, Clifford.

Phyllis was formidable. She reminded Skelton of Miss Halford, a teacher at St Saviour's Elementary School in Leeds who, with a single glance from her left eye, could make tough boys wet themselves. Phyllis used both eyes in an expression combining rage, contempt and remorseless determination that drilled to the core of your being. Her voice boomed, like a roadhouse barmaid's at closing time on a wet Saturday night.

Early on in her marriage to Bottomless, she had become something of an expert in salting away the proceeds of his escapades out of sight and out of reach of the judiciary, with the result that she now enjoyed a comfortable life. She ran a bric-a-brac and second-hand jewellery shop and owned a sizeable house in Chingford, where she was a well-respected member of the community.

Neither Skelton, Edgar, nor indeed Aubrey Duncan, quite understood the power that Phyllis exerted over them. Guilt was something to do with it – for failing to secure an acquittal on the Ponders End job – but mostly it was plain animal fear. Clifford, the son, played some part in it too. He was a smart, likeable lad. You had to admire him if only for his ability to stay cheerful with a mother like that. All three took an avuncular interest.

Phyllis's visits to 8 Foxton Row were thankfully rare and always left everybody in the building, from Mr Clarendon-Gow, head of chambers, down to the lowliest office boy, feeling shaky.

'Where did you get these chairs?' she asked.

The chairs and the low table were Skelton's only personal additions to his room. The desk, bookcases, cupboards and all the other furniture had probably been there for the past hundred years. His aversion to conducting meetings from behind a desk had prompted the new acquisitions.

'I can't remember,' he said. 'Can you remember, Edgar?'

'Might have been Heal's.'

'How much did you pay at Heal's?' Phyllis asked.

Edgar knew exactly how much he'd paid at Heal's but suspected it was a trick question. Whatever he said, Phyllis would try to humiliate him by suggesting the sum was either pathetically small or reprehensibly large.

'I really can't remember,' he said.

'Because you could have got better quality at half the price in Whiteleys. This upholstery won't last, you know.'

'Won't it?'

'Not a chance. You can feel, there's no weight to it at all. I'm not sure this arm's walnut either. Dressed-up deal.'

Phyllis shuffled her weight in the chair. Her stately physical presence was a triumph of modern corsetry. Many whales had given their lives to make her the woman she was, but the creaking, each time she moved a muscle, could be deafening.

'Anyway. On to the matter in hand,' she said. 'Clifford's in trouble.'

'I hope it's nothing too serious,' Skelton said.

'He's in Durham.' The word 'Durham' carried a note of accusation. It was, after all, Skelton's fault that Clifford had gone there at all.

The lad had done well at school, got a distinction in his School Cert, stayed on for his Highers and had shown great promise as a historian. When he failed the entrance exams for Oxford or Cambridge, Skelton had pointed out that those two institutions were not the only universities in the country and had helped him with his application to read Mediaeval History at Durham.

'I didn't realise term had already started,' Skelton said.

'It hasn't,' Phyllis said. 'He said he wanted to go back early to get ahead with his work. I should never have believed him. Is that silver?'

Phyllis was pointing to the inkstand on Skelton's desk.

'I'm not sure,' Skelton said.

'Plated, I think,' Edgar said.

'I thought it might be. Plated gives a bad impression. There's no point having silver unless it's sterling. I've got a beautiful Georgian inkstand in the shop. I could do you a very good price.'

'I'll bear that in mind,' Skelton said.

'You're a fool then. Be gone tomorrow. Thing like that gets snapped up in no time.'

'What kind of trouble is Clifford in?'

'He's bought himself a motorcycle.'

'Oh dear.'

'Been running with a gang.'

'In Durham?'

'Late at night they rode their motorcycles across the turf of Durham City Cricket Club, then set up bottles on a fence and shot at them with an air pistol.'

'Is he in custody?'

'His case comes up on Monday.'

'I'm sure it'll be no more than a small fine and a telling-off,' Skelton said. 'He'll learn his lesson and mend his ways.'

Phyllis leant forward with the sound of a galleon changing tack. 'I only wish I shared your optimism, Mr Skelton,' she said. 'My son is in a police cell. Can I remind you that my husband died in a prison cell? I don't want the same thing to happen to Clifford.'

'There's very little possibility of a charge of vandalism leading to a prison sentence.'

'Very little possibility is a long way from being sure, though, isn't it? These matters need to be attended to properly and personally. If you were to go to Durham—'

'I'm afraid there's—'

'Would you please have the courtesy not to interrupt, Mr Skelton.'

Skelton gestured an apology and she continued. 'I promised Charlie before he died that Clifford would have the best. The best of everything. And that means the best suits, best education and, when the need arises, best brief money can buy.'

'While it's not unknown for a barrister to attend Petty Sessions,' Skelton said, 'there is in fact very little point to it. I should also mention that, I do have many engagements on Monday—'

'Such as?'

Skelton hadn't thought it through this far and had to improvise. 'There's the . . . Edgar, what are the important things I have to do on Monday?'

'I'm afraid Mr Skelton is extremely busy at the moment,' Edgar said, playing for time while he tried to invent some immutable commitments. 'He's busy all day Monday, all day Tuesday . . . and Wednesday . . .'

He petered out. Phyllis was glaring at him with rage, contempt and remorseless determination.

Immediately Edgar crumbled and found himself saying, 'But I'm sure there's nothing we can't postpone or cancel.'

Skelton gave him the look that Caesar gave Brutus when the knife went in. Edgar came back with an apologetic shrug.

'Good,' Phyllis said. 'That's settled then. Probably best for you to go up to Durham on Sunday to be sure of being there first thing Monday morning, but I can leave all that to you.'

She finished her tea and pulled a face.

'Cheap tea turns to acid when it gets cold, don't you find? Now, there was something else . . .'

Skelton and Edgar held their breath. 'Something else' was ominous. The chances of her saying, 'I'd like you to live with bears in the forests of Siberia,' were strong, and they knew they would be powerless to refuse.

'That's it,' she said. 'I'm chairman of the Women's Charity League. Just in Chingford. And next week we've got the national committee coming to visit from all over the country and we were supposed to have Julia Chatterton in to give us a talk. Do you know her?'

'I'm afraid—'

'Me neither. She collects folk songs.'

'Does she?'

'And she was supposed to be giving a talk about a collecting trip she'd been on in Albania. But she's come down with something. So, I thought you could do it instead.'

'I'm afraid I've never been to Albania and I know nothing of folk songs,' Skelton said.

'You can talk about your famous cases.'

'Mr Skelton is very busy on Thursday,' Edgar said.

'No, he isn't. You distinctly said he was busy Monday, Tuesday and Wednesday.'

'Zuh . . .' Edgar said, hoping the sound might develop into a word and the word into a sentence.

Skelton stepped in. 'I'm not really very good at public speaking.'

'So what d'you call all the nattering you do in the courtroom, then?'

'That is a different sort of—'

'Mrs Chatterton was going to bring lantern slides. I don't suppose you've got any lantern slides, have you?'

'The thing is—'

'I expect we can manage without. Just talk for an hour. Not just murders. Chuck a couple of divorces in. Have you done much with film stars?'

'I don't think—'

'You did the bloke off the wireless. I saw that in the paper. He'll do. Just keep it peppy, eh? And nothing about Charlie. That's important. I'm a respectable member of the community, and what Charlie did and didn't do is none of their business. I don't want them knowing he ever went to prison. And Clifford, neither. Oh, and Clifford likes Palethorpes Pork Pies. Don't think you can get them in Durham, so make sure you take two or three up with you. Artillery Hall, Chingford, Thursday, quarter to seven. Don't be late.'

She creaked away.

'Hear that?' Edgar said, when she'd gone.

'What?'

'The quiet.'

It was true. Usually 8 Foxton Row was clamorous with the bray of barristers, the joshing of lads and the rattle of teacups. But when word got round that Phyllis Pitt was in the building, a frightened silence fell. It was rumoured that Clarendon-Gow hid under his desk until he was sure she'd gone.

There was a knock on the door, and Daniel, one of the lads, showed Rose in.

'I was hiding in Temperley,' she said. Temperley was the waiting room, off the lobby.

'You've encountered Mrs Pitt already?' Skelton asked.

'No, but Mr Duncan's warned me about her. He said I should come round and give you this.' She handed him a slim file.

'What is it?'

'It's a preliminary report from Vernon Goodyear on his entomological findings on the remains of Edna Aziz.'

Skelton, puzzled, took the file. 'Take off your coat,' he said. 'Sit down.'

Rose was aware that Skelton had not seen her in her new clothes and felt a little self-conscious. She didn't want him to think she was suddenly putting on airs.

'Miss Summers said I had to get new things for the office.'

'Of course. Very correct. Good quality wool, too.' Skelton liked to think that coming from Leeds gave him a right to be an appraiser of woollen fabrics.

'Bourne & Hollingsworth,' she said. 'Four guineas.'

'I told her she'd have paid six at Fenwick,' Edgar said.

Skelton opened the file and began to read.

'Do you know Mr Goodyear?' Rose asked.

'I can't say as I do,' Skelton said.

'He's a postgraduate student at Imperial College doing research in the field of forensic entomology.'

She gave them a potted version of Vernon's discoveries and told them about the strange coincidence that she was a Ranger guide and Vernon had been a Boy Scout in Wolverton, and how Vernon had once camped in Yorks Wood and so had she. She told them about the importance of forensic entomology and how it could completely revolutionise police investigations.

Skelton had reamed, filled and lit his pipe, and Edgar had finished a Gold Flake and was thinking of lighting another before Rose got to the point. 'And he thinks that at some point she was in a greenhouse or perhaps a warm house with potted plants in it.'

'This is because he found these tiny bugs?' Skelton asked. Vernon had including little drawings in his report. They were very nicely done, with cross hatching.

'So, Mr Duncan telephoned Dr Aziz's receptionist, Miss Devereux,' Rose said, 'and she told him that the doctor doesn't have a greenhouse, and neither are there any potted plants in the house. So that means he can't just have killed her in the house, cut her up and dumped the suitcase in the quarry. Either he took her somewhere else first or he didn't do it.'

Skelton exchanged a glance with Edgar. Could a defence be built on such a thing? On one side of the balance was the bloodstained rug, late-night screams and ample opportunity. On the other, the almost invisible larvae of the greenhouse whitefly discovered by a student entomologist.

'It's an excellent start,' Skelton said, nodding.

Edgar nodded, too. 'If you see him again, please give him our thanks and congratulations.'

Rose blushed. 'I will certainly do that,' she said. A cloud passed. 'If I see him again.' She glanced at the clock. 'Oh, my goodness, I'll have to run.'

And she was gone.

Edgar lit the second Gold Flake and picked a shred of tobacco from his tongue.

'Has she had much to do with boys, do you think?' Skelton asked.

'She might have engaged with one from time to time on a strictly patrol leader to patrol leader basis or appreciated the timbre that their broken voices brought to a campfire song, but I've never had the impression that her beating heart has been fully awakened.'

'You don't know this Vernon Goodyear at all?'

'Never heard of him.'

'I mean, what sort of job might a forensic entomologist end up doing?'

'Might work for the police, I suppose, or . . . university don?' Edgar said. 'She's a sensible girl.'

'Yes, of course she is. But that sort of thing can knock you sideways when you're twenty.'

'It can knock you sideways at any age.'

'Exactly,' Skelton said. 'And she hasn't got a mother or father.'

They smoked, ruminatively.

'*In loco parentis,* then,' Edgar said.

'At school we always used to say *in loco parentis* was Latin for "my dad's a train driver",' Skelton said. 'It was a joke.'

'We never did Latin at the George Street Board School,' Edgar said, remembering the squeak of the slate pencils and the savage beatings with surprising fondness. 'Or jokes.'

CHAPTER TWELVE

Though there was no need for Edgar to accompany Skelton to Durham, he felt an obligation as Clifford's honorary uncle. The Sunday train took nearly seven hours. They sat for a long time in the restaurant car, waiting for their meal and listening to an extended argument going on just off stage between a waiter and a chef.

'I can't serve these potatoes.'

'Why not?'

'They're wetter than the gravy.'

It was past midnight when they arrived at their hotel.

At court the following morning, Clifford was first up. The presence of a famous London barrister at Petty Sessions put the wind up the magistrate who, terrified that any breach of procedure might bring complaints and consequences, stumbled and mumbled his words. Skelton convinced him that Clifford was of good character, a keen and industrious scholar who had been led astray by bad company, and it would be a tragedy if anything happened to jeopardise his future at the university. Without fine, remonstrance or warning, the magistrate dismissed the case and moved on.

Skelton and Edgar treated the boy to a late breakfast and tried to give him a jolly good talking-to, but his charm got in the way. He'd been doing a lot of 'reading around' in his history course and told them filthy stories about Jean Buridan, a French mediaeval philosopher who had an affair with Queen Marguerite de Bourgogne. Then he showed them some magic tricks he'd learnt with spoons and bits of string.

They gave him the Palethorpes Pork Pies.

'Did Mum tell you to get these?' he asked.

'She did, yes,' Edgar said.

'I mentioned once I liked 'em, and I've been inundated ever since. Do you want them?'

They'd bought three, so let the lad have one and kept the other two.

After a second cup of tea, he told them he had an important engagement he needed to keep.

'With your tutor?' Skelton asked.

'With a waitress from Lil's Cafe on Saddler Street.'

There was a stiff, cold breeze blowing off the river. It felt cleansing.

'We've almost two hours before the next train back to London,' Edgar said.

Skelton suggested they follow a late breakfast with an early lunch, but Edgar, who had just had a boiled egg and one slice of dry toast, said lunch was out of the question.

Skelton looked at the sky. Here and there he could see patches of blue, not quite enough, as his mother would say, to make a pair of sailor's trousers but plenty for a peg-leg. 'Do we have many appointments for tomorrow?'

'No. Nothing important except a meeting with Bernard Gregory about the Cheeseman divorce.'

'We'll send him a wire. I was just thinking we might go to the seaside.'

'Why?'

'Whitley Bay's not far. Change at Newcastle, I think.'

They booked into the Waverley Hotel, sent telegrams to the people who needed to know they would not be home that night, then took a walk in the freezing wind along The Links. The North Sea looked evil; black, mostly, dotted with dirty yellowish spume. The town's most glamorous attraction, the Spanish City, evoked Grimsby more accurately than Granada. Gulls did not screech. They sat wherever they could keep hold and looked miserable.

It rained. Umbrellas were blown inside out. Hat brims were freezing reservoirs.

'Viking sailors,' Skelton said, 'used to think that whales fed on rain and darkness.'

'Where did you read that?'

'A book that Lawrence got for Christmas. They'll all have bellyaches in the morning, getting through this lot.'

'Why exactly have we come here?' Edgar asked.

'I can't remember.'

Skelton had eaten both of the pork pies on the train but now he was hungry again. Out of season, most of the shops and cafes, and even some of the pubs, were closed. Eventually they found a sit-down fish and chip shop and basked in its greasy warmth.

'I wonder if they'd do a salad.' Edgar said.

'It's a chip shop.'

'I'll just have fish and peas, then. No chips.'

The waitress, to whom an order of fish and peas without chips could only be a mistake, brought the chips anyway and two big mugs of tea.

Edgar didn't make a fuss about it or about the tea coming with the milk already in it, even though he'd got his lemon and knife at the ready.

There was a surprising amount of coming and going on the street outside. People ducked and dodged as a newspaper hoarding flew along at head-height, threatening to decapitate the unwary. Further up the road, out of sight, there was a crash as the flying object collided with a car or a window.

'It wasn't nearly so blowy in Durham,' Skelton said. 'I suspect I was so elated to have brought the Clifford business to a satisfactory conclusion that I momentarily went barmy.'

'Easily done.'

'I thought a trip to the seaside might make a pleasant change.'

'Have you ever known any part of the North Sea to be pleasant?' Edgar asked.

'I seem to remember Bridlington being all right. Once.'

They ate their chips and drank their tea. Unwilling to risk being beheaded by a headline, they lingered, smoking and watching the struggles of those less fortunate than themselves.

Skelton suddenly brought up his hand to the side of his face. 'Hide yourself,' he said.

'What?'

'Jimmy Coyle.'

'Never. Where?'

'Too late. He's seen us.'

It is an occupational hazard of all those involved in the law. From time to time, they will encounter somebody they last saw being taken down for a long sentence. Jimmy Coyle was a left-handed riveter. This, Skelton had been informed, was a desirable asset in the shipyards, possibly because right-handed and left-handed riveters could work as a team without getting in each other's way. When Jimmy had had to leave Belfast because of some trouble, he had crossed the sea from Ireland and easily found employment on Tyneside.

He was caught stealing from the yard, on commission from an organised gang. When the police raided a pub in Wallsend to arrest three of the gang's leading lights, Jimmy happened to be there. The 'gangsters' resisted arrest. Two of them were armed. Nobody was hurt, but pistols were fired.

If it hadn't been for the gang and the nature of the arrest, Jimmy might have been charged with petty theft and given a light sentence or even a fine. As it was, he was sent down for three years.

Skelton had defended. He could perhaps have done a better job. Jimmy knew he could have done a better job. It's never the jury they blame, nor, perversely, the prosecution counsel. It's the judge and the defence counsel. Sometimes they bear a grudge. They get vindictive.

Jimmy, hands in pockets, head ducked either against the wind or in anger, crossed the road, entered the cafe and approached them.

Edgar flinched when Jimmy took his hands out of his pockets, but no violence was offered. Instead, Jimmy pulled off his cap and his face broke into a big smile. He greeted them like long-lost pals.

'D'you remember me, Mr Skelton, Mr Hobbes? I'll bet you don't.'

'Of course we do, Jimmy. How are you?'

'I'm very well, Mr Skelton. And how's yourself?'

'A little windswept, but none the worse for wear. Can I buy you a cup of tea or something?'

Jimmy took charge and called to the woman behind the counter, 'All right, Flo?'

'Oh, hello, Jimmy, didn't see you there.'

'Bring us three teas, can you?' Jimmy sat down. 'I'm glad to see you, Mr Skelton, because I've given the matter a good deal of thought down the years and I've come to realise I owe you a lot.'

'I can hardly think that possible, Jimmy.'

'No, it's true. Remember when you came to see me before the trial? That's what I'm thinking of. You asked about how I'd got caught up in all that terrible bother. And then in court you said I was a weak man who was easily led. That was the meat of what you said anyway, but you might have used different words. A weak man who was easily led. Well, you were right, Mr Skelton, you were absolutely right, and I took what you said to heart. All the time I was in prison, I found myself thinking about it, and I thought about how I'd never been my own man and how I had to be. I had to be my own man. Well, you meet all sorts of people in prison, don't you? People who want you to do this and people who want you to do that. But I decided I'd had enough. I was not going to be at anybody's bidding ever again. I stood my ground. I got beaten up a couple of times, but a beating only

131

lasts so long. If you say yes to these people, that can be the rest of your life.'

Skelton listened patiently, remembering next to nothing about what he had and hadn't said during the trial, simply thankful that Jimmy hadn't come at him with a knife.

Their tea arrived. They smoked.

'I couldn't get my job in the yards back when I came out,' Jimmy said. 'But that was to be expected. So, I went on the tramp for a bit, you know? All the way down south and Wales and all over. Then I signed up with the Royal Corps of Dregs.'

'What's that?'

'The Lynch Mob. Lynch is a big contractor. Gets gangs of navvies together, the dregs of England, Scotland, Ireland and Wales, ships them all over the country for roads, tunnelling, big buildings, all that sort of thing. I saw a lot of the country with them. It's rough work, though, and the people can be very nasty. Lunatics. Mad for the drink a lot of them. And the fighting can be terrible. I don't expect you've done any navvying, have you?'

'Is the work regular?' Skelton asked.

'You do it till you can't stand it any more, then you move on. There's always something if you don't mind moving around and sleeping rough. Fruit picking's not bad, or hop picking. You get women doing that so it's nice to have the company, if you know what I mean. I took up with a lovely Italian woman for a bit. We travelled around together. But she was a terrible drinker and ended up being more trouble than she was worth, so I left her in Ipswich. I did a bit of scaffolding. Now, scaffolders are a really hard people. Pirates. You don't want anything to do with them.'

'You've never taken a permanent job, then?'

'They'd ask for references and find out I've been in prison. And, anyway, I prefer the freedom to up and go whenever I get fed up. And if all else fails, I always know I can find work in the Lynch mob. Have you ever done any tunnelling?'

'To be honest, I don't think I've ever done a proper day's work in my life.'

'You're a lucky man, Mr Skelton.'

'I helped put up a shed once, for my landlady in Swiss Cottage,' Edgar said.

'There you go, then, hands like steel hawsers.'

Edgar held up his hands. A princess would have been proud of them.

They laughed.

'What are you up to in Whitley Bay?' Skelton asked.

'Here I have my bum in butter, Mr Skelton,' Jimmy said. 'I'm at the Royal. The Royal Hotel. They're rebuilding. Moving rooms around. New staircase. Lifts. Indoors practically all day. Sleeping in a hotel room, proper bed. Three meals a day. Never had it better. And look at the weather. Can you imagine digging footings outside in this? Up to your knackers in cack? Worst of it is, we've only got a couple of weeks left and then I'll be out on my arse again. And there's only so much you can do to slow things down. If they catch you slacking or messing something up, they dock your pay. Are you just here for the day or staying over?'

'We're at the Waverley.'

'Oh, they're all right up at the Waverley. I drink with some of the porters from there. Very good money to be had there in the summer for the porters. I've been trying to swing a job with them, but, you know, everybody wants a portering job, don't they? Have you ever done any portering?'

Skelton and Edgar both began to feel ashamed of themselves.

'Are you here on business or what?' Jimmy asked. Then it dawned on him. 'You're doing the suitcase lass. She used to come here?'

'Yes, that's right.'

'I read in the paper she'd been up this way. I don't know what you expect to find out now.'

'Her husband's been getting postcards from here.'

'Still? She's sending them from the suitcase?'

'He thinks they might have made a mistake and it's not his wife in the suitcase at all. He thinks his wife is still alive and living hereabouts somewhere, possibly in disguise.'

'Sending him postcards from here? I could ask around if you like, see if anybody's seen her. Have you got a picture I could show to people?'

'Not with me, no. There have been several in the papers.'

At this, Edgar stood up and had a word with Flo. She invited him to join her behind the counter, where he rummaged through the pile of newspapers they used for wrapping the chips until he found what he was looking for.

'Here you are.'

'She looks a real sourpuss,' Jimmy said.

It was true. Edna Aziz had the look of a woman who thought a smile would break her face.

'I'll ask around,' Jimmy said, 'but I wouldn't hold out much hope. Very few people left out of season.' He folded the newspaper and put it in his pocket. 'Is it nearly half past five?'

Skelton checked his watch.

'It's twenty to six.'

'I'm in trouble. Meeting a chap about a horse. I wanted to pop in and say thank you. You can get me at the Royal if you need anything.'

Jimmy left.

Skelton and Edgar finished their tea, then reluctantly forsook the warmth of the cafe to walk back to the hotel.

It was dark and still very cold.

The Waverley was serving dinner, but Skelton and Edgar had had enough chips to last them the rest of the week, so they sat by the fire and drank Bass.

Outside the wind howled and lumps of wet ice began to smack against the windows.

'I think "beside myself with glee" would probably be stretching a point,' Edgar said.

It took a second or two for Skelton to spot that his clerk was quoting 'I Do Like to Be Beside the Seaside'.

'Tiddley-om-pom-pom,' he said, making up for the dearth of brass bands.

The following morning, as they ate a breakfast as mournful as the sleety drizzle that was still falling, Jimmy appeared, sat down at their table and helped himself to toast and butter.

'So, me and this chap were in the Stanford last night and then we went to the Globe where a lot of the staff from the various hotels drink when they're off duty. Not many there out of season, as I said. But I showed them the picture. And this one chap recognised her and said last summer a woman who looked like her gave him a pile of postcards she'd bought and written on and stamped and addressed and said she

135

wanted him to post them, but not all at the same time. She wanted him to keep them all safe and post just one a month. Beginning of the month, didn't have to be on the same date. And she gave him two pounds for his troubles and said she'd give him another two pounds in a year – there were twelve of the cards – if he did it right. He's still got eight of them left and every one of those cards was addressed to the same person. Dr I. Aziz.'

'Had he read about the case in the papers?' Skelton asked.

'Oh yes. He knew all about it.'

'So why hadn't he mentioned all this to the police?'

'He's still hoping to collect the other two pounds, isn't he?'

'Even though she's dead?'

'Some of the papers said the body might be somebody else. He's an optimist.'

'What's this man's name?'

'I promised not to mention his name or the place he worked.'

'Could he be persuaded to give a witness statement and possibly appear in court if he knew a man might hang if he didn't?'

'He might do it for, say, double what the woman was going to pay him. Four pounds?' Jimmy said.

'You know as well as I do, Jimmy, that witnesses don't count if money's changed hands.'

'There are ways and ways, though. You can tip a hotel porter however much you like and nobody's the wiser.'

'I'll bear that in mind. And if the worst comes to the worst—'

'If the worst comes to the worst, I'll give you the name of the hotel where he works, so you can pop in, ask him to clean your shoes or tell you the way to the station and leave him a generous tip.'

'I wonder if *you* could tell us the way to the station, Jimmy.'

Jimmy told them and Skelton transferred two ten-bob notes when they shook hands.

'An affair, then,' Edgar said, when they were back on the train.

'Seems likely,' Skelton said. 'Which leaves two . . . no, three possibilities. Either she's alive and well and living the high life on the Boulevard des Anglaises and it's somebody else in the suitcase. Or that *is* her in the suitcase, murdered and dismembered by her lover. Or Aziz found out about the affair and killed her.'

'Doesn't leave us any closer to a defence than we were this time last week, though, does it?'

There were less than five weeks to go before the trial.

The fields of Northumberland rolled by, grey with drizzle, like a murky photograph. It was stuffy in the carriage. Edgar pressed his face against the window to feel the cold on his cheek. He suddenly had a craving for a stick of rock but was glad he hadn't bought one.

CHAPTER THIRTEEN

c/o The Cross Keys Public House, Fetterick

Monday 13th January, 1930

My dear cousin Arthur,
Thank you for your letter. What you had to say about
the postcards reminded me of a consumptive young
man we once knew in Rhyl, who was in love with
Gertie Gitana of 'You Do Look Well in Your Old
Dutch Bonnet' fame. This was not long after the
war. He wrote to Gertie Gitana twice, I think, asking
for her photograph, and was ever so disappointed
when he received no reply. So, his mum – he would
have been about nineteen at the time but practically
bedridden he was that poorly – cut a photograph out

of a magazine, stuck it on a bit of cardboard and sent it to him with a lovely letter she wrote pretending that she was Gertie Gitana. It really bucked him up, that did. But the trouble was that he wrote back to her, so his mum had to write another letter back to him. And this kept going until in the end the poor boy thought that he was having some sort of romance with the singer.

The thing never had a chance to get completely out of hand because the boy died not long after his twentieth birthday. I have little doubt that he died much happier as a result of his mother's innocent deceit.

Mendacity is a complicated sin. I think it is, at any rate.

I think I told you in my last letter about the frozen chapel. Well, on the Tuesday morning we set to work.

Coal was not a problem. We found a huge pile of it and some kindling sticks under a lean-to at the back of the chapel. It was all frozen up, but a little hacking with a spade broke enough free to get us started, and I had some scraps of paper, pamphlets of one sort or another and old raffle tickets left over from Carlisle, in my pockets.

We were afraid that the stove doors would break off at the hinges, they needed such a lot of levering to get them open. After a lot of coaxing, though, we got the fires going and fetched more coal.

Then we realised the danger that we were in. The icicles began first to drip then to fall from the ceiling. I have never felt threatened by a falling icicle before so may be overstating the danger. All I can say is they looked lethal, as if archers and pikemen were hiding up in the dark by the roof.

We retreated and stood outside, listening to them fall. After half an hour or so we decided we had not heard one for a minute or two, so risked a return. It was then that we realised the advantages of a tin shack. Metal walls conduct heat beautifully. Though the areas nearest the stove would almost burn you if you were to touch them, those a few yards distant were just lovely and warm. By the afternoon, the warmth filled every corner. We basked in it.

The cement floor was awash. We found brooms and a mop in a cupboard at the back and started cleaning up. The stoves burned fiercely, consuming a hodful of coal every hour. They seemed to have no damper to control the airflow, so we had no choice but to let them burn. As I say, there was no shortage of coal.

Having got the place so warm, it seemed a pity just to walk away and let it get cold again, so we decided to see if we could rally a few people together for our first meeting.

We had had nothing to eat since breakfast, so we walked back into the village centre and had a hurried meal in the Eccles. We have a supply of posters and pamphlets we use to advertise the meetings with spaces left to fill in the time and place by hand, so we did a couple of posters, one for the pub and one for the local shop, and then went up the main street back towards Abbotsbank, putting pamphlets through the doors.

It was dark by the time we got back to the chapel. We had left the door unlocked, and, when we went in, though it was not much after five and the meeting was not supposed to start until six, there were already ten or twelve people waiting there in the dark.

We lit the oil lamps. They looked like ghosts. Skeletal bodies. White faces. Some of them had no shoes and had wrapped their feet in rags. The state of the children, solemn, their faces aged by want, made you want to weep.

We tried to chat but did not get much more than one-word answers. They seemed frightened of us, as if we might throw them out or offer violence.

Two of the little ones, whose names I learnt were Martin and Owen and might have been anything between eight and twelve, looked as if they were in urgent need of a doctor. They were barely able to stand, and when you spoke to them, they did not seem able to focus on where the sound was coming from. I told the mother I could perhaps ask May Balfour, the minister's sister, where to find a doctor, but she told me that the only medicine her children needed was bread.

I asked her how she had heard about the meeting. She told me she did not know anything about a meeting. Somebody had told her that the chapel was open and warm.

In couples, families and small groups, more people arrived, all of them ragged, cold and starving.

Before one can engender the joy of Jesus in one's fellow human beings, one must first ensure that certain basic necessities are provided. Among these are food and warmth. The two stoves provided plenty of warmth and you could see limbs unbend as it found its way into muscles and sinews. But we had no food to give them. Preaching to these people felt somehow heartless, like showing lantern slides to the blind. Singing would have been an insult. It was warmth they had come for, anything else was a silly distraction from its meagre comfort.

One man, more talkative than the rest, said his name was Easy, although this could be wrong; his accent was very strong. He told me that many people in Abbotsbank had been without income for many weeks. The ironworks had closed down a year ago and, apart from the farms, that was the only work in the village. I asked whether there was work in Fort Blaine and they said that factories had closed there, too. What about poor relief? He told me that for a time they were allowed a small pittance, but then the rules changed and in order to claim assistance you had to prove you were genuinely seeking work. But you cannot prove that you are genuinely seeking work when everybody, including the officials, knows that in Fetterick there is no work to seek.

In the newspapers you read of businesses and factories closing down all over the country – the result, they say, of the stock-market crash in America last autumn, but here in Scotland industry never really recovered after the war. The system of poor relief is different to that which operates in England. Or it seems to be, anyway.

I asked whether there were any poorhouses, workhouses or soup kitchens they could go to. He told me there were, but only in Fort Blaine. Some people had walked there last week – a journey that would be no more than a step for me but a considerable undertaking for somebody with no coat or shoes. When they got there, they were turned back by the police and came home hungry.

I am, of course, paraphrasing. Lacking both the nationality and the literary skills of Burns, Scott or Stephenson, it would be as pointless and erroneous for me to try to transcribe each 'cannae' and the 'didnae' and 'O wad some pouer the giftie gie us, tae see oursels as ithers see us' as it would be for you to begin your letters to me 'Annwyl gefnder Alan'.

I said it seemed strange to me that, with the weather being so cold, the pile of coal round the back of the chapel had not been filched for the hearths of home, and I asked Mr Easy whether the people were perhaps too respectful or too afraid to steal from a church. Mr Easy gave me a gappy smile and said, 'You should have seen the size of it last week.'

Just after seven, three new people, well-fed and well-dressed – by which I mean not fashionably or expensively dressed but wholesomely inasmuch as they had garments that actually looked like proper coats, shoes and hats – popped their heads around the door, seemed alarmed at what they saw, but nonetheless entered and stood at the back warming themselves. I approached them.

They were Jack, Beryl and Margaret, who live in the village, had seen the posters and had come hoping, as the posters had promised, music, song, good cheer and joy. I told them that that was usually the general idea but here we seemed to be faced with something of an emergency. They agreed and were ashamed to admit that they had no idea how grave the problem had become in Abbotsbank, even though it was in their own village, under their noses.

Jack and Beryl told us to find a big pot or several pots and put water on to boil. They disappeared into the night.

I asked Mr Easy if he knew where we could find big cooking pots. He had a word with one or two of the others and they left, to return a few minutes later, two carrying a great washtub and another two – they looked half-dead with the effort – carrying something that looked like a witch's cauldron in a storybook.

Someone had thoughtfully lagged the pump outside with layers of sacking, so it was not frozen, and we were able to fill the washtub and cauldron.

We set them on the stoves. Presently Jack and Beryl arrived carrying bags filled with oats and barley and some tinned peas and butter beans that they had got from somebody called a local shopkeeper. I do not know whether the goods were given freely or whether Jack and Beryl paid for them, but my goodness they were welcome and made a good thick soup, almost stew. We sent the people home then to fetch bowls and spoons.

Jesus fed the five thousand with five loaves and two fishes. We managed twenty-two with a washtub and a cauldron.

Afterwards, Norah got her accordion out and I the banjo, and we sang 'That Old Irish Mother of Mine', 'Tipperary' and 'When Father Painted the Parlour'.

Nobody joined in. I overheard somebody say, 'What are they doing that for?'

We did not mind. Sometimes it is good to see people go home filled with the joy of Jesus and sometimes it is better to see them go home filled with soup.

There was some talk of people bedding down for the night in the warmth of the chapel, but the lack of a lavatory made this inadvisable. A promise that there would be more food tomorrow made their going a little less reluctant.

As we were clearing up, Beryl asked why we had chosen to bring our mission to Fetterick of all places and we told her that the tragic death of Edna Aziz had brought us here. Places where tragedy has struck often suffer a spiritual ache for which we hope to bring relief. Beryl smiled and told us that Edna's death would not have caused much of an ache in Fetterick. Apart from her father's funeral, eighteen months ago, she had barely set foot in the place since before the war. Mr Easy, whom we had met earlier, might know more about her because, from time to time, he used to do bits of work up at Aldwin House, where she had lived as a girl. But otherwise, Beryl doubted whether many people in Fetterick, or Fort Blaine for that matter, would even have recognised Edna Aziz if she had bumped into them in the street.

It is strange the way in which the Lord guides our feet. We came to offer spiritual comfort to the bereaved but find there is no need for it. Thus, the signs seem to indicate that we will be unable to offer much help with your case – for which I can only extend my apologies.

Nevertheless, the Lord has led us to a new and indubitably worthy mission. With help from Jack, Beryl, Margaret and anyone else we can find, we shall feed the hungry and warm them, and, if possible, find them clothes.

I am ever yours faithfully in the joy of Jesus,
Alan

CHAPTER FOURTEEN

Thursday started badly.

Aubrey Duncan had done his best with Reggie Ashworth and Lennie Jeanes, the two lads in the Luton 'motor bandit' wages snatch. He had equipped them with new collars and ties from Woolworth, and made sure they'd combed their hair flat with brilliantine and polished their shoes. He'd even prompted them to mention their mothers, which they did with monotonous frequency.

The police evidence was flimsy: a scrape on a mudguard; a blue flannel cap that a witness thought she recognised; there were doubts about the reliability of their alibis. The prosecution counsel, a young chap, mumbled, dropped his notes and muddled names and dates.

Skelton thought he had it in the bag.

Trouble came when the doctor, giving evidence about the

victim's injuries, said that some of the bruising suggested a violent push to her sternum. The judge asked whether, for the sake of the jury, he could clarify whereabouts on the body the 'sternum' was to be found. The doctor told the court it was 'the breastbone'.

The two defendants sniggered because he'd said 'breast'.

Skelton blamed himself. He should have warned them about the dangers of sniggering, smirking or grimacing in court. Smirking at any time can be enough to lose a case. Do it when your alleged victim's injuries are being described pretty much guarantees a guilty verdict and a couple of months added to your sentence.

And so it came to pass. Reggie and Lennie each got six months hard.

Afterwards Skelton and Edgar popped into the King of Denmark to drown their sorrows with halves of mild.

Detective Sergeant Kimberley, who'd provided the police evidence, was in there. They fell into conversation.

He agreed that it was the smirk that did for them, but he said that Skelton shouldn't worry if the conviction was a bit dicey. Even if the boys hadn't done this one, there was a string of other jobs the police knew for certain they'd done but had never been able to get enough evidence to collar them. They were bad boys.

Under normal circumstances, putting them away would halve the crime rate in Luton, giving him and his mates more time to practise their snooker. They had a big match coming up in a couple of weeks.

The curious thing was, though, he said, that crime had actually gone up since the lads had been taken into custody. Three houses and a shop had been done just in the past week. Word was out that two other chancers, possibly from London, had moved in to take the place of Ashworth and Jeanes. This raised the possibility that there was a London gang sending boys up to Luton to rob on commission – most likely the Italians or Captain Musgrave's lot.

Skelton had never heard of either the Italians or Captain Musgrave's lot.

'It's the same all over these days, though, isn't it?' Kimberley said. 'Little independent traders and craftsmen being sucked up by big business. Like all the little grocers' shops all over the country. You see them everywhere with the new sign hanging up outside: "Home and Colonial Stores". Every High Street, every town you go to. "Home and Colonial Stores". Then next door you're going to have a Woolworth putting all the "everything shops" out of business. It'll happen to us all in the end, you wait and see. Home and Colonial Police Station. Woolworth Old Bailey.'

Skelton and Edgar expressed their sympathy and bought another round.

In the taxi to Chingford, he could feel dread in the pit of his stomach. Knowing there was no sane reason why the words 'Women's Charity League' should inspire such terror didn't help. *What's the worst that could happen?* he asked himself. *It'll all be done in a couple of hours and you'll feel stupid for worrying. You're actually quite good at this sort of thing.*

The Artillery Hall was a welcome surprise. Instead of paint, mould and rot, it smelt of fresh tobacco, new tweed and Lifebuoy soap.

Phyllis Pitt was at the door waiting for him, a monolithic presence in forest green barathea with matching hat and pink flounces. As he approached, she smiled at him like a gourmet addressing meat and pumped his hand.

'This is so very, very kind of you,' she said, and introduced him to several other women, all of whom seemed to be called Mrs Snasby, apart from one who was called Miss Snasby.

'We can furnish you with tea,' one of the Mrs Snasbies said, 'or, if you would prefer, we have a secret bottle of sherry.'

Skelton accepted a glass of water and allowed himself to be led to the stage where a table, chair and lectern had been arranged.

Mrs Pitt went to the lectern. 'First of all, we would like to welcome our visitors from the national committee and give them a rousing Chingford welcome.' *Hooray.* 'Now, tonight, ladies, we are honoured . . .' She spoke for a good fifteen minutes while Skelton looked out on the sea of hats. Some had ornate pins. Some feathers. Some flowers. One had fruit, a miniature kingfisher and an artistic arrangement of autumn leaves. 'Distinguished . . .' Mrs Pitt said, and 'celebrated'. *Could her fifteen minutes be deducted from his hour?* Skelton wondered. '. . . *The Times* described him as . . .'

And he was on.

It happened every time in court and it happened now. It was a knack he had learnt, he supposed, in school debates. 'This house believes that school holidays should be shorter', 'This house believes that military service should be compulsory'. Tell him which side he's on. Stand him up. Give him a lapel to grasp and off he went. Thoughts found words and words found thoughts. A subject would find its verb and the verb its object and, as long as he kept those three elements in mind, he could spin any number of subsidiary clauses and even parentheses. His voice went up here, down there. Here comes a joke or a pleasantry, here a note of awful tragedy and here a thumping conclusion.

So painfully good was he at this sort of thing that he despised his own fluency. It was the trivialisation he hated most. In court it meant doing away with nuance and turning complex greys into harsh blacks and whites. It meant turning tragedy into melodrama and humour into stupid farce.

He told the Women's Charity League the story of Mary Dutton, a case from a year earlier. Her husband, Ted, a brutal man who had beaten her, threatened her with a gun, mistreated the children and bashed out the brains of her puppy dog, had died of arsenic poisoning. There were sniffles – particularly when he spoke of the poor children. Several women in the front row took handkerchiefs from their handbags, wiped their eyes and discreetly blew their noses.

Thankfully there was a clock at the back of the room. Five minutes before his hour was up, he adopted a 'concluding remarks' tone and finished by saying that on the whole it's best to avoid the courts because the one thing you can guarantee about a lawsuit is that it's going to cost you a lot more than the suits you get at Burton. This got a laugh and a round of applause. He sat down. Phyllis Pitt glowered because he had deducted her fifteen minutes from his hour and now she felt short-changed. She asked if anyone had any questions. One brave woman asked what the difference was between a solicitor and a barrister. Skelton did his usual routine about the solicitor being the organ grinder and the barrister the monkey. The lady in the kingfisher hat asked why judges wore long wigs and barristers, short ones. He said it was because judges got paid more and so could afford a few extra inches of horsehair. Some people laughed at this while others made humourless, 'My goodness, I'd never have guessed' faces.

Mrs Pitt said that if there were any more questions, she was sure that Mr Skelton would be glad to answer them informally over a cup of tea, and brought the meeting to a close.

A hatch was opened at the side of the room and the audience queued up for tea, biscuits and cake.

Skelton tried to find a moment to say, 'I really should be getting off. It's a long way home to Lambourn, and I'm in court tomorrow morning,' but Mrs Pitt made sure he never found one.

A sprightly woman with a fascinatingly mobile mouth asked what the best way was she could encourage her son to go into the law.

A thin, miserable-looking lady with deep vertical grooves everywhere asked how long a neighbour's privet could grow over your side of the fence before it counted as trespass.

A tiny woman – one of the national committee – very shyly asked him whether he could remember somebody called Doris Maybury, who, she said, had been at St Saviour's Elementary with him. The woman's voice was so quiet he had to bend down to hear. She had a soft Lancashire accent. He told her that he vaguely remembered the name but suspected that Doris would have been a bit older than him and was possibly in his sister's year. He straightened up. Then he realised that the woman was saying something else and he had to bend down again.

'You're doing the suitcase one, aren't you?' she said.

'Yes, I am, but I'm not really allowed to talk about it before the trial.'

'It's just – I saw the picture of the label thing in the paper.'

She was talking about the tiny gummed label that had been found inside the lid of the suitcase. Pictures of it had appeared in the papers. It was presumed to be a stock number from the shop or some such, but nobody had recognised it. It was just a nondescript scrap with the number '428' written on it in indelible ink.

'I recognised the handwriting,' the woman said.

Whatever the case, there are always scores of people who believe they have some valuable insight, a clue that will lead, Holmes-like, to the unravelling of a great truth.

'It's really the police you should be talking to, not me,' Skelton said.

'I promised I wouldn't.'

'Why was that?'

'Because the chap who wrote that label takes bets.'

'He's a bookie's runner, you mean?'

'He takes bets in the shop. The police'd shut him down if they found out.'

'What does the shop sell?'

'Suitcases and trunks like that one. Well, he sells all sorts of stuff. Hardware and suchlike. But the suitcases as well. And I recognised the handwriting. It's the way he does his twos. Like a loop on its side.'

'Well, as I say, Mrs—'

'Reynolds.'

'As I say, Mrs Reynolds, if you do have any information you think might be important you really should go to the police.'

'If I write the address of the shop down on a piece of paper, will you take it to the police for me? Only they mustn't know it was me who gave it to you.'

'I'd be happy to do that for you.'

Skelton's back was beginning to ache with all the bending. He straightened and looked around for Phyllis Pitt so as to make his goodbyes. Mrs Reynolds was saying something else. He bent down.

'I'm sorry, were you saying something?'

'I was saying I've got pencil and paper in my handbag over there, if you could wait here a minute.'

'Of course.'

He stood, saw Phyllis Pitt and made his way over to her.

'I really—'

But Phyllis introduced him to a Mrs Hennessy, who wanted to draw his attention to certain inconsistencies in the new Rating and Valuation Act. It was another ten minutes before he was able to make his escape.

Near the door, Mrs Reynolds pressed a piece of paper into his hands.

'Remember—'

He bent down.

'I'm sorry?'

'Remember,' she repeated, 'you didn't learn this from me.'

CHAPTER FIFTEEN

Skelton had spent the following morning coming to grips with a defamation case in which the libel had been perpetrated on a tombstone.

A Mr Staplehurst had left his wife some years before and run off with Lilian Doggett, a woman from his office. They lived together as man and wife, and even though Mr and Mrs Staplehurst had never divorced, Miss Doggett passed herself off as 'Mrs Staplehurst'.

When Miss Doggett passed away, Mr Staplehurst had continued the fiction and the words 'Lilian, loving wife of Wm. Staplehurst' were engraved on her tombstone.

The real Mrs Staplehurst, now a successful businesswoman running a chain of ladies' outfitters in south London, was outraged and claimed that the suggestion on the tombstone that she, rather than Miss Doggett, was the imposter, could damage her reputation and that, since, apparently, reputation is all in the ladies' outfitting trade, this could have severe financial consequences.

Both were wealthy. Mrs Staplehurst had Sir Astley Snow KC leading her prosecution of the libel. Mr Staplehurst had Skelton.

The meeting, called by the solicitors of both parties to negotiate an out-of-court settlement, was incendiary.

Mr and Mrs Staplehurst had been separated for almost twenty years, yet both bore what should have been ancient scars like fresh-made wounds. Eventually Skelton, Snow and the solicitors, tired of trying to intervene and bring some order to the proceedings, simply sat back and let them get on with it.

The accusations that filled the air quickly strayed from the matter of the tombstone to conflicts of a very personal nature that brought a blush to Skelton's cheeks. But man and wife could not be stopped until Mrs Staplehurst's solicitor found just enough pause to say, very loudly, 'Well, I think we've all made a great deal of progress in resolving this matter and perhaps any details that still remain can be cleared up by an exchange of letters. Thank you very much for your attendance. Good day, gentleman, lady.'

Everybody stood and shuffled papers. The solicitor shepherded Mrs Staplehurst out of the room and into the corridor where she continued shouting.

Edgar, who had been dealing with some other business, met Skelton outside, saw the expression on his face and said, 'Kembles, I think.'

Skelton fell into step with him.

* * *

They were slightly too late for the midday rush and far too early for tea, so Kembles was agreeably empty. Norman gave them an effusive welcome and showed them to their favourite table. They ordered: veal and ham pie for Skelton and an egg salad for Edgar.

Skelton was wondering whether he should encourage Edgar to order a bread roll to go with the salad when he saw Rose scurrying towards them with an envelope in her hand.

He and Edgar stood.

'How nice to see you, Rose,' Skelton said.

'I went round to Foxton Row, but somebody there said I might find you here. Mr Duncan did want to get this to you as soon as possible.'

Rose gave him the letter.

'Do, please, sit down, Rose. I'll be a few minutes anyway and there may be a reply. Have you had lunch?'

Rose looked around. She had not had her lunch. Like Skelton when he was her age, she'd only just learnt to call it 'lunch' rather than 'dinner' and certainly had never eaten a meal in a place as grand as Kembles.

'Mrs Westing made me some sandwiches,' Rose said. 'I'll have them when I get back to the office.'

'A cup of tea, then.'

'I won't, if it's all right with you,' Rose said. 'I told Miss Summers I'd only be five minutes.'

'You shouldn't let Miss Summers boss you around,' Edgar said. 'You're an articled clerk, not an errand boy.'

'Oh, that is interesting,' Skelton said, passing the letter to Edgar.

'What is it?'

'Note from Aubrey. Dr Aziz may never come to trial. The Egyptian government are demanding his extradition, as an Egyptian citizen who allegedly murdered an Egyptian citizen, to face trial in his own country.' Skelton turned to Rose. 'Any idea when Aubrey heard about this?'

'A gentleman from the Egyptian legation came round in person, earlier today,' Rose said. 'Huge car with a flag on the front.'

'Isn't Egypt ours?' Edgar asked. 'I'm sure it's coloured red on the map.'

'There was an uprising some time just after the war,' Rose said. 'Theoretically it's been an independent nation ever since, although I'm not sure the British government has ever fully accepted that.'

'Have you had much to do with extradition, Edgar?' Skelton asked.

'Nothing.'

'Does the native country always have first call? Does the severity of the crime have anything to do with it?'

'No idea,' Edgar said.

'Rose?'

'I could look it up.'

'Is Mr Duncan in the office?' Skelton asked.

'He was just going out when he asked me to find you with the letter, but he said he'd be back at about four if you wanted to talk over the implications.'

'Good,' Skelton said. 'We're free at four, aren't we, Edgar?'

The food came and Rose left them to it.

The pie was substantial. It came with potatoes and cabbage. The egg salad looked like the sort of thing that Mr Gandhi might have eaten as a form of protest.

Edgar waited impatiently for Skelton to finish, desperate for a cigarette to take the edge off his hunger.

Two lovers sat at the worst table in the cafe, the one in the gloom by the kitchen door. Glad of the gloom, they joined hands and spoke of love. Skelton saw Edgar watching them and turned to look himself.

'I noticed that Rose didn't mention Mr . . . what was his name?'

'Goodyear, Vernon Goodyear.' Edgar seemed annoyed, or at least distracted. He hadn't been thinking about Rose and Vernon at all.

'I can't finish these spuds,' Skelton said. 'I don't suppose you want them, do you?'

Edgar shook his head and hurriedly lit a cigarette. Lowering his voice to a confidential whisper, he said, 'There is something I've been meaning to talk over with you.'

A personal note was being struck. Perhaps even a confession. Skelton wanted to say, 'Whatever it is it's none of my business,' but modified it to an ambiguous, 'Hmm?'

'You might have been wondering why I've been doing all this,' Edgar said, 'not eating and so forth.'

'You said – it was because Norman used the word "portly" in an unwarranted way.'

'I'm thinking of getting married.'

'To Rose?'

'Good God, no.'

'I just thought—'

'She's a child,' Edgar said.

'You read every day of men in their forties marrying eighteen-year-olds.'

'Well, they shouldn't.'

'So . . . who . . . ?'

'I haven't quite decided yet.'

Edgar had never married and, as far as Skelton knew, neither had he ever been engaged or had a sweetheart.

Mila had once suggested that he might be homosexual, and Skelton, to the extent that he'd given the matter any thought at all, had supposed she might be right.

He had twice defended clients accused of 'gross indecency'. One who was caught importuning an undercover police officer in a public toilet in Camden Town and one caught 'behaving in a lewd manner' with several friends on Clapham Common. He found it difficult to see the sense in any of it. Other than rape and anything to do with children, what people chose to do with their private parts was none of his business, and he didn't see why the law should be bothered either. He'd known boys at school who'd stuck it in beer bottles and thought as long as the beer bottle doesn't mind good luck to them.

Edgar was a kind man – he knew that – who would go to endless trouble to make sure another person had a chance of being happy. Without even wanting to enquire, Skelton had always hoped Edgar had found or would one day find happiness himself, the same kind of happiness he'd found with Mila. But he'd never been sure.

'So, are there various options?' Skelton asked.

'I don't really know many women.'

'What brought this on?'

'All sorts of things. Being forty-five. Getting fat. And Christmas. I spent it with my sister, as always. She has five children and a loving husband. She's younger than me, but the way she treats me, it's as if you can't be called a grown-up until you've had children. Then, Rose came to stay at Mrs Westing's, and at breakfast every morning I see myself through her eyes, an elderly, portly bachelor still living in furnished rooms because he never had a proper home of his own. I'm sorry, I really shouldn't be bothering you with all this.'

'No, please, go on.'

'It's embarrassing.'

'There's no need to be embarrassed. Look, I'll order you an ice cream. Ice cream doesn't make you fat.'

'Really?'

'I read it in a magazine.'

'Must be true then,' Edgar said.

Skelton called Norman over and ordered two bowls of mixed strawberry and vanilla.

'To be honest, Edgar, I'd have thought you'd have your pick of the field. Practically every woman you come across these days between the ages of thirty-five and fifty is a widow. Or had a fiancé killed in the war. They'll be queueing up to marry a man like you. You're well mannered, beautifully dressed, you like the theatre, you have an encyclopaedic knowledge of fashion.'

'I wouldn't call it encyclopaedic.'

'You're an authority on the correct use of byocks and spadones. You're catnip for the ladies.'

'Where does one meet them, though? Socially.'

'Can you dance?' Skelton asked.

'I have twice-weekly consultations with a chiropodist about my deformed feet.'

'I just thought—'

'It's out of the question. I was wondering . . . people advertise in newspapers. And there are agencies.'

'I think you'd need to be careful.'

'I'm sure some of them are quite above board.'

'I'll ask Mila, see if she knows any likely contenders.'

'You make it sound like prizefighting.'

'And you, Edgar, are the prize.'

The ice cream came.

Skelton saw the expression on Edgar's face when he looked at the pink of the strawberry and yellowish white of the vanilla. He was glad to have brought this moment of exquisite pleasure to his friend's troubled life.

CHAPTER SIXTEEN

The furnishings at Aubrey Duncan's office could have come straight from Kembles. His desk and shelves were steel, the chairs constructed cunningly from what looked like a single length of tubular metal, bent this way and that, with leather upholstery screwed in place. The telephones – there were two of them – were white.

Aubrey was one of those people who radiates a glowing good health. Skelton and Edgar had often discussed how he did this. Edgar had mentioned his skin, which had a pinker and more even hue than most people's – a good step or two up from Skelton's putty grey and nowhere near as blotchy as Edgar's mixed geranium. Shaving probably had something to do with it, too. The only way to get that permanent sheen was to do it three or four times a day, and they wondered whether he'd added a quick shave to his going-to-the-lavatory routine

– button up, flush, wash hands, lather, neck, cheeks, chin, lip. He was, of course, expensively tailored and his shirts could cause snow blindness. Probably most significant was his habit of leaning slightly forward, with the weight on the balls of his feet, as if he was just about to run somewhere very fast. Even when sitting, there was a reluctance to commit himself. He perched, ready to jump up at a moment's notice and, again, run somewhere very fast.

He was perching now, his bottom barely touching the windowsill as he held forth on the subject of extradition.

'I've phoned Jowitt and Sankey and had a brief word with the Permanent Secretary at the Home Office. I don't know how much you know about the situation in Egypt at the moment. They've technically been independent since following the recommendations of the Milner Commission after all that nasty business in '19. But the British still have a considerable military presence, ostensibly there to protect the Suez Canal. The King is broadly pro-British but the Wafd Party, which won a massive majority in parliament at the election just before Christmas, is anti-British. There are also a lot of smaller factions and splinter groups – fascists, communists, anarchists. And, of course, there are some extremely powerful business interests at play whose politics are entirely dependent on profit. Anyway, the upshot is that our Egyptian doctor might easily become a pawn in a rather complicated game of diplomatic chess.'

Aubrey stopped and looked around, possibly expecting applause for his erudite summary of complex issues. He was disappointed. Edgar looked at his feet. Skelton sucked his unlit pipe thoughtfully and asked, 'So, what does this boil down to?'

'Well, for instance, we – the British – would not want to be seen agreeing too readily to the extradition, lest it be perceived by our empire and dominions as a sign of weakness at a time when many might argue that our position, not just in Egypt, but also in – to name but one – India, might be better served by a clear demonstration of unwavering strength and resilience. On the other hand, one can only imagine the anti-British sentiments that could be whipped up if we were to refuse the extradition and hang an Egyptian citizen.'

Skelton had followed about half of Aubrey's argument – Wafd, Jowitt, Sankey, Milner were all complete mysteries – but he'd got the gist. And there was only one thing that mattered, anyway.

'Would he get a fair trial in Egypt?'

'Again, hard to say, but there'd be no political axe to grind once they'd got him extradited, so I see no reason why not. Oh, and there's this.'

Aubrey stood, practically ran to his desk and, with a balletic twist, picked up an envelope and handed it to Edgar.

The envelope was gold-rimmed and had crest on the front, with a crown, drapery and an upturned crescent moon holding three stars. Inside was an invitation to a cocktail party at the Egyptian Legation printed on what could have been a sheet of ivory and dribbling with gold leaf. He passed it to Skelton.

'Very impressive,' Skelton said.

'I suspect it's basically a misplaced bribe,' Aubrey said. 'They think if they ply us with drink, we'll be more likely to give them a thumbs up about the extradition. As if any of *us* had a say in the matter at all.'

'It's tomorrow night,' Skelton said.

'Suggests we were something of an afterthought,' Aubrey said. 'Will you go?'

'It's not actually addressed to me, though, is it?'

'It's not actually addressed to anybody, but apparently the chap who delivered it said it was for whoever was in charge of the Aziz case.'

'Well, that's you, isn't it?'

'I would have thought, in these matters, it's the barrister they want rather than the solicitor.'

'But you have a much greater understanding of the implications than I do.'

'I'm sure Mrs Skelton would relish a chance to dress up in her finery,' Aubrey said.

'She doesn't like finery. She probably disapproves of the current regime in Egypt, too.'

'Why would that be?'

'She makes a habit of disapproving of regimes. You go.'

'I can't I'm afraid. I'm have a dinner engagement.'

'One you can't cancel?'

'With the Prince of Wales.'

'Oh.'

'Do you know him?' Aubrey asked.

'No,'

'Nice chap.'

Skelton turned to Edgar. 'You go. You're just as much in charge of the case as either of us.'

'Don't be preposterous.'

'I think it's an excellent idea,' Aubrey said.

'Well, I am free tomorrow evening,' Edgar said.

After another glance, Edgar carefully slid the invitation into his briefcase.

'Oh, one other thing,' Skelton said. He passed over the address that Mrs Reynolds had written down. 'A lady at the Women's Charity League gave me this last night. It's a shop in Manchester where she seemed to think the suitcase may have been bought. I doubt whether there's anything in it, but it might be worth a look.'

'Is it worth getting the police in?'

'I promised not to. The chap who owns the shop takes bets.'

'I'll see if Stanhope's can do something.'

Stanhope's was a private detective agency that Aubrey used from time to time.

'As I say,' Skelton said, 'I doubt whether there's anything in it.'

On the way back to 8 Foxton Row, Edgar said, 'Have you ever wondered about his hair?'

'Whose?' Skelton asked.

'Mr Duncan's.'

'What about it?'

'There's such a lot of it.'

'What d'you mean?'

'He's fifty-eight.'

'He never is.'

'He is,' Edgar said.

'I thought he was about my age.'

'I saw his date of birth on a thing once. 1871. And it's not even grey. I don't know whether you've ever noticed, but dipsomaniacs nearly always have a very full head of hair.'

'You think Aubrey's a drinker?' Skelton asked.

'That would be one explanation.'

'He doesn't look or act like a drinker.'

'They never do. The other explanation would be that he wears a wig.'

'It looks very real.'

'Few people properly appreciate the wigmakers art because, of course, when you see a really good example, you don't realise it's an example at all.'

'I never thought of that. What's Wafd?'

'I think, sometimes, he just makes words up to sound clever.'

CHAPTER SEVENTEEN

Mila found her Saturday morning archery class particularly tiring. A stiff breeze was blowing. Trying to teach the girls how to adjust their aim in order to take its effect into account was a thankless task. Bows were pointing dangerously in all directions.

'But you said we had to aim to the left, Mrs Skelton.'

'Not ninety degrees to the left, Hermione. You're poking Virginia's eye out as it is and once you let go of the string, that arrow will fly all the way through her head and hit the pavilion windows.'

At home, she begged tea from Mrs Bartram and took her newspapers into the sitting room where the fire was blazing comfortably.

Selfridges, she read, the big department store on Oxford Street, was planning to open an aeroplane department.

'Our belief,' said a director of the firm, 'is that flying in this country is as far advanced as motoring was in 1908.'

It was worrying. With every Tom, Dick and Harry popping down Oxford Street and picking out a Supermarine S.5, by the time she had trained, got properly equipped, bought an aeroplane and flown to Australia, the whole venture could have become as commonplace as driving to Slough.

Mrs Bartram came in with the tea and told her that Primrose Moorfield had escaped.

'Who is Primrose Moorfield?' Mila asked.

'The guinea pig.'

'I thought its name was Giselle.'

'Elizabeth decided to change it on Thursday.'

'Why?'

'I don't know.'

'Does she know a person called Primrose Moorfield?'

'I don't think so. I just went in the conservatory and the cage was empty. Elizabeth had fed it and changed its water before she went for her ballet lesson this morning, and you have to be ever so careful when you're closing the door because the catch can be tricky.'

'Are you sure it's not just lurking in the conservatory.'

'I've had everything out,' Mrs Bartram said. 'I've looked all around the house and I can't find it and neither have I seen any droppings, so I think it'll be outside somewhere.'

'Where is Mr Skelton?'

'He went for his walk.'

Mila weighed the inconvenience of getting out of her chair and going outside to look for the damn thing against that of dealing with Elizabeth's tears and decided that the former would be more bearable.

'Vic Walton said that guinea pigs have a home range of no more than a few hundred yards,' Mrs Bartram said.

Mila was about to ask who Vic Walton was but thought better of it.

'So, it'll most likely be in the garden or next door's garden or the back lane. I can't spare the time because I've got a pie half made.'

Mila put on her outside shoes, coat, hat, scarf and gloves and went into the garden.

She looked under shrubs and behind things making kissy noises and calling 'Primrose Moorfield', then, remembering that the creature had had only two days to get used to 'Primrose Moorfield' switched to 'Giselle'.

She felt weary. How, she wondered, could a little bending and standing make her so tired so quickly? For three weeks last summer she had been persuaded by the parish council to run a 'Physical Beauty and How to Keep it' class at the village hall. The class had been so popular that in the end she'd had to run three one-hour sessions on Saturdays with only five-minute breaks in between. The exercises were sometimes strenuous, yet her heart rate rose only a little above that of a Sunday stroll and, far from being out of breath, she'd had plenty with which to exhort and encourage the class.

She sat down on the little bench at the bottom of the garden by the sheds and found herself, despite the cold and the wind, wanting to stay there for quite a long time. Her throat felt scratchy.

After a while Skelton appeared, back from his walk.

'Mrs Bartram said the guinea pig's lost,' he said. 'Did you find it?'

She didn't reply.

'Are you all right?'

'I feel a little peculiar.'

'What sort of peculiar?'

'Unwell.'

'Stomach?'

'Throat. Fluey.'

'It's this wind, I expect. Takes it out of you. There it is.'

He ran around the back of the sheds and returned stroking the guinea pig.

'Just saw it out of the corner of my eye. Come on. Cup of tea'll see you all right.'

Mila barely touched her lunch. Afterwards she took a couple of aspirin, sat huddled in front of the fire and asked for a blanket.

'You can't be cold.'

'I think I'm feverish.'

Skelton remembered that not long after Christmas, when he was worried that the children would catch Dorothy or Mrs Bartram's colds, he had bought a thermometer at the chemists. They had all taken each other's temperatures and then he'd put it away somewhere safe.

It took him a good half hour to find it at the back of the drawer in his bedside cabinet.

He took Mila's temperature and said, 'Just over 98 degrees. Just by the little red arrow. You're fine. Out in the cold too long and you've taken a bit of a chill, I expect.'

'I do not take a chill when I get cold.'

'I expect the aspirin'll start working in a minute.'

Lawrence was at the table. On the way back from his

piano lesson he'd bought a balsa wood kit to make a station for his railway and was putting it together.

'Did you shake it?' he asked.

'You don't have to shake the aspirin. It's pills, not medicine.'

'No, the thermometer.'

Skelton remembered. You had to shake it until the mercury moved down the scale. He did so and took Mila's temperature again.

'One hundred and two. That's quite high, isn't it?'

'It's very high,' Lawrence said.

'Is it high enough to send for the doctor, do you think?'

'Not on a Saturday afternoon,' Mila said.

'It's high enough to go to bed, though.'

'I don't want to go to bed.'

The argument took a lot of time and energy. Eventually Mrs Bartram came in with her hat and coat on to say she was off now and she'd left the things out for tea.

She looked at Mila.

'You should be in bed.'

'I'm fine here, Mrs Bartram.'

'None of your nonsense, come on.'

Skelton watched Mrs Bartram take control and remembered how his mum used to be the same as Mila. Take no notice of anything his dad said, ever, but if one of his sisters told her to do something, she was putty in their hands.

Lawrence was scratching his arm. 'Can we get a piece of plywood eight feet by six?' he asked.

'What for?'

'So I can do a permanent layout with the train set and

won't have to get it out and put it together and break it up and put it away all the time.'

'Eight foot by six?'

'For two separate lines with points and stations.'

'Where would you keep it?'

'In the conservatory.'

'There isn't room.'

'There is. I've measured.'

'There wouldn't be room for anything else.'

'We hardly ever go in there.'

'We do in the summer.'

'I could move it in here in the summer.'

Lawrence scratched again.

'Are you all right?'

'Yes. I'm fine.'

'You keep scratching.'

'I'm a bit itchy.'

'Where's that crystal set thing I got you for Christmas?' Skelton asked.

'It's in the cupboard in my bedroom.'

'We should get it out, have a go at putting it together.'

'To be honest, I don't want to sound ungrateful, but I don't really see the point.'

'Why not?'

'We've already got a wireless set.'

'I know but it's—'

He was scratching again.

'Roll your sleeve up.'

Lawrence did so. He had a rash on his arm.

'How long have you had that?'

'I don't know.'

'Show me your other arm.'

The rash was there, too.

When they'd had their tea, Skelton took a cup and a piece of cake up to Mila.

'You haven't got a rash, have you?' he asked.

'I don't think so. Where?'

'On your arms.'

She pulled her arms out from beneath the bedclothes. There was no trace of a rash.

'No itching anywhere?'

'No.'

'Lawrence has got a rash on his arms.'

'It's probably the glue he's been using with his model,' Mila said.

'Can that give you a rash?'

'Maybe. What do you think it might be?'

'I don't know. He's got a rash and you've got a fever.'

'Yes.'

'A rash and a fever,'

'Yes?'

'I was just a bit worried it might be typhus.'

'Have you been reading *The Home Doctor* again?'

'I glanced.'

'We should burn that book.'

Mila buried herself under the bedclothes.

'Don't forget your cake,' Skelton said.

There were muffled sounds suggesting she didn't want it.

CHAPTER EIGHTEEN

'I had heard that it is proper to arrive slightly late for these embassy affairs,' Edgar said, 'so I asked the taxi to set me down in Curzon Street and walked very slowly so as to arrive twelve minutes late, which, going by the crush at the entrance, was exactly right.'

It was Monday, and they were in Kembles. Skelton, having finished a slice of sandwich cake, lit his pipe and sat back to listen.

'Extraordinarily impressive interior,' Edgar said. 'Marble, silk, real Tiepolos on the ceiling, wonderful wrought iron balustrades. In the French style. Louis Quinze? That sort of thing anyway. Fussy and very expensive-looking. And nothing Egyptian at all, except the servants all wore tarbooshes and long white cotton coats down to their knees. And then there was the smell.

You know how sensitive I am to smell: Shalimar, Arpège, magnesium from the flash bulbs, Turkish cigarettes and of course mothballs. Although the mothballs may have just been me. My dinner jacket gets frequent outings, but my proper evening clothes had hung unused since the first night of *Don Giovanni* last year. I worked hard on them with a wet cloth and iron, but I fear that did more to release the smell than remove it.'

Edgar sorted through the slices of lemon that Norman had provided and chose one for his tea.

'I was ushered into the ballroom,' he said. 'There was a string quartet playing, but no dancing. I think other rooms might have been in use, but I didn't want to explore too much for fear of straying out of bounds, so I just managed one peek into an anteroom where servants were doing things with food. Looked like offal mostly. And some big fish. Dates, but not like the ones you have at Christmas. So, I went back into the ballroom, stationed myself against one of the pillars and drank in the spectacle . . . and two passionfruit cocktails.'

'Who else was there?' Skelton asked.

'Lots of politicians and business people whose pictures you see in newspapers but whose names you can never remember. A gentleman with a big moustache and small glasses who you could tell was very important by the gaggle of admirers around him and who I thought might have been either Theodore Roosevelt, the former American president or Rudyard Kipling.'

'I think Roosevelt died about ten years ago.'

'Must have been Kipling, then. There was an awful lot of that sort of thing going on.'

'What sort of thing?'

'People looking at other people and wondering whether they were T. S. Eliot or the Bishop of Nyasaland. Lots of soldiers as well, in uniforms, some of whom may have been sailors.'

'Did you speak to any of these people?'

'Some. There seemed to be a lot of young men who had letters instead of jobs. Like in the war when everybody was ADC to the DFO at the MOA. Usually their first question was to ask what connection I had with Egypt. Well, saying I was clerk to the barrister leading the defence of an Egyptian chap accused of cutting his wife into little pieces didn't seem quite right, and saying 'None at all' tended to bring a halt to further conversation, so I said that I worked for a firm representing the interests of certain Egyptian citizens currently residing in England and that seemed to make people think I was perhaps an important businessman or a spy.'

'And was that better?'

'Yes, it had the happy consequence of precluding further questions of that nature, which meant we could move on to more pressing matters.'

'Like what?'

'All sort of things. One chap, whose name I didn't catch, had an interest in theatre, so we spoke of Gerald du Maurier's rather *too* casual performance in *Peter Pan* at the St James's. I think we may have touched on the ubiquitous tyranny of the wireless, too. Then the string quartet was joined by a group of men with sort of zithers and clarinetty things and lutes. They *all* looked like Kipling. And a stately matron came on – she looked more like Kipling than Kipling. And she sang. A contralto. Sounded like a felled bison to me, but she went down very well. An Egyptian lady standing next to me kindly translated the lyrics. "He taught me to regret" was one of the lines, and then there was quite a lot about acacia trees, and then some more about regret. You've got coconut on your tie.'

Skelton pulled his tie from his waistcoat and examined it.

'I haven't been eating coconut. I think it's icing sugar.'

'It's much too coarse for icing sugar. It's desiccated coconut,' Edgar said.

'I haven't had any . . .' Skelton licked his finger, dabbed at the detritus and tasted. 'No, you're right. It is coconut. Where did that come from?' It had smeared. He rubbed. 'Go on. You had the lady singing about regret and trees.'

'Yes. Then my feet began to trouble me, so I sat down on a little gold chair next to a crumpled gentleman who was very morose and very drunk. I asked him what connection he had with Egypt and he told me that he had recently been there on his honeymoon. So, I asked him whether his wife was present and he said that soon after their return to England she'd asked for a divorce. He was a writer. You know that book that everybody said was very funny.'

'Which one?'

'Came out a year or so ago. Everybody said it was very funny.'

'A novel?'

'Yes. I think so. Anyway, he wrote that. Although, having met the man I can't believe it can have been at all funny.'

'Perhaps it was very sad, and people took it the wrong way,' Skelton said.

'Possibly. Then an Egyptian gentleman came and expressed deep admiration for the drunk writer and the drunk writer swore at him and the Egyptian gentleman said he was something of a writer himself but had never dared embark on anything as ambitious as a novel. And the drunk writer said that given pen, paper and six weeks with no telephone and no wife, anybody can write a novel.'

'Is that true, d'you think?'

'I meet all the requirements and I've never written one.'

'Have you ever had the six weeks?'

'There is that. Anyway, the drunk writer went away so I struck up an interesting conversation with the Egyptian gentleman. Mr Turnbull,' Edgar said.

'Doesn't sound very Egyptian.'

'Jabari Turnbull. His mother's Egyptian. His father's English. From Burnley. Mr Turnbull is a reporter, for the *Manchester Guardian* mostly, I think, who has spent a great deal of time in Egypt, so he knows all the ins and outs of who's who and what's what. He in fact brought up the matter of the little diplomatic flurry that Dr Aziz is causing, which meant that I could declare my interest in the matter without overstepping the bounds of good taste.'

'And what was he able to tell you?'

'It is very interesting and could be useful, I think. Dr Aziz is from a very wealthy, very well-connected family. Mr Turnbull in fact pointed out two of his brothers who were standing with the most glittering company – men with medals and sashes and ladies in Lanvin and Schiaparelli.'

'What does that mean?' Skelton asked.

'Lanvin and Schiaparelli are dress designers. He told me that possibly the family is behind this extradition request.'

'What, they spirit him home to Egypt, a pretend trial and an acquittal?'

'That's one possibility.'

'What other . . . ?'

'It's all very murky. Mr Turnbull suspects that Dr Aziz may indeed have been framed for the murder.'

'Who by?'

'Most probably by some anti-British faction in Egypt. Remember Aubrey said that if Aziz were to hang, it could be used to stiffen resistance against the British oppressors. So, in order to promote this anti-British feeling, some assassin murders poor Mrs Aziz, cuts her up and dumps her in a suitcase in the nearby quarry.'

'Bloody hell. So the killer could be an Egyptian assassin?'

'Like a Sax Rohmer story, isn't it?'

'But the family won't stand for that, will they?' Skelton said. 'They can push through the extradition, he can go back to Cairo, safe and sound, and Egypt will remain on good terms with Britain.'

'Well, I think it's a little more complicated than that.'

'In what way?'

'I don't know. Mr Turnbull was about to say something else, but then there was a kerfuffle because Gloria Swanson turned up.'

'The film actress?'

'Yes.'

'You met Gloria Swanson?'

'Well, I didn't meet her. I saw her. She made a spectacular entrance in a gown of vivid green crepe that flowed over her like a waterfall. Feathered turban, gloves above the elbow in matching green, emeralds as far as the eye can see and a brown paper carrier bag.'

'A brown paper . . . ?'

'The sort you get from a greengrocer.'

'What was . . . ?'

'Mr Turnbull told me it was her food. She'd presumably dropped in on her way to a dinner party. She's a vegetarian apparently. Always takes her own food in a paper bag.'

'You didn't get a chance to . . . ?'

'Chat to her? Good lord, no.'

'No, you didn't get a chance to look inside the carrier bag?'

'No.'

'I was just wondering what she'd have for dinner.'

'I've heard that vegetarians eat a lot of beans.'

'Not raw. They'd be poison.'

'Perhaps cooked, in little jars,' Edgar said.

'Could be. Celery?'

'Without a doubt.'

'What happened to Mr Turnbull?'

'There was a bit of a press forward to see Gloria and when I turned back, he was gone.'

Skelton was plunged deep in thought.

'D'you think, if the extradition doesn't go through,' he said, 'any of this could be fashioned into a defence?'

'It would depend, I would have thought, on Mr Turnbull. If he's got actual written evidence that some Egyptian political faction has framed Aziz . . .'

'Even convincing hearsay might be enough to cast doubt. He works for the *Manchester Guardian*?'

'I think that's what he said.'

'Can't be that hard to get hold of, then. Have a word with Aubrey. See what he can do.'

CHAPTER NINETEEN

Skelton had written to Hughes and Bowers, the estate agent in Slough, and they had sent him details of the new bungalows outside Maidenhead. They were on a bit of a hill above the flood plain, overlooking an expanse of meadow down to the river.

In Hunslet, he showed them to his mum and dad.

'There's a proper bathroom and a kitchen and an electric immersion heater for the hot water and the garden's easily as big as your allotment. And the thing is, I'd only be a fifteen-minute drive away so you can come and have Sunday lunch with me and Mila and the kids, or we could pop over and see you.'

His mum kept staring at the details from Hughes and Bowers, not looking up once. His dad was filling his pipe, very slowly, very carefully. Neither of them was listening, they were just trying to think of the politest way to say 'no'. But still he persisted.

'I know from the times you've visited before you've never thought much of being down south, but when you're living there you really start to appreciate the differences. The weather for a start. I mean, it gets cold in the winter – everywhere does – but it's not that sharp cold you get here. D'you remember those times you've come home from work and you couldn't move your face it was that cold? It's hardly ever like that down south. And the air's ever so clean. Up London you get the fog and everything, but out by Maidenhead there's none of that. Bit of river fog, but not the filthy, dirty stuff you breathe in London, and nothing like the soot and smells you get up here. You've said it yourself, Mum. All the days when you hang your washing on the line and it comes in dirtier than it went out.'

His voice trailed off. His mum turned the estate agent's paper over. There was nothing written on the back.

'They look lovely, don't they, Ernie?'

Skelton's dad looked up, slightly alarmed, worried that his wife might actually mean what she was saying. Reassured by the look on her face, he turned back to the fire and said, 'All right.'

'Only, the thing is,' Mum said, 'There's our Winnie and everybody, isn't there? And Amy and Jean pop in nearly every day, and I'm supposed to be making Jean a frock on my machine.'

'What do you think, Dad?' Skelton asked.

'Your mother's right.'

'I just thought . . . you've worked hard all your life. I wanted to do something for you. It really is very nice.'

'Well, it's ever so kind of you, Arthur,' his mum said. 'Isn't, Ernie? Lovely of Arthur to think of it.'

Dad took a spill to light his pipe but couldn't get it to catch on the hot coals. He tried in another place and then another, but still it wouldn't take. Skelton gave him his matches, and Mum saw the look on her son's face as he watched his father fumbling to strike one. She knew he was worried. She knew why he was worried. She knew he was doing everything he could, wanting to spend all this money trying to put things right. But things couldn't be put right. Not like they were ten years ago. They never could be.

The following afternoon, Skelton met Edgar at the station in Leeds, and they took the tram to Armley. Edgar had brought Dr Aziz some packets of Player's, matches and a copy of *The American Journal of the Medical Sciences* he'd spotted in the bookshop next to the Charing Cross Hospital. It looked like the sort of thing Dr Aziz would like. He had flicked through it on the train and found himself momentarily diverted by a paper on the use of the vermilion spotted newt – *Diemictylus viridescens Rafinesque* – for mosquito control.

The warder brought in chairs for them and Edgar presented his gifts.

Aziz thanked him and glanced briefly at the contents of the magazine, then with a certain regret at having to delay the pleasure of reading it, he addressed himself to the business in hand.

'I believe that Mr Duncan has already been in touch with you about the latest request from the Egyptian government,' Edgar said.

'Indeed he has,' Aziz said. 'My first question is, when you

say "the Egyptian government", who exactly do you mean?'

'Well, my understanding is that your family has a degree of influence in these matters,' Skelton said.

'This is what I suspected.'

'Now, the decision as to whether the British government accedes to this request is entirely out of my hands,' Skelton continued, 'but it might, to some extent, depend on your wishes. They will take into account your opinion on whether or not you'll receive a fair trial in Egypt.'

Aziz fell silent. He opened one of the packets of Player's that Edgar had brought, offered one to Edgar, lit both cigarettes and pulled the ashtray on the wooden stand around so that it stood equidistant between them. Then he turned back to his table and spent a while smoothing the silver paper from the Player's packet.

When the silence grew worrying, Skelton asked, 'Do you know a journalist called Jabari Turnbull?'

'I don't think so,' Aziz said. 'Should I?'

'He seems to believe that you may have been "framed" for the murder.'

'By whom?'

'By some anti-British faction in Egypt – a political group or some such – who might want to make political capital out of your arrest and possible execution.'

'Am I really so important?'

'Your family is. If you were to come to any harm at the hands of the British, I can't imagine that it would pass unnoticed,' Skelton said.

Aziz turned to his desk again and, taking his time, squared some papers, spotted a note he'd made on a scrap of paper, opened a book and found the place where the note belonged.

'My father is a cotton trader who expanded into shipping,' he said. 'He owns a sizeable fleet of steamships. Business held no interest for me. I wanted to become a doctor. My father thinks he controls the world and all who live in it, especially his sons. My mother had a brother, Uncle Ozzie, the black sheep of the family. He lived in France and sometimes in Algeria. As you know, I was sent to school here in England. At Rugby. The last time I came home from school, in '08, instead of going to Cairo, I jumped ship in Algiers and went to see my uncle. He played cards and had been doing well at the casino. He gave me three thousand francs – more than a hundred pounds – and said every man had to make a choice to become a free man or a slave. I took his money and studied medicine at the University of Edinburgh. I have been a free man ever since. Even in this prison cell. Nevertheless, because I defied my father's wishes, he disowned me more than twenty years ago.'

'But all the same, family ties . . .'

Aziz stiffened. 'A terrible thought has occurred to me.'

'Yes?'

'My family has very sound monetary reasons for wanting the British to leave Egypt. If the Egyptian government were to seize Suez and perhaps extend preferential treatment and possibly even a monopoly to Egyptian ships wishing to pass through the canal, my father could become, without exaggeration, the richest man in the world.'

'I'm sorry, Dr Aziz,' Skelton said, 'are you suggesting that your own family might have been responsible for your wife's death?'

'I'm afraid so.'

'Even though you might hang for it?'

'As I say, my father disowned me twenty years ago and now has dogs and horses upon whose lives he places a higher value than mine. If I hang, he will, as you say, use my death as a focus for unrest – he owns newspapers and no doubt provides funds for many political movements – fascist, communist, Muslim, Christian – doesn't matter as long as they want the British out.'

'And if the extradition goes through?'

'He will use it as a demonstration of how he can make the British do his bidding and how he saved his beloved son from the injustice of their courts. Not quite such a satisfactory outcome, but useful all the same.'

'And would you receive a fair trial?'

'No. I would not receive a fair trial. I would receive no trial at all,' Aziz said.

'You mean, the charges would be dropped?'

'Yes. But in my father's eyes I would be crawling home with my tail between my legs, a failure, living vindication of his view of the world and proof that those who disobey suffer the consequences.'

'And the consequences . . . ?'

'He will condemn me to some small part of his mighty empire, somewhere in the south, and put me in an office where I will spend my days juggling pieces of paper and arguing with traders. And if I refuse, he will remind me that with one word he could have me imprisoned or executed. And while I accept that such a fate might be preferable to the hanging shed, I must also stress that I am innocent of any crime. If I go to Cairo, I will never have an opportunity to prove that fact in open court. For the rest of my life the reputation would be a cloud above my head: "There goes the man who cut up his wife." I would prefer to stay here and prove my innocence in an English court.'

'I should warn you that the way things stand at the moment, your innocence will be very hard to prove.'

'Even if my wife is not found alive and well, and I still most certainly believe that she will be found, I trust that British justice will run its course, prosecution and defence will argue their cases, the judge will advise, the jury will decide and I will walk free.'

'Innocent people have been hanged.'

'Possibly they did not have the benefit of your advocacy, Mr Skelton.'

Skelton felt the hair on the back of his neck rise. Once there had been a seventeen-year-old girl, accused of murdering her baby. She, too, had had blind faith in his ability to secure her acquittal. They had dragged her from the court screaming, and still she screamed in his dreams.

'I very much fear that your faith in my powers and in the British judicial system may be dangerously misplaced,' he said.

'In which case "how weary, stale, flat, and unprofitable seem to me all the uses of this world" and I am better off hanged.'

They rode in silence on the tram back to the station. Skelton was absorbed in his thoughts and Edgar thought it best not to intrude.

Indeed, they barely spoke a word to each other until Doncaster. Then, when he was sure they were alone in the compartment, Skelton said, 'Bugger.'

'Indeed,' Edgar said, and lit a Gold Flake.

'He doesn't *know*, does he, that he'd be stuck in a smelly

office all his life? He's a qualified doctor. How old is his dad?'

'No idea. Aziz isn't the oldest child and he's nearly forty, so sixty or seventy at least.'

'The father will die,' Skelton said. 'Anything could happen. But Aziz prefers to stay here. Now, I don't know about you, but there's only one reason anybody in their right mind would make a choice like that.'

'What's that?'

'He really is innocent, isn't he?'

'Seems like it.'

'Of course he is. And we haven't got a scrap of evidence to prove it.'

'Perhaps Jabari Turnbull can save his bacon.'

CHAPTER TWENTY

c/o The Cross Keys Public House, Fetterick

Monday 20th January, 1930

My dear cousin Arthur,
Thank you for your letter.

We are doing our modest best here in Fetterick. Most of our days are spent getting the evening meal ready for the people of Abbotsbank with help from Jack, Beryl and Margaret. Actually, Jack works for an insurance broker in Fort Blaine and Margaret is the school secretary at the girls' high school, so they have very little time during the day to do anything, But Beryl, Jack's wife, is an industrious and resourceful woman.

She has butchers, bakers, grocers and greengrocers all saving stuff up for us: trimmings of meat and bones that would have otherwise gone as dog food, three-day-old bread, vegetables that you can cut the rotten parts away from, damaged sacks of flour that the mice have been at. We start early and I drive Beryl around in the Morris. We miss out Fort Blaine itself because they have their own charities, but Beryl seems to know all the towns and villages within a twenty-mile radius, some of which are quite prosperous. You soon learn what you need to feed the forty or so people who turn up.

We go out scrounging in the mornings, then, around one o'clock, we get the stoves going and put on the big pots to boil. We do not use the washtub and cauldron any more. Margaret has borrowed two big proper cooking pots from the school. We put them on early because it takes a lot of boiling to get the goodness out of bones.

Beryl keeps us entertained as we drive around with stories about local people. The other day, as we passed Aldwin House, I mentioned that I heard poor Edna Aziz had once lived there and wondered whether Beryl had known her.

She had not. She knew Edna's mum and dad by sight, but never to speak to. Otherwise, all she could tell us was local gossip which I am sure you have already heard, but I shall record it here just in case you find any of it useful.

Edna's parents, Mr and Mrs Goldie, were wealthy. From the linoleum that I am sure I have already told you about.

They had just the one child. Mrs Goldie was too ill to have any more.

Edna was clever. She went to the girls' high school in Fort Blaine. Beryl had the impression that she did not have many friends but kept herself to herself, devoted to her studies.

After she went to Edinburgh University, she never returned home, or did so very rarely. Again, Beryl did not know why, but suspected that it was because the parents disapproved of her marriage. The first time Beryl laid eyes on her was in 1928, when Mr Goldie died, and Edna came back to attend his funeral and to deal with the estate. Her mother, was very ill by this time and had a live-in nurse. Edna wasted no time selling off the house and dismissing the servants – there were a lot of them, cook, nurse, maids and a gardener or two – and moving her mother to a nursing home in Edinburgh. Beryl did not know what she did with the family business. Presumably she sold that off, too, but she had heard it had not been doing well, so there may have been debts.

We had forty-three for tonight's meal and we were able to provide them each with a large piece of bread, a bowl of stew and cups of tea. It is good, nourishing food. It has not been two weeks since we first began to boil up the stew but already you can see people putting flesh on their bones. Norah and I are thriving on it. Martin and Owen, the two lads who, the first time that they came, seemed to be at death's door, now run their mother ragged, and she, who could barely lift her head to speak, has the strength to give them a good clip around the ear whenever they deserve it.

As we were eating, Beryl mentioned that Mr Easy used to know some of the people at Aldwin House and got him talking about them. He said he was particular friends with the gardener, a man called Ben Murcheson. And thereby hangs another tale that may be of interest to you.

There is slum housing in Fort Blaine as bad if not worse than that on Abbotsbank in Fetterick, but forty years ago there were even worse slums in a place called 'The Burgess'. This was an accretion of wooden hovels sometimes built one on top of the other like tenements. That was where Ben Murcheson was born.

His parents died when he was seven or eight, leaving him in the care of a brother and sister. He took to the streets, begging for farthings and evading the police, who would have shipped him off to the workhouse or an orphanage.

One of his regular spots was just outside A. W. Goldie's offices on Hunter Street in Fort Blaine. He was a good beggar who, rather than playing the sick and starving innocent, always retained a sort of solemn dignity, sometimes engaging passers-by in very formal conversation, like a maiden aunt over the teacups. 'And how are you today, sir? The weather is unusually inclement for the time of year.' Mr Goldie would usually give the lad a couple of pennies and, if he had time, stop for a chat. Then one winter's day he happened to see Ben not at his usual pitch but crouched in an alleyway at the side of the building. He was white-faced and shivering and clearly ill. Mr Goldie brought him into the office and tried to get him to eat or drink, but the boy fainted clean away, so a doctor was called. The doctor ascertained that Ben had a bad fever and a weak pulse and spoke of burial arrangements. It seemed to the doctor that, since the boy had neither home, nor bed, nor shoes, there could be no other outcome.

But Mr Goldie took him home, gave him a bed and organised the maids to nurse him and keep him warm and fed. The boy recovered and stayed around the house, making himself useful, fetching coal for the fires, taking out the ashes, running errands. Always willing, always industrious.

Ben was a few months older than Edna. They played together. But, when she went to the high school, she grew out of him and he ran away.

He stayed away for a year. He went to sea, walked to Eyemouth and got a job with the herring fleet.

When he returned, the Goldies took him back as an assistant gardener, and then head gardener when the old gardener died. He lived in the old boathouse down by the lake, which he furnished with a stove and a bed and one or two other things.

Then the war came, Ben went off with the King's Own Scottish Borderers. It hardened him. When he came back, he had, sad to say, become a drinker, who, in his cups, often got into fights. He still kept Mr Goldie's gardens, but spent longer and longer travelling all over – off with the fishing boats and road gangs, digging sewers, gutting fish, Aberdeen to Plymouth.

You said in one of your letters that you wondered whether Edna Aziz had a lover. It did occur to me that this Ben Murcheson could be a candidate for that role. I dismissed the thought at first as too fanciful by far, but then, later in the evening, when everybody had gone home leaving just Beryl, Jack, Margaret, Norah and myself clearing up, we talked about Mr Easy's story. The idea that Edna and Ben may have been lovers seemed far from fanciful to others.

Norah told me to read *Wuthering Heights* by Emily Brontë, which, she said, tells just such a story of a rich man bringing a poor boy into his house and a love growing between the poor boy and the rich man's daughter – a love that endures even though they marry other people, that endures even after the woman dies and it is her ghost he loves.

I told her not to be so soft.

Beryl said that I did not understand passion.

I smiled at that and said she was probably right.

Beryl offered to show me what passion was like.

This made me nervous. I think it made Norah nervous as well.

Beryl smiled at Jack, and they both smiled at Margaret.

Margaret asked to borrow Norah's accordion.

'You play the accordion?' Norah asked.

'She's very good,' Beryl said.

So, Norah passed over the instrument. Margaret strapped it on and played an impressive flourish.

Beryl and Jack joined hands as if to dance a waltz, except that they stood too close, Beryl leaning into Jack with her head turned up, her lips close enough to kiss.

Margaret began to play four to the bar *chum chum chum chum* rhythm in a minor key, then added a wailing sort of a melody. They were off.

Perhaps you can remember the big tango craze from before the war. For two or three summers in Rhyl, the dance halls were full of it. Then it came back again for a while after the war, when all the gentlemen thought that they were Rudolph Valentino and ladies thought that they were Beatrice Dominguez. It was as popular up here in Scotland as it was down south. Beryl and Jack used to give demonstrations and teach the tango in Edinburgh. For a while they ran tango-teas in Fort Blaine, too, but the church and the council decided that the dance was an affront to human decency and banned it.

When they had finished the dance, Norah and I applauded enthusiastically. Beryl and Jack asked us if we would like to have a go. I was not at all sure, but before I could say so Beryl had grabbed me and Jack had grabbed Norah. Thankfully the postures they adopted were a good bit more seemly than the way they had held each other. They taught us one or two basic steps. We both have good rhythm, Norah and I, so we picked it up in no time and were dancing around the room.

It is not just a matter of learning the steps. You also have to have the right attitude. There really is nothing indecent about it at all. It is the dignity that matters. The holding yourself secure, precise and majestic.

It brought a new depth to my understanding of joy.

I am ever yours faithfully in the joy of Jesus,
Alan

CHAPTER TWENTY-ONE

Skelton was late getting home after his visit to Dr Aziz in Leeds. It was half past nine by the time his train pulled into King's Cross. Then he missed the five past ten from Paddington and had a half-hour wait for the next one, a stopping train that lumbered into Lambourn well after 11.30 p.m.

The house, he could see from the end of the road, was blazing with light. Mrs Bartram and Dorothy opened the door before he could get his key out.

'We were watching for you,' Mrs Bartram said.

'It's gone midnight,' Skelton said. 'What's . . . ?'

'Mrs Skelton took a turn for the worse. I sent for the doctor. He took one look at her and took her to the hospital in Reading.'

'The Royal Berkshire?'

'The big one.'

'Are the children all right?'

'They were already in bed when the doctor came. Dorothy's telephoned to her mum and dad and they say she must stay, so both of us'll be here all night. Have you had your dinner?'

'I ate on the train. I'll get the car out and—'

'I don't think they'll let you see her at this time of night. Visiting hours are two and six. I'll make you some tea,' Mrs Bartram said.

Skelton came inside and put a call though to the hospital. He was answered by some sort of emergency desk and the chap said he didn't have any information about patients who'd just been admitted. He told Skelton to phone back in the morning after 8.30.

'I'm sure they'd telephone you if there was any news,' Mrs Bartram said.

'What time did all this happen?'

'Would have been half past eight or nine.'

'I'll drive round to Dr Spencer's,' Skelton said.

'It wouldn't be kind getting him up this time of night.'

The phone rang. It was Dr Spencer, only just back from Reading.

'She's comfortable,' he said. 'But her fever had risen again. She was delirious and having trouble catching her breath. I thought she'd be better off in a hospital bed.'

'But it's just a . . . what, a chest infection?'

'I'm afraid it could be pneumonia. Are you still there?'

'Yes, of course. Thank you for telephoning, Doctor, and thank you for your prompt action.'

* * *

He didn't sleep. In the morning he endured the sympathetic glances from Dorothy and Mrs Bartram and tried to stay cheerful as he explained to the children that their mother might have to stay in the hospital for a few days.

Lying to children is wrong. Mila had always been very firm on that point. Children, she believed, have robust minds that can withstand all kinds of shocks and setbacks. Shielding them from war, pestilence, plague, death and illness, telling them fairy tales, telling them that all is bright and beautiful in a perfect world, is a crime. Untold harm is wrought when they discover that the adults whom they have trusted without question have been telling them lies.

Nevertheless, he told Lawrence and Elizabeth there was nothing to worry about and lied so well that he almost believed it himself, which was a comfort. Elizabeth asked when her mother would be coming home.

'Hard to say. Next week, I expect.'

This, to a child, was an eternity. Elizabeth's face fell.

'Or probably much sooner than that,' Skelton said.

She brightened a little and went to put her coat on.

'Have you fed Primrose Moorfield?' Skelton asked.

'No, she hasn't,' Lawrence said in an undertone. He wasn't telling tales, just pointing out a problem that the men of the family possibly needed to take in hand. 'She keeps forgetting.'

'I'll do it when you've gone to school,' Skelton said.

'It's all right,' Lawrence said. 'I've already done it. And I changed the water and cleaned the cage on Tuesday.'

'Good man. As long as it gets done.'

'It is her guinea pig, though.'

'It's everybody's guinea pig.'

Dorothy took them off to school.

At 8.30 on the dot, Skelton put a call through to the hospital in Reading. The operator told him that the number was engaged. He asked her to try again and call him back when she got through.

The phone rang after fifteen minutes. The woman at the hospital was forbiddingly efficient. She said she could not connect him with the ward nor to the doctor in charge of Mila's case, but she could assure him – he heard her refer to a list and turn over a couple of pages – that Mila had passed a comfortable night. She confirmed that the afternoon visiting hours were between two and three and the evening six till seven. Skelton asked whether exceptions were ever made in urgent cases. In a voice suggesting that she made the same reply a hundred times a day, she told him that if anything occurred that might require his immediate attention, the hospital would be sure to get in touch with him.

Mrs Bartram offered him breakfast and he accepted a cup of tea and a piece of buttered toast. He drank the tea but left the toast with one bite taken out of it. He thought of going up to his study and trying to do some work. In his briefcase he had notes and references that he needed to go through, but there was no telephone extension in his study. For three months he had been waiting for the post office to put one in, but extensions, it seemed, were available only to personal friends of the Postmaster General.

What if the hospital rang and he didn't hear the ring? What if he limped downstairs so slowly that the phone had stopped ringing by the time he got there, or rushed too much, slipped and broke his neck, leaving the children without a father and possibly without a mother?

To make sure, he brought a chair out to the hall and sat by the phone in his overcoat because there was no fire out there.

Realising he'd better let Edgar know what was going on, and not wanting to tie the phone up, he asked Mrs Bartram to pop down to the post office and send a telegram to 8 Foxton Row: MILA IN HOSPITAL STOP PLEASE REARRANGE ALL STOP. He could have had another half-dozen words for the shilling it would cost, but Edgar would understand what he had to do without lots of 'postpone this' and 'cancel that'.

He tried to resist the temptation to fetch *The Home Doctor* but succumbed. It told him that pneumonia was caused by certain germs getting into the lungs. The outlook depended on the resistance of the patient and the virulence of the germs. '*If the infection is by a very virulent germ then death may occur in an apparently perfectly healthy individual.*'

Mila's oilskin coat, the one she wore on particularly wet days, was hanging in the hall. He stared at it for a while. When he could bear it no more, he looked away. He could still smell it, though.

There are two sorts of pneumonia, he read, lobar pneumonia and bronchopneumonia. Both are awful. The progress of the disease lasts for seven to ten days.

Skelton wondered whether the seven to ten days would be measured from the previous Saturday when she had first fallen ill, or from yesterday when she was taken into hospital.

Mrs Bartram came back and made him another cup of tea.

'Aren't you cold out here? There's a lovely fire in the dining room.'

'I'm worried I might miss the telephone ringing.'

'It's very loud. I can usually hear it when I'm right down the bottom of the garden burning rubbish.'

'All the same.'

He looked at his wristwatch, the Omega that Mila had given him for Christmas. It was almost ten. It would take him forty-five minutes to get to Reading. Perhaps a little longer if there was a hold-up in Maidenhead and perhaps even longer if, for example, he got stuck behind a hay cart or some such. There are no hay carts in January, of course, but the point still held. Best leave it an hour so as not to be late. Leave at one to be there by two. Or an hour and a quarter. Or a half. He would leave at half past twelve.

He made sure he had his car keys in his trouser pocket and felt inside his jacket for his wallet. He only had to put his hat on and his scarf and gloves. The scarf was hanging in front of him. The hat and gloves were on the hall table. He put them all on. No point leaving everything to the last minute.

At twelve, Mrs Bartram asked whether he would want lunch before he left. He told her he wouldn't have time.

At a quarter past twelve he left. There was no hold-up in Maidenhead and neither was there a hay cart on the road. He was opposite the hospital, parked at the end of Princes Street just before one. He found a florist and bought flowers. At a fruiterer he bought apples and bananas. They had no grapes. Then, realising that Mila would not be getting her supply of four newspapers a day, he found a newsagent and bought six of them, a *Spectator* and a copy of *Aeroplane*.

By a quarter to two, loaded down with parcels, he was waiting in the hospital foyer for the bell that marked the start of visiting time to ring.

A nurse took him to Mila. Curtains were drawn around her bed. A cylinder of oxygen stood to one side. She had an arrangement of rubber tubes strapped to her head and disappearing up her nostrils.

He put down the flowers, fruit and reading material and gave her a cheerful hello. She did not respond. She did not open her eyes. He felt her forehead. She was very hot.

He went to find a nurse.

'She seems to be unconscious.'

'The doctor has given her something to make her sleep. It's best that she saves all her energy for getting better.'

He returned to Mila. The charts at the bottom of the bed were difficult to decode, but the lines that possibly showed pulse rate and temperature seemed to be even, which he hoped was a good sign.

None of the other patients on the ward were unconscious. Some of them seemed quite well, chatting happily with their visitors.

Skelton sat and looked at his wife, glad every time she breathed.

When they were first married, she used to like him to read to her. They had fallen out of the habit.

He opened the copy of *The Times* he'd bought and read: 'CONVICT'S JUMP TO DEATH. TEMPORARY INSANITY. EFFECT OF TEN YEARS SENTENCE. The inquest on the body of James Edward Spiers of Delancey Street, Camden Town, a carpenter who, after being sentenced to ten years' penal servitude and the "cat" jumped over the balcony outside his cell in Wandsworth Prison, was held yesterday by Mr Ingleby Oddie in the Visiting Justices' Room at the prison.'

He kept reading until the bell went.

On the way out, he spoke to the nurse again and asked whether he could see the doctor to discuss Mila's case. She told him it wouldn't be possible. He asked whether they'd determined whether Mila had lobar or bronchopneumonia, and hoped he'd got the pronunciation right. Her manner changed slightly. It's a wonder what a couple of technical terms can do.

'Lobar,' she said. 'The illness was detected too late to try the serum treatment. She's being given morphia for the pain and to help her rest.'

'Does she wake up at all?'

'We wake her every four hours to feed her.'

'She's eating?' Skelton asked.

'Fluids: milk, cream, sugar, raw eggs.'

'She doesn't like raw eggs.'

The nurse smiled.

What Skelton wanted to ask was *Will she still be alive in five minutes' time, five days' time, thirty years' time?* but he knew the nurse couldn't answer questions like that.

He left.

The Home Doctor had said that there would be a 'crisis' when the temperature would quickly drop and the patient feel much better. There is a danger, though, that the temperature may continue to drop to subnormal levels, resulting in general collapse and death.

He was home in time for the children's return from school. They were surprised to see him. He said he'd been to see their mum and she would have to stay in hospital for another night, but that she sent lots of love and had asked him to remind Lawrence to do his piano practice and to ask Elizabeth whether Primrose Moorfield had everything she needed or would a trip to the pet shop be necessary.

Lawrence said that Primrose Moorfield had food and straw, but again this was no thanks to Elizabeth.

Elizabeth drew with her crayons. Lawrence got on with his homework.

'Anything I can help you with?' Skelton asked.

'Not really, no. It's the Hundred Years' War.'

The Hundred Years' War lasted more than a hundred years. The Battle of Agincourt was in 1415. That was all he knew about the Hundred Years' War.

At five he set off to see Mila again. Elizabeth had wanted to come with him, but he had told her that patients were only allowed one visitor each and children weren't allowed at all. She sulked, so he gave her sixpence and said that it could only be spent on sweets. To be fair, he gave Lawrence sixpence too, with the same condition. This was, he knew, a terrible thing to do, but desperate times call for desperate measures.

Mila was unchanged. Her temperature was unchanged. Her pulse was unchanged. He read to her.

'"PARROT DISEASE". WOMAN'S DEATH IN LONDON. MEDICAL EVIDENCE AT INQUEST. The first inquest to be held in London on the body of a supposed victim of the present outbreak of "parrot disease" (psittacosis) took place at the London Hospital, Whitechapel, yesterday.'

At seven, the bell rang. He gently kissed Mila's forehead. On the way out, Skelton saw the nurse again.

'It couldn't be parrot disease, could it?' he asked her.

'Does she have a parrot?'

'No.'

'Has she been near parrots?'

'Not as far as I know.'

'It doesn't seem likely, then, does it?'

He could see that any respect he'd garnered from knowing words like 'lobar' and 'broncho' had evaporated.

He left, walked slowly back to his car and drove home.

Mrs Bartram had left him a plate of ham sandwiches. He made himself a cup of cocoa and ate them while staring at the embers of the fire.

For some reason he found himself thinking about Ibrahim Aziz in his cell in Armley prison.

He'd lost his wife, too.

CHAPTER TWENTY-TWO

On the Friday morning, Skelton decided to go into work. Just for the morning. He could still easily be at the hospital for the afternoon visiting time. Anything would be better than sitting at home and worrying. And besides, if he took another day off work, the children would know that something was seriously wrong and start to worry.

'Do I take it that Mrs Skelton is back at home and all is well?' Edgar asked.

'No.'

Skelton gave a short account of Mila's condition. Then he noticed the expression on Edgar's face.

'I'd rather you didn't look at me as if I was a fragile piece of porcelain. What have you told Clarendon-Gow and everybody else?'

'I told them that your wife was ill.'

'Did you say she was in hospital?'

'No, but they will assume it's something quite serious, otherwise you wouldn't have taken a day off.'

'I'm just a little leery of everybody saying "How is everything, old chap?" in a concerned voice, not least because it'll be the same concerned voice they use in court and thus raise immediate questions of sincerity.'

'I'll do what I can to make sure nobody gives a fig,' Edgar said, with just enough of a smile to make a difference.

'That's very kind of you.'

'I'll go and hurry the tea along.'

Skelton stood at the window. The postman was sitting on the wall opposite, sorting through his bag. He'd either lost something or got it all in a muddle.

Edgar returned with the tea. Aubrey Duncan was with him.

'Mr Duncan has some urgent business he wishes to discuss,' Edgar said. And he straightened his mouth into a line and cocked his head almost imperceptibly on one side to indicate, 'I'm sorry there was nothing I could do to stop him coming up.'

In reply Skelton raised an eyebrow to ask, 'Does he know about Mila?', and Edgar made a tiny shake of the head.

'Come in, Aubrey,' Skelton said. 'I see Edgar's brought three cups.'

Skelton sat in one of the low chairs. Aubrey perched a tiny fraction of buttock flesh on the edge of the desk and still managed languidly to stretch his legs without falling over.

'I have excellent news,' he said. 'I've spent most of the morning on the phone to Gerry Danvers and he's been raising seven kinds of ruction at the FO and the HO with the result that we have at least a provisional agreement to extradite Aziz. There's a lot of toing and froing still to be done of course and—'

Skelton stood and said, 'No.'

'I'm sorry?'

'No. He mustn't be extradited.' There was an edge in Skelton's voice. Edgar looked up, alarmed. 'I have spoken to him about the matter. He's innocent of the crime and wishes his innocence to be properly proven and made public in an English court of law.'

'But if he goes to Egypt—'

'If he goes to Egypt, there will be no trial. His family will spirit him away to some backwater and he will carry the slur of being a wife-murderer with him to the grave.'

'But—'

'I am aware . . .' Skelton had raised his voice. 'I am painfully aware that the evidence against him is formidable, but nonetheless the man is innocent, and it is your job—'

'My job is to serve my client and defend his interests as best I can,' Aubrey said, 'and your job is exactly the same. It seems to me the best way of serving his interests at the moment is to get him out of the country and to safety. And can I remind you that if you insist on taking this matter to court, you have nothing to counter the overwhelming weight of prosecution evidence except for – what? – some whitefly larvae. And if you think you're in with the slimmest chance of finding anything else, can I also remind you that the trial begins in less than three weeks.'

'You're wrong,' Skelton said, shouting now. 'Your job and my job and the job of the police too is . . . he didn't do it and if he is not given the chance to prove his innocence, or, worse, if he hangs for a crime he did not commit, then everything that you do and everything that I do and everything that this country stands for and everything that happens in life is a complete and utter nonsense.'

Skelton was out of breath, almost sobbing.

'My dear fellow,' Aubrey said, 'are you . . . ?'

'Get out, please,' Skelton said. 'Go away, get out.'

Edgar ushered Aubrey out of the room muttering, 'Mr Skelton is under a certain strain. I'll explain outside.'

Skelton stood rooted to the spot, helpless. Ten minutes passed. Edgar returned.

'I've sent one of the lads out to find you a taxi to take you to Paddington. I'll come with you. Will you go straight to Reading? Aubrey understands completely and—'

'Don't let them send Aziz to Egypt, will you? You have to make sure of that. He'd rather hang than that. He as good as said so. And I have to do this, Edgar. I have to make sure the jury understands. I have to do these things. I have to keep everybody—'

Skelton cleared his throat and pulled himself together. Edgar looked out of the window. The taxi had arrived. He picked a pile of papers from the desk.

'Do you need any of this at home?' Edgar asked.

'No, I don't think so.'

Edgar smiled. 'I had a closer look,' he said.

'At what?'

'The edges, particularly around the sides above the ears. My big disappointment is that at no point did either you or he say "Keep your hair on."'

CHAPTER TWENTY-THREE

It had already begun to feel like a routine. At two he was back at Mila's bedside.

'MISHAP ON LMS RAILWAY. PASSENGER AND GOODS TRAIN IN COLLISION. A passenger train and goods train on the London, Midland and Scottish Railway came into collision near Whitehaven today. Considerable damage was done to rolling stock and the permanent way, but no one was seriously hurt. Mr A. Trevallion, a commercial traveller of Rathbone Place, London, suffered from shock.'

He didn't go home after the visit. He couldn't face the children, and anyway, it was important that they should stick as far as possible to their usual routines and he was never usually home when they got back from school.

He wandered around Reading instead. He looked at some hats and gloves, bought some model railway track and a signal for Lawrence and, guiltily, because he knew Mila would disapprove, *Flower Fairies of the Spring* and *Flower Fairies of the Summer* for Elizabeth.

He had two cups of tea at two separate cafes and a bun at the second, where he also had a long conversation with the proprietor about the quality of milk. The proprietor, who said his name was Jeb, thought it wasn't as good as it used to be. Skelton had to say that he hadn't really noticed any difference but deferred to the proprietor's judgement because a cafe owner would have had a great deal more to do with the product than he had.

'How many pints of milk does a cafe like this get through in an average day?' he asked.

'You'd be measuring it in gallons not pints,' Jeb said.

And Skelton said, 'That much, eh?'

Jeb thought the decline in standards was something to do with what they fed the cows on. Skelton was surprised to learn that cow food had changed. He had assumed that they still mostly ate grass. Jeb told him that grass is what they eat in the summer, but in the winter there is no grass and it's what they feed them on in the winter that you have to keep your eye on.

It was the steamiest cafe Skelton had ever been in, and the wet warmth and the know-it-all prattle brought a welcome comfort.

At six he was back at his post.

'BEAUTIFICATION OF ROADS. GROUPS OF SCULPTURE SUGGESTED. The progress made towards beautifying roads with trees and sculpture, and particularly securing the assistance of young people in sowing flower seeds in the hedgerows, was reported at the annual meeting of the Roads of Remembrance

Committee held under the presidency of Lord Ullswater last night at the Faculty of Arts Gallery, Golden Square.'

The following morning, Dorothy took Lawrence to his piano lesson and Elizabeth to ballet. While they were out, Dr Spencer called round to ask after Mila. He told Skelton that she was in the best possible hands and that although her temperature was still high, the fact that there was no fluctuation and that she was taking nourishment and keeping warm and rested was the best that one could hope for.

Skelton wanted to say, *No, it isn't.* The best that one could hope would be for Mila to be taking her archery class at the school like she always did on a Saturday morning and for her to come home in a foul mood, then insist they go on a ridiculously long walk that made his leg hurt so much he'd have to take aspirin and go to bed.

Lawrence and Elizabeth returned home. Dr Spencer said the usual things people say to children they don't know very well, and the children made the usual set of responses.

'Oh, before you go, I wonder if you'd have a look at this. Show Dr Spencer the rash on your arm, Lawrence.'

Lawrence took off his blazer and jumper and rolled up his sleeves. Dr Spencer examined the rash and asked, 'How long? How itchy? How persistent? Has it got worse? Have you been putting anything on it?'

Skelton told him that calamine lotion eased the itching, that it had got considerably worse and they had first noticed it when Lawrence was making a model using glue. This led to another string of questions about hobbies, new subjects at school, new gym or sports kit.

'There's that,' Skelton said, and pointed at the green and

black mould under the peeling wallpaper in the corner of the room. Dr Spencer looked at it, and then at the rash.

'You haven't been climbing up there and touching it, have you?'

Lawrence looked up at the mould. He'd never noticed it before. It did look worthy of further examination, though, and he resolved to get a chair and have a proper look as soon as the opportunity arose.

'No,' he said.

'Do you go riding? Have anything to do with animals?'

'Just the guinea pig,' Lawrence said.

'This is a new guinea pig?'

'We got it at Christmas,' Skelton said.

'She's called Primrose Moorfield,' Elizabeth said.

'Really, and why is that?' Dr Spencer asked.

'Because it's her name.'

'Where is she kept?'

'In her cage.'

'And where is the cage?'

'In the conservatory.'

'And who feeds Primrose Moorfield?'

'I do,' Elizabeth said.

'No, you don't,' Lawrence said. 'She's supposed to, but she forgets so I have to do it.'

Dr Spencer wrote a prescription for some zinc ointment and, in the hallway as Skelton was showing him out, said that he should keep Lawrence away from the guinea pig and it would probably be best to get rid of the thing altogether.

Skelton had read in some magazine that, when worry makes it impossible to sleep, you should write down your worries

216

because often you'll see they're not really worth worrying about at all. His were. His wife was dying, his father was dying, an innocent man had been falsely accused of a terrible crime. And there was nothing he could do to save any of them. On top of that, for the sake of his son's health, he had to take away his daughter's guinea pig. All of these things were well worth worrying about.

In the same magazine, he'd read that Sir Edwin Lutyens had built, or at least designed, a magnificent dolls' house for the Queen. It had many rooms and furniture and tiny ornaments, even food.

He decided to approach Lutyens and ask him to do something similar for Elizabeth. She'd like that. Possibly even more than a guinea pig.

How satisfying it must be to build things. Not to make drawings, not an architect, but to be a bricklayer or stonemason. Wasn't that the most honest thing a human being could do? Bricklayers make solid structures that serve a useful function. They provide shelter, a basic human need.

He'd been right when he told Aubrey it was all nonsense. The courts were nonsense factories peopled by barristers, judges, solicitors and clerks who were all employed to manufacture the nonsense needed to keep the myth of justice alive. There never was such a thing as a 'fair trial'. Only a fool could think there was.

In the final analysis, advocacy and cross-questioning was all just a lot of pantomime that had nothing to do with the outcome of a trial. Ashworth and Jeanes, the 'motor bandits', had gone to prison because they smirked at the wrong time. Thomas Winthrop, the ostrich feather thief, had gone to prison because he was good at organising football matches.

And both, it seemed, were stand-ins, scapegoats for real criminals. Or maybe that was an illusion, too. Perhaps the 'criminal mastermind' was as much a myth as the 'fair trial'. Something we like to believe in because it makes the world a more comfortable place in which to live. The myth that there are good people and bad people. And bad people aren't like 'us'.

Or perhaps it was time to start believing that other forces shape our destinies, darker forces for whom we are but playthings, the darker forces that had shoved a germ into his wife's lungs for no reason other than to bring endless grief to a family that could not have been less prepared for it; devils, demons, ghouls and hellions, djinns and banshees, avenging furies, Viking fiends and the all-knowing, all-seeing, all-possessing Home and Colonial Stores.

He took the children out for a walk on the Sunday morning and managed to look as if he was eating a hearty lunch before driving to the hospital.

'LORD BEAUCHAMP AND UNEMPLOYMENT. Lord Beauchamp, speaking last night at the annual dinner of the Manchester Reform Club, said that Mr Thomas had no plans to offer to cure unemployment. He was like a man floating to the rapids and seemed almost to have given up any hope of escaping them.'

It had been more than a week since the first symptoms. What would happen if there was no 'crisis'? Could she stay like this, eating raw eggs and absorbing morphia, indefinitely?

He turned back to *The Times*.

'MANCHESTER GUARDIAN JOURNALIST FOUND DEAD.'

CHAPTER TWENTY-FOUR

Skelton was exhausted, but still he dragged himself into work on Monday morning.

'Head in the gas oven, apparently,' Edgar said, skimming through the newspapers.

The *Manchester Guardian* journalist was Jabari Turnbull, whom Edgar had met at the Egyptian party, who had first mooted the possibility that Dr Aziz had been framed by some anti-British faction – or even his own family.

'Aubrey put a call through to the Manchester police first thing this morning,' Edgar said. 'He says he'll telephone when he has any news.'

Thankfully Skelton had no court appearance, but he had opinions to write and a complicated brief to master concerning a money-lending scheme in which, Edgar was sure, the key legal principle was the interpretation of *promissory estoppel* implied in Lord Cairns' judgement on *Hughes versus Metropolitan Railway Co. (1877).*

Skelton had no concentration for such matters. After the third attempt to explain it, Edgar resorted to drawing pictures.

The call from Aubrey came just before eleven. Skelton answered.

'Er . . . how is . . . ?' Aubrey asked.

'No, first I must apologise for my outrageous behaviour on—'

'Please don't say another word. How is she?'

Skelton thought before answering, then said, 'Comfortable.'

'I'm very glad. If there's anything I can do . . .'

'Thank you. Now, tell me, what have you learnt about Jabari Turnbull?'

'Little more than was reported in the papers. He took his own life at his flat somewhere off the Oxford Road. The police are not regarding his death as suspicious. He left a note saying his heart had been broken by a woman called Betty, an optician's assistant who lived in the flat upstairs. Nothing suspicious about her either. I've told them the death could have some bearing on the Aziz case, and they've agreed, with the family's permission, to bundle up any notebooks and diaries and send them down.'

'Good. Do you really think it might have some bearing on the Aziz case?' Skelton asked.

'Well, that's the thing, you see. I got the report in from Stanhope's, the detective agency, about that luggage shop, which of course also gives us a Manchester connection.'

'They found something?'

'They sent a stringer in, and he showed photographs of the suitcase and the label to' – Skelton heard Aubrey turn over pages in a report – 'Mr Pickering, the owner of the shop. He – as you were told – is an illegal bookie so was at first unwilling to talk. Money changed hands.'

'How much?'

'Ten pounds.'

'Is that the going rate these days?' Skelton asked.

'For information in a murder enquiry it's very reasonable. Anyway, Pickering recognised the suitcase as a model he'd sold three or four of and the label as a stock number written in his own handwriting. He was able to look up the sale in his ledger. He keeps excellent records, apparently.'

'Presumably he'd have to if he's bookie.'

'And he could confirm the date of purchase as Saturday 7th September 1929 but had no record of the name of the purchaser,' Aubrey said.

'Blast,' Skelton said. 'Could he remember anything about the transaction? Describe the person who bought it?'

'Apparently not.'

'Did the stringer show him a picture of Dr Aziz?'

'Yes. And one of Edna Aziz. He didn't recognise either of them.'

'That's something, I suppose,' Skelton said.

'In what way?'

'He'd have remembered an Egyptian coming in, wouldn't he?'

'Possibly.'

They said goodbye and Skelton replaced the receiver. Edgar had heard enough of both sides of the conversation to get the gist.

'I'm just trying to piece it together,' he said. 'So – the hypothesis here is that Mr Turnbull may not have taken his own life but may have been murdered by an Egyptian assassin . . . because he knew too much.'

'That sort of thing. Possibly.'

'And this would be the same Egyptian assassin that killed Edna Aziz.'

'Hypothetical Egyptian assassin,' Skelton said.

'So why would the hypothetical Egyptian assassin have bought the suitcase in Manchester?'

'What?'

'Does he live in Manchester?'

'I'm not with you.'

'I can see why he'd go to Manchester to kill Mr Turnbull, but why would he have gone there to buy the suitcase *before* killing Edna Aziz?' Edgar asked.

'Still not with you.'

'Either he lived in Manchester or he was visiting Manchester because he was a friend of Mr Turnbull's . . . *or* the plot to kill Edna Aziz and discredit Dr Aziz was hatched in cahoots with Mr Turnbull or . . . *or* . . . Mr Turnbull *is* the Egyptian assassin.'

Had Edgar lost his reason, Skelton wondered, or was the fog of exhaustion turning all words to mush?

'Who killed Turnbull, then?' he asked.

'Another Egyptian assassin, to make sure he wouldn't spill the beans.'

'So now we've got two mystery Egyptian assassins?'

'Or perhaps he killed himself because he was racked by guilt.'

Skelton closed his eyes and wished he'd stayed at home,

'Betty isn't an Egyptian name, is it?' Edgar asked.

'I wouldn't have thought so. Who's Betty again?'

'The woman in the flat upstairs who'd given him the elbow,' Edgar said. 'The other difficulty is that, when I met Mr Turnbull, he didn't seem much like an assassin.'

'How many assassins have you met?'

'Three.'

'Really?'

'Hired killers anyway.'

'And did they all conform to a type?'

'No.'

'There you are then.'

Skelton wasn't able to get to the hospital for the two o'clock visiting hour. He had been co-opted by a committee set up to discuss changes in the patent law. In the previous year he had been involved in a case about rubber processing, details of which were deemed relevant to the committee. Edgar had said he could postpone at the last minute, but Skelton had already decided that his sitting reading the newspaper out loud wasn't helping Mila's recovery so best press on as planned.

The gentlemen on the committee discussed at length such matters as the quantum and quale of a patent's subject matter and the vexed issue of disconformity. At school, Skelton had mastered the knack of falling asleep with his eyes open and an intelligent expression on his face. So that is what he did.

He wasn't called upon to say much to the committee and wouldn't have wanted to anyway; when you can see the pleasure others take in self-important babbling, you don't want to be a spoilsport.

There was just one moment when he became aware that he'd been asked some sort of a question and was expected to reply. He had the sense, from the drone that had been going on and from the expression on other people's faces, that it was a complicated question and not something like, 'What's your favourite colour, Arthur?' It would demand a considered answer.

So, he reached for his stock of platitudes and, assuming the expression that lawyers and their like put on when they make a 'joke', said, 'I think, when addressing oneself to all matters of this nature, the principle one should bear in mind is the fundamental axiom that "not only must justice be done, it must be seen to be done". Except that in this case' – short pause to let them know the punchline was coming – 'the latter most certainly predicates the former.'

It was utterly meaningless, but it was joke-shaped enough to get a grunt of a laugh and even a *sotto-voce* 'Hear, Hear'. They hadn't listened, anyway. Why would they want to do a thing like that? They were on a committee.

They talked some more, and he went back to his waking sleep.

The law and everything to do with it was indeed a heap of nonsense. Much better to be a bricklayer. He'd seen them using a spirit level. Imagine the pride you must feel when you'd made your wall eight feet high and still it was dead level, the mortar neat, the bricks flat and even.

Then, with a start, he remembered.

Was it like the war? he wondered. *Did they send a telegram?*

* * *

As soon as the meeting was over and he was back in his room, he telephoned the hospital. Again, the endless wait for the call to be connected. Then another 'comfortable'.

At six he was at her bedside.

'RIVAL SCHEMES FOR MERTON BYPASS. MINISTER OF TRANSPORT TO DECIDE. Rival schemes to relieve temporarily the congestion caused on the Kingston Road by the level crossing near Merton Park station have been laid before the Minister of Transport by the Surrey County Council—' and on and on.

Sometimes, when people are asleep, their eyes move beneath the lids. He'd read somewhere – possibly *The Home Doctor* – that this is thought to indicate that they are dreaming. Mila's eyes weren't moving.

He left her bedside for a moment to see if he could catch a word with the nurse.

'She's still eating well, is she? The raw eggs and cream?'

'Oh yes. Very well.'

'And you wake her up for that?'

The nurse didn't quite know how to answer. 'We wake her enough so that she can swallow safely.'

'Does she open her eyes?'

'I'm afraid I couldn't tell you. I haven't been supervising the proceedings.'

They were 'proceedings', were they?

Some crisis at the other end of the ward called the nurse away.

Skelton went back to Mila's bedside and reopened the newspaper.

'AIR CRASH IN SURREY. NO SERIOUS INJURIES. CATERHAM. An accident occurred at Whyteleafe near

Caterham today to an aeroplane containing a pilot and passenger. Both escaped serious injury. The pilot, Mrs Cecily Pemberton, was under instruction from the passenger, Flight Lieutenant J. C. Millard. They—'

'Read that again,' Mila said.

Her eyes were open.

Skelton couldn't speak.

'Cissy Pemberton's crashed her kite,' Mila said, and made a little chuckling sound. She cleared her throat and winced with the pain of it.

'I think I'd better get the nurse,' Skelton said.

He found the nurse at the far end of the ward and told her what had happened. The nurse hurried and took Mila's pulse and temperature.

'I'll telephone for the doctor,' the nurse said. 'Then I'm afraid you'll have to leave.'

It was, Skelton realised, the 'crisis'. He remembered what it said in *The Home Doctor*. The temperature would quickly drop and the patient feel much better, 'but there is a danger, that the temperature may continue to drop to a subnormal level, resulting in general collapse and death'.

While they were waiting for the doctor, he did what he could to straighten Mila's bedclothes.

Mila was looking around, examining her surroundings suspiciously.

'It this a hospital?' she asked.

'It is,' Skelton said. 'You've had pneumonia.'

'Don't be silly.'

'You have. Ask anybody round here.'

'I'm never bloody ill.'

'You bloody just have been. But you're on the mend now.

The main thing is to keep warm, get plenty of rest and eat a lot.'

'I am quite hungry.'

'Good.'

Mila looked at a spot on the ceiling with intense curiosity. 'Who's that?'

'Where?'

'Up there. Is there a creek?'

'I can't hear one,' Skelton said.

'No, not a creak. You were in a creek with a tiger . . . no, what do I mean . . . a tenant.'

'You've had a very high temperature and a lot of morphia.'

'That's all right then. No tiger.'

'Everything's all right. All you've got to do is lie there and stay calm and the doctor'll be here in a minute.'

'I am very hungry.'

'I expect they'll get you something to eat.'

'And the little buzzing things on the . . . terraces . . . that's the operative word.'

'No, I think the operative word is something more like morphia. There aren't any buzzing things or creeks or tigers or terraces.'

'Does Elizabeth have a guinea pig called Primrose Moorfield?'

'Yes, that is real.'

'I feared as much.'

There was a long pause. Skelton wondered whether she might have drifted back to sleep, but her eyes were still open, staring at the ceiling.

Suddenly they turned to look at him, with what he hoped was great fondness.

'And the other thing's true as well, isn't it?' she asked.

'Which other thing?'

There was a trace of a smile. 'Cissy Pemberton's crashed her aeroplane.'

CHAPTER TWENTY-FIVE

Skelton endured another restless night, haunted by that phrase from *The Home Doctor* – 'general collapse and death'.

At 8.30, he was at his desk at 8 Foxton Row and managed to put a call through to the hospital.

'Comfortable.'

She had survived the night. It had been fourteen hours since she had opened her eyes and spoken. He wasn't sure how long the 'crisis' was supposed to last, but this, surely, gave him licence to hope.

Edgar wasn't in. Daniel, one of the lads, said he'd mentioned before he left the previous day that he wouldn't be in until after twelve.

Skelton opened his post, wrote a few letters and addressed himself to *promissory estoppel* and *Hughes versus*

Metropolitan Railway Co. (1877). Edgar's diagrams were very useful indeed.

Daniel brought him tea. He drank a cup, lit his pipe and stood by the window. It was so dark and miserable out it could still have been night-time.

He still had to prove Dr Aziz's innocence, do something about his dad and get rid of the guinea pig without Elizabeth bursting into tears that might last the rest of her life, but Mila, for now, was alive.

He said it out loud, quietly, so that they wouldn't hear in the other rooms.

'Mila is alive.'

He puffed so hard on his pipe that the smoke caught in his throat and he found he couldn't stop coughing.

'Are you all right, old chap?' Edgar had entered. 'Do you need me to smack you on the back?'

'No, I'm fine,' Skelton said. Edgar was dressed for a funeral, black suit, black tie. 'You're jumping the gun a bit, aren't you?'

Edgar started to explain but Skelton pre-empted him. 'Mila's much, much better. Chatting almost coherently and pleased as punch because an old school friend almost died in an air crash.'

'Well, that is good news. Not about the air crash obviously. But the . . . that's marvellous news. You must be—'

'Yes, I am.' Skelton waved his hand at Edgar's suit and tie. 'What is all this, anyway?'

'Oh, poor Miss Dundridge. The lady who used to have the second-floor back at Mrs Westing's before Rose.'

'Yes, you said she was ill. Big funeral?'

'No. That was the awful thing. There was the vicar, the undertaker, a lady from the nursing home where she died, Mrs Westing and me.'

'No family at all?' Skelton asked.

'None that came to the funeral.'

'That is awful. Poor thing.'

'Makes you think, doesn't it?' Edgar felt the teapot. There was still warmth in it, so he poured himself a cup, then, no lemon having been provided, took out his oilcloth bag and penknife and set to work. 'It is a terrible thing to die alone and unmourned.'

'Fat chance of you doing that,' Skelton said.

'Is it?'

'You've got brothers and sisters, nieces and nephews.'

'I think Miss Dundridge has at least one sister and several nieces and nephews.'

'Perhaps they're in – I don't know – Inverness or Canada or somewhere and couldn't spare the time.'

'Bromley. They live in Bromley. In Kent.'

Edgar sipped his lemon tea, pulled a face as he swallowed, then bravely took another sip.

'According to the weighing machine at Swiss Cottage Station,' he said, 'I've lost a pound, which is coincidentally the amount I've put into the machine over the weeks, a penny at a time.'

Skelton could see the train of thought. Being less portly would lead to marriage and possibly children: marriage and children would lead to a better turnout at Edgar's funeral.

'What was the lady from the nursing home like?' Skelton asked.

'Socially unyielding.'

With an expression of disgust, Edgar put his teacup, still half full, back on the tray. 'It's not nice unless it's very hot,' he said. 'I think it's because burning the tongue makes the taste buds less sensitive.'

'Some people put honey in their tea,' Skelton said.

'Some people wear slipovers and grow beards.'

CHAPTER TWENTY-SIX

c/o The Cross Keys Public House, Fetterick

Monday 27th January 1930

My dear cousin Arthur,

I am so sorry to hear your news about Mila. You were not clear in your letter what was wrong, but it must be something quite grave to merit her having to be in hospital. Mila always seems to enjoy such good health. I know that the Royal Berkshire Hospital is one of the best in the country so I am sure she could not be in better hands, and hope that, by the time you receive this letter, she will be well on the road to recovery.

Our prayers are with her and with you and little Lawrence and Elizabeth, and I do not need to add that if there is anything we can do to help, we would be more than happy to drive down from here to Lambourn and could be there in two or three days.

The rest of this letter is taken up with the usual account of what we are getting up to. I could perfectly understand if you are not in the mood for such trivia, but who knows. Once I sat with a woman in great pain and showed her a map of Africa. Naming the countries and geographical features brought her a strange sort of comfort. Perhaps our mundane doings might have the same effect on you.

Last Wednesday night, at the chapel, I noticed Margaret brought along her own accordion. When the meal was over and Norah and I led everybody in 'Jesus Bids Us Shine', Margaret played, too. We sang some more songs, then Mr Easy said, 'Now play us some of the other music.'

'What other music?' I asked.

'The music you were playing the other night after we'd all gone.'

He meant, of course, the tango music.

'I did not realise you could hear that,' I said.

'They'll have heard it in Galashiels,' Mr Easy said.

Margaret did not need asking twice. She played the flourish that summoned Beryl and Jack to their feet, and then launched herself into the tune which I now know is called 'La cumparsita'. Norah joined in on her accordion and I on the banjo.

When we had finished that tune, Beryl and Jack gave some simple instructions and soon had everybody dancing along. Even the children. Martin and Owen, the two lads who had seemed so ill when they first appeared, partnered each other, exchanging punches between steps precisely in time with the music.

I watched, wondering at the strange turn our mission has taken and hoping that the Reverend Balfour did not get wind of what was going on. I am sure he would have no complaints about us providing the food, but he might have reservations about our using his chapel to teach the indigent unemployed how to dance the tango.

It does the heart good, though, remembering that first night these ragged people came in, sick with hunger, and comparing that to them now, capering and laughing.

If that is not the joy of Jesus in action, I do not know what is.

On Saturday afternoon, we left Mr Easy and some of the other five thousand and took ourselves off to the boys' high school for the joint school choirs' concert. Margaret, who, you may remember, works at the girls' school, had told us about it and provided us with tickets. As the name suggests, the joint choir is the massed voices of the two schools, boys and girls, and the concert is precursor to a competition that takes place at York Minster later in the month. As school secretary, Margaret has been very busy sorting out charabancs and accommodation for that.

Norah and I are always a little careful when we go into Fort Blaine, keeping our heads down, as it were, because the last thing either of us wants is a repetition of that little set-to with the police we had the first night we arrived. We presented our tickets and slipped in apparently unnoticed.

The Great Hall at the boys' school is very grand indeed, wood-panelled with vaults above like a church. Along the sides are boards recording the names of boys who have achieved distinction in one or other of the universities, with two special ones memorialising those who gave their lives in battle.

The proceedings were opened by the headmaster of the boys' school, Mr Gordon Innes, who is also, we are told, the Provost of Fort Blaine – the Scottish equivalent of a mayor. One look at him is enough to tell you why the tango is banned in this town and why we were moved on when we first arrived.

The singing was magnificent.

There is no sound to beat a choir in four-part harmony, so much more than the sum of its parts. There is – I cannot think of any other word for it – a grunt somewhere in the middle where the harmonies blend that elevates the chest and fizzes the head. They did an extract from Handel's *Messiah*, but the highlight for me was undoubtedly a piece by Johannes Brahms called 'How Lovely is Thy Dwelling Place', which stabs the heart with joy and glory.

During the interval, on the way out to the refectory for tea and biscuits, my eye was caught by one of the 'honours' boards which recorded the names of those who had won certain prizes and scholarships. Down the years, four students had won something called the

James Adamson-Adie Scholarship for Mathematics, three of them boys and the fourth, in 1906, a girl, Edna Goldie. I pointed it out to Beryl and asked whether she knew anything about it. She did not, but Margaret did.

The brightest students from all over Scotland compete for the James Adamson-Adie Scholarship and, in '06, there had been a good deal of argy-bargy about whether a girl should be allowed to take the examination at all. And then there was outrage when Edna had had the cheek to win the thing. Margaret said that the story had been in the papers at the time, so you could probably look it up if you think it might have any relevance to your case.

The refectory, in contrast with the grandeur of the hall, reminded me of one or two workhouses I have visited. As we drank our tea, Margaret introduced us to Miss Bryce, the head of music at the girls' school, who had been conducting part of the concert, and to Miss Shawcroft, a younger music teacher who had been playing the piano.

In the corner we could see the forbidding headmaster, sitting at a table, holding court, as it were, surrounded by flatterers and supplicants. A woman stood by his side; her face fixed in a frown of great disapproval. Margaret told me she was Mrs Innes, Gordon's wife. I asked why she seemed so angry. Margaret said she was not angry at all. She always looked like that.

My attention was then diverted by the man from the hat shop who knew so much about frogs. He hailed me from across the room – 'Hello, there' – in a voice so loud that everybody turned. As I say, we had been trying to attract as little attention as possible, but now you could see people turn to their neighbours, point and enquire.

'I forgot to tell you,' he said, barging his way through the crowd to get to me, 'about the differences between frog spawn and toad spawn.'

Frog spawn is laid in a lump like jelly. Toad spawn comes in strings, like a necklace. Just in case you were wondering.

We were given a sack of rotten onions today and found that they can be completely black and stinking on the outside, but when you take the outer layers off, there is goodness inside. I might work that up into a sermon.

I am ever yours faithfully in the joy of Jesus,
Alan

CHAPTER TWENTY-SEVEN

There was a kerfuffle in the main office at Hogg's Yard that Wednesday. Miss Summers was on the rampage. It had been brewing, Rose knew, all morning.

Miss Summers had doubled-booked Mr Felstead, setting up a meeting at the same time as he was supposed to be in court. His absence from the meeting almost caused the loss of an important client.

She didn't admit the fault, of course. She was trying to put the blame on Roland, one of the office boys, only fourteen and young for his age, and giving him a public, and entirely unjustified, dressing-down.

Roland was almost in tears. As politely as possible, Rose rallied to his defence, pointing out that he had nothing at all to do with the appointments books or the court diary, but Miss Summers said he'd distracted her with his constant chatter.

Rose pointed out that Roland was not a chatterer but one of the quietest, most efficient and well-mannered people she had ever known. This caused Miss Summers to turn her fury on Rose.

She did not mind. Rose had learnt from both Pelmanism and from her Girl Guide training that names could never hurt her, and that injustice is best faced with quiet dignity. Besides which, she was an articled clerk and thus not strictly under Miss Summers' jurisdiction but directly answerable to Mr Duncan himself. And she knew, and Miss Summers knew, that Mr Duncan thought very highly of her and, as Mr Skelton had pointed out, she was not Miss Summers' errand girl.

Despite which, when, a few moments later, Miss Summers said, 'Somebody needs to go to Bart's to pick up some photographs,' Rose found herself saying, 'I'll go.'

She ran on her toes to the hospital, dodging through the traffic as she crossed Farringdon Street.

Chas – she assumed it was Chas anyway – was in his little ticket booth.

'I'm from Aubrey Duncan, the solicitors,' she said. 'Come to pick up some photographs from Mr Goodyear.'

'Do you know the way?'

'Yes, thank you.'

She went through the big swing doors, made her way to room B29 and knocked. There was no answer, so she knocked again, then tentatively opened the door and popped her head round. No corpse was in residence. She crossed to the door of Vernon's room. It had a glass panel, backed on Vernon's side, with black paper that acted like a mirror. She was wearing her hat. She removed it. Her hair was a mess. Her face looked pasty. She was spending too much time indoors. At the weekend she would take a bus east and explore Epping Forest.

She knocked.

'Come in.'

The room was a jungle of tanks and vivaria with Vernon in the middle of it all, his jacket off, sweating slightly. He seemed pleased to see Rose and wiped his hands with a tea towel before shaking hers.

'Sorry about the mess. I'm doing a bit of reorganisation. I was running an experiment to see the effect of different temperatures and chemical agents on the life cycle of *calliphora vomitoria*, but I'm beginning to realise that from a forensic point of view air pressure might be a more useful line of enquiry.'

He indicated a bell jar with a rubber hose and a gauge attached.

'You connect it up to an electric pump and you can add or subtract air to create any pressure you want – top of a mountain to the depths of an ocean. I'm trying to make room for it, but it means moving everything around.'

He picked up a tank from the bench in the middle of the room and carried it over to one of the side-benches.

'You have some photographs I'm supposed to collect,' Rose said. 'To do with the Edna Aziz case.'

'Of course. They're upstairs. I'll get them for you.'

'There's no hurry. Do you need a hand?'

'Oh yes, please. If you could bring some of those flasks over. They're not heavy.'

The flasks were crawling with maggots.

Rose, oddly nervous, found herself talking too much. She wittered about a conversation she'd had with Mr Felstead at the office. Felstead didn't think much of barristers. As far as he was concerned, solicitors did all the hard work, then barristers put their wigs on, spouted a few clichés in court and took all the credit. Essentially, they were actors, paid to say the lines solicitors wrote for them. More like music hall turns, really. Nothing they like more than a rabbit they can pull out of a hat.

An unbearable silence fell. Rose felt her pulse and wondered if she might have the same heart condition that had carried off her father. What to say, what to say?

'Oh, I know what I wanted to ask,' she said. 'I'm not getting enough fresh air stuck in an office all the time and I was wondering if Epping Forest would be a good place to go.'

'It's all right,' Vernon said, 'but there are much better places. Where do you live?'

'I'm in Swiss Cottage.'

'Oh, I'm in Maida Vale. We're practically neighbours. I could cycle over on Sunday, if you like, and show you the way round to Richmond Park. Takes just over an hour and the hills aren't too bad at all. Have you got a bike?'

She'd left her bike at her aunt's house in Castle Bromwich. There would be no time to fetch it before the weekend. On the other hand, on the previous Monday some of her father's money had come through from the solicitors in Birmingham and she'd paid nearly a hundred pounds into her bank. She passed a bicycle shop every evening on her walk from the Swiss Cottage Underground station to Mrs Westing's. They had a second-hand Raleigh in there with good Dunlop tyres and Sturmey-Archer three-speed gears for £3 12s 6d. She could easily afford that.

'Yes,' she said. Her voice came out strangely. 'That would be very nice.'

Vernon passed his notebook and a pencil. 'Write your address on there and I'll come over, what, half past eight, nine o'clock?'

'Half past eight would be grand,' she said. Her voice still wasn't working properly.

Next to the flasks she'd been moving was a larger tank sealed with a metal lid that seemed to be filled with dead leaves.

'Do you need any of this?' she asked.

'I wouldn't have thought so. It's more rubbish from the Edna Aziz suitcase. Nothing's emerged yet, but I just wanted to go through it to make sure nothing's been missed. I can't think there will be.'

Vernon took off the lid of the tank and poked around among the dead leaves.

'The goal is to take the research smaller and smaller until you can make a full bacteriological analysis of every item. Different forms of life contain entirely different—'

He broke off suddenly. Rose was standing very close, looking over his shoulder. Vernon turned and looked her in the face. He seemed transfixed, fascinated. Rose blushed, avoiding his eyes. Very gently, Vernon reached up and stroked her hair.

'*Erebia epiphron*,' he said, 'I think.'

'I'm sorry,' Rose said, 'we only did a little Latin at school . . . or is that Greek, because we . . . ?'

She saw that he had a butterfly in his cupped hands. Quickly he transferred it to a jar and sealed it with a rubber stopper.

'Or *maniola jurtina*. I'll have to get the book. It must have emerged from its chrysalis in the last couple of hours, flew out and landed in your hair. Completely the wrong time of year, of course, but with it being so warm in here . . . here we are.'

From the bookshelf he took down Spuler and Hofman's *The Lepidoptera of Europe* and a couple of other reference works, found a magnifying glass in the drawer and began comparing observations with descriptions and pictures.

Rose stood near and watched. Her hair, where he'd touched it, felt as if it was fizzing.

'Definitely not *maniola jurtina*, he said. Wrong wing shape entirely. I think if you spent ten years studying lepidoptera you'd still never . . . and nothing like *erebia epiphron* either. This is a bit more like it.'

He fell silent as he examined tiny details of the creature in the jar. '*Aricia artaxerxes* is the most likely suspect.' He took down another book and checked a couple of pages. 'Yes, that's the one, *Aricia artaxerxes*. Northern brown argus.'

'Is that rare?'

'I've never come across it before, but that means nothing. Lepidoptera is a very specialised—' he had noticed something in one of the books. 'Now, that is interesting,' he said.

CHAPTER TWENTY-EIGHT

'It's Scottish,' Rose said. Aubrey had sent her round to 8 Foxton Row to break the news.

'In what way?' Skelton asked.

'It's a Northern brown argus. Found in the north of England and Scotland. But this one has a white spot on each of its wings.'

'What does that mean?'

'It means it's almost certainly one of the Scottish ones. The ones further south have brown or black spots. At some point either the suitcase or the body or both must have been in Scotland. And the caterpillar crawled in and pupated, then in the warmth of the laboratory at Bart's, it decided it was time to emerge.'

'And . . . what's the entomologist's name?'

'Mr Goodyear. Vernon Goodyear,' Rose said.

'Mr Goodyear is sure it definitely came from the suitcase?'

'The chrysalis was among leaves and muck from the suitcase, all kept in a sealed container. And Dr Aziz says he hasn't had a day off for a year and has an appointments book, a receptionist and presumably several hundred patients who could bear witness to that, so he cannot have been to Scotland.'

'And Mr Goodyear still has the butterfly?'

'He wasn't sure it would be more useful as evidence dead or alive,' Rose said, 'so he's keeping it alive for now.'

Skelton gave his empty pipe a couple of sucks to make sure it was clear from bowl to lip, then said, 'Crikey. A greenhouse in Scotland, then.'

Edgar, returning some books to their rightful places on the shelves, sniffed.

'What is it?' Skelton asked.

'I'm just imagining the prosecution's reaction to the assertion that the murder cannot have taken place in Wakefield because a butterfly has white spots on its wings rather than brown; the thousand ways in which they could suggest the chrysalis might have arrived at the doctor's surgery; and the stories they will tell of reticulated pythons being found in King's Lynn council offices and tarantulas on trains to Bognor.' Edgar noticed the crestfallen look on Rose's face. 'Although, having said that, as a piece of forensic investigation, Mr Goodyear's discovery is most definitely touched by genius.'

'I've had two cases that swung on a good bit less than that lately,' Skelton said. 'I've had two lads got sent down because they smirked and one poor chap who got twelve months for running a football team. Compared to that, a whitefly larva and a white spot on a butterfly count as irrefutable evidence. And anyway, who knows where it might lead? Cousin Alan has already turned up a couple of likely suspects in Scotland. Well, one vaguely likely and one not very likely at all. Unless Dr Aziz mentioned anything about his wife being a devil-worshipper to you, Edgar, did he?'

'Not as I remember, no.'

'Has Aubrey been in touch with the Scottish police about this?' Skelton asked.

'He says he will,' Rose said, 'but he says there is very little for them to investigate, even if they were willing to do so.'

'He's right, I suppose,' Skelton said. 'No suspect, no line of enquiry. Have a look through these anyway.' He handed over a bundle of letters from Alan. 'My cousin Alan – you remember, the one whose van burnt down in the Collingford case – is up near Fort Blaine at the moment. I'm sure he won't mind you filleting through his letters to see if they turn up anything useful. There's never anything personal in them. Alan doesn't have a private life. Might be some use. No mention of Egyptian assassins in kilts though, I'm afraid.'

There was a knock at the door. Edgar opened it.

Daniel, the office boy, announced that Mrs Pitt had arrived.

'Oh God, is it that time already?' Skelton asked.

Edgar told the boy to show her up and to bring tea.

'I'd make myself scarce if I were you, Rose, unless you particularly wanted to meet Mrs Pitt.'

'I think I can forgo that pleasure,' Rose said. She picked up the file of Alan's letters, made a hasty goodbye and slipped out of the door. A few seconds later, after a cursory knock, Phyllis marched in, almost pushing poor Daniel out of her way.

'The worst has happened,' she said.

'Good afternoon, Mrs Pitt,' Skelton said. 'How nice to see you again. Do take a seat. Daniel will bring tea in a moment. How are you?'

'He's burnt a factory down.'

'Oh dear.' Skelton sat in one of the low chairs, hoping that this would encourage Phyllis to do the same. Instead, she creaked towards the window, blocking the light and turning her substantial form into a looming silhouette.

'My Clifford has burnt down a factory. I thought you were going to have a word with him.'

'We had a very nice chat,' Skelton said.

'Well, it didn't do a blind bit of good, did it? What did you tell him? Ignore your studies? Spend more time with your motorbike pals? And why don't you burn a factory down while you're at it? He's up on a charge of arson.'

'Perhaps you'd like to tell us exactly . . .'

Skelton nodded to Edgar, who took out his fountain pen and notebook.

'They're saying him and his pals broke into a factory just outside Durham somewhere.'

'What kind of factory?' Skelton asked.

'Stebbings and Dodd, paper factory. The police are saying Clifford and his pals broke in, took some money from the office and mucked the place up. Then they set fire to it.'

'Was the factory badly damaged?'

'Burnt to the ground.'

'And was anybody hurt?'

'The night watchman's in hospital.'

'Burned?'

'I don't think so. Inhaled a lot of smoke. He's old. If he dies, that's murder, isn't it?' Phyllis leant forward, suggesting that Skelton himself had blood on his hands.

'That would depend on many circumstances. When you say Clifford and his pals, how many pals were there?'

'There were three of them. Clifford and two others.'

'And have the other boys been arrested?'

'I couldn't give a monkey's arse what's happened to the other boys. Clifford is in prison and I want you to get him out.'

'If the charge is arson and possible manslaughter or murder, I'm afraid bail is out of the question,' Skelton said.

'Well, it certainly is if you just sit there on your arse doing nothing about it, isn't it? He's in the police court tomorrow morning. Go and get him bail.'

Edgar knew from childhood that all that stuff about 'the only way to deal with bullies is to stand up to them' was nonsense. He had a clicky nose and occasional tinnitus to prove it. But there comes a moment when a man must make a stand and he thought that, as long as he averted Phyllis's gaze and addressed his remarks to the artist's impression of the Old Bailey that hung on the wall, he might be able to finish a sentence without wilting.

'I'm terribly afraid that is out of the question, Mrs Pitt,' Edgar said. 'Mr Skelton has to go to Leeds tomorrow and it cannot be rearranged.'

There. He'd done it.

Phyllis moved out of the shadows, crossed the room and, in full light now, gave them her famous look of rage, contempt and remorseless determination.

'That is very unsatisfactory,' she said.

Skelton's heart was in his mouth. He'd never seen anybody stand up to Phyllis Pitt before. The full capacity of her power had never been tested. Forces which, once unleashed, were unstoppable might be revealed.

Edgar kept his eyes on the Old Bailey.

'If you think there is anything to be gained, Mrs Pitt, from having a barrister present at your son's preliminary hearing, then I'm sure that there are many 'locals' in Durham whom Mr Duncan would be more than happy to instruct. However, as Mr Skelton has already pointed out, if the Lord God almighty were to appear at your son's preliminary hearing, he would not be able to persuade a magistrate to grant bail on a charge of arson and possible murder. The trial itself is, of course, a different matter entirely. If Mr Duncan, your solicitor, agrees, I'm sure Mr Skelton would be more than willing to appear for your son.'

Phyllis opened her handbag to look for something. Edgar risked a glance. His thoughts ran to a tiny dart tipped with curare which she would fling with deadly accuracy and smirk as she watched the poison take its effect. As it was, she took out a compact and powdered her nose with enough force to break it.

'I'll have a word with Mr Duncan, then, shall I?' She said this as if it was a threat. 'And might I add, Mr Skelton, that despite my asking you to speak to the Women's Charity League for an hour, you sat down after just over forty-five minutes, so I have to inform you that you will *not* be asked again. And with that, gentlemen, I bid you good morning.'

On her way out, she collided with Daniel, who was bringing in the tea, causing him to wobble. He managed to save the pot, but cups skittered off and smashed.

Mrs Pitt turned back and nodded triumphantly.

CHAPTER TWENTY-NINE

The following day, Rose had a long list of tasks.

First, she read through Alan's letters, taking careful note of any nugget of information she thought might be useful.

The parcel containing Jabari Turnbull's papers had arrived from the Manchester police the previous afternoon. She opened it. A bundle of notebooks and diaries fell out, all different sizes and colours, some smeared with dirt. Choosing one at random, she turned to the first page and was immediately dismayed. '*Eryngium*,' she read. '*Hippeastrum, Zantedeschia, Moluccella, Strelizia, Dicentra spectabilis, Trachelium.*'

It seemed a jumble of languages. 'Spectabilis' she learnt from a Latin–English dictionary could mean a whole range of things, including 'notable' and 'gaudy'. There was no trace of 'Zantedeschia' in the Latin dictionary, though. She began to wonder whether it might be Italian and not Latin. Or even something more obscure like Albanian or Romanian. Or a code, perhaps. She'd done some straightforward letter substitution codes at Guides and knew the rudiments of deciphering.

Deciding to come back to it, she turned the page.

Turnbull's handwriting was atrocious. The heading on the page read 'COSY'. A date was written underneath it: 3rd November 1929. The rest of the page was an illegible mess. She managed to make out a few phrases. 'British Isles', something that may have been 'from what it has in Falmouth', although the 'Falmouth' was little more than a wild guess, and then a word that could have been 'Bew', 'Kew' or 'Hew'. Then it occurred to her that 'COSY' might in fact be 'COPY'. Could this be his copy for the newspaper?

She turned another page. This one was even worse. Not one letter in twenty was legible.

Perhaps, she decided, if she could find a copy of the *Manchester Guardian* for 3rd November 1929, something, at least, would become clear.

Mr Felstead told her that the British Museum Reading Room would have old copies of the *Guardian*. A letter written on office notepaper would be enough to get her a reader's ticket. She typed the letter. Felstead signed it.

Before she could leave the office, Mr Duncan came in and asked her to look up some things in preparation for the Clifford Pitt arson case, so she took down the big street directory and found the address and telephone number of the National Union of Printing, Bookbinding and Paper Workers, phoned them and made an appointment to visit the following afternoon.

* * *

The Reading Room was magnificent. She'd always been impressed by the Reference Library in Birmingham, but that was almost poky compared to this place. It was a huge circular room roofed by a single dome, with the catalogues in the middle and desks for the readers radiating out like the spokes of a wheel. All around were bookshelves, twenty-five miles of them according to the information sheet she'd looked at while she was waiting to get her ticket.

She looked around at the desks to see if anybody famous was there, then realised that if there was, they'd be famous philosophers, mathematicians, politicians and historians, and she wouldn't be able to recognise them anyway. Einstein she could probably do, or George Bernard Shaw, but neither of them seemed to be present.

She tiptoed across the Reading Room and found the newspaper room. A helpful librarian showed her how to use the catalogue and pointed out that anything she ordered would have to be brought down from the store, so wouldn't be available until tomorrow. She ordered the *Manchester Guardian* for October, November and December of 1929, then was delighted to find a newspaper called the *Fort Blaine Weekly Chronicle*, which was also available.

She was back in the Reading Room as soon as it opened on the Friday.

The *Fort Blaine Weekly Chronicle* was, thankfully, a shoestring affair. Most issues had no more than ten pages, only three of which were devoted to proper local news, so you could flick through a year's worth in no time at all. The controversy over Edna Goldie's triumph in the James Adamson-Adie Scholarship for Mathematics was mentioned in practically every edition from March to April 1906. Nothing significant, just the facts that she did terribly well, tempered by the usual outrage about girls even being allowed to enter for such a thing because education is wasted on them. Even the mathematics teacher at the girls' school, a Miss Benningford, had had her doubts, although the boys' mathematics teacher, Mr Gordon Innes, had been all for it.

Rose assumed that this was the same Gordon Innes that Alan had mentioned, who was now headmaster of the boys' school and Provost of Fort Blaine – perhaps a more forward-thinking man than Alan's description of him had given her to believe.

Alan's letters had also talked about Ben Murcheson coming back from the war as a drinker who 'often got into fights'. Rose's attempts to find out whether he had a prison record had not met with success. Prison records were notoriously ill-kept. The local paper was her last resort.

She turned to the issues for 1918, starting at the end of the war in November and working steadily through the pages, scanning the headlines. In May 1919, she came across what she was looking for. Ben Murcheson was reported as having been in court on a charge of assaulting a man outside the Fort Blaine Picture House. He was fined 12s and bound over to keep the peace. Less than a year later, in February 1920, he was in court again. This time the fight, in a pub, involved a woman. Murcheson had laid into her and her companion, wounding both. It took the pub's landlord and four other men to restrain him. This time he got three months and £10 costs.

There it was then. Ben Murcheson was a violent man, even to women.

In the issue for July 1928, she found pictures of Edna's father's funeral. It was a big civic affair with a solemn procession, a hearse drawn by black horses and the Provost, Gordon Innes, in his chain of office, chief among the mourners with Edna Aziz.

Finally, she turned to the *Manchester Guardian*, starting with the 3rd November 1929, the date from the page in Jabari Turnbull's notebook labelled 'COPY'.

In the back pages she spotted the words 'Falmouth' and 'Kew'. The rest of the story fitted the gist of Turnbull's scribble. 'After all,' she read, 'hardiness is a relative term, and that which makes Kew the standard is convenient for the Home Counties, for any plant which outlasts a hard winter there is safe almost anywhere. There is a great variety of climate in the British Isles and the word "hardy" has a very different significance, say, in Eastern Northumberland from what it has in Falmouth.' The heading on the column read 'Gardening Notes'.

Outside the museum she found a telephone box and called Edgar.

'He was indeed a journalist,' she told him. 'I found one of his stories in an old copy of the *Manchester Guardian*.'

'Was it about Egypt?'

'It was about hardy annuals.'

'What?'

'He wrote the gardening notes.'

There was a pause at the other end of the line.

'All the same, he could have had a deep knowledge of Egyptian affairs and . . .' Edgar petered out. After another pause, he went on, 'But . . . it is unfortunate. I can't help feeling that, even if we were to find references in his notebooks to the Aziz affair, in court, the written testimony of a dead author of gardening notes would not carry quite as much weight as that of an illustrious foreign correspondent.'

'Are we left with anything then?' Rose asked.

'About the hypothetical Egyptian assassin?'

'Yes.'

'Other than Dr Aziz's own suspicions . . . it would appear . . . no.'

Rose walked to Euston, took an Edgware, Highgate and Morden Line train to Clapham South and made her way to Nightingale Lane, headquarters of the National Union of Printing, Bookbinding and Paper Workers. Mr Hesketh, the gentleman she'd spoken to on the telephone the previous day, had sought out everything she'd asked for and even had the courtesy to show her to an office where she could study the files without being disturbed.

Stebbings and Dodd, she learnt, owners of the factory that Clifford Pitt was alleged to have burnt down, was not run with the neatness or efficiency required to keep its workers safe and healthy. The list of complaints, inspections and reports dated back to the turn of the century. Rose opened the soft leather cover of her notebook and began to record them all.

It was five to five by the time she left. If Miss Summers asked on Monday where she'd been all day today, she decided she would try her best to look and sound like an articled clerk rather than an office junior and say, 'I really don't think that's any of your business, Miss Summers. I was acting on Mr Duncan's instructions,' and flounce out. She'd never flounced before but hoped to have time over the weekend to practise.

* * *

The Raleigh was still there at the bike shop on the Saturday morning. Rose looked it over. The shop assistant, who was trying to grow a moustache like Ronald Coleman's but had shaped it crooked, told her that it had seen a bit of wear and tear, but had been thoroughly renovated and was in tip-top condition. Rose pointed out the bent spokes and misaligned brake callipers, then turned the bike upside down and demonstrated that the gears slipped. He said that the mechanics must mysteriously have overlooked those defects and offered to reduce the price from £3 12s 6d to £3 10s. She offered £3. He tried £3 7s 6d. She said she'd give him £3 5s if he'd throw in oil, a spanner, a puncture repair kit and a pump. A deal was struck. As she was paying, she added a cheap 'cyclists' map. Ordnance Survey Maps were always unwieldy when cycling.

On the way home from the bike shop, she bought cakes, bread, butter, ham, cheese and two bottles of lemonade, then spent the rest of the afternoon adjusting, oiling and cleaning the bike.

She had known lots of boys before and had often taken part in joint activities between Guides and Scouts. It was inevitable, she supposed, that, having arrived alone in this great city where she knew no one except for Mr Skelton and Mr Hobbes, she should be excited about finding somebody more her own age with whom she could share her interest in trips out to interesting places, outdoor activities and picnics.

She studied the map until she had memorised the route.

Vernon, thank God, was five minutes early.

Richmond Park was a much better idea than Epping Forest, not least because the route took them through Hyde

Park and Chelsea and lots of other bits of London that Rose had read about but never visited. Early on a Sunday morning, there wasn't much traffic about, either. Even in the middle of London they had the roads pretty much to themselves.

As they crossed over Putney Bridge, the sun came out and the Thames, which had looked like gravy at Waterloo, twinkled. They saw deer in the park and Vernon's pathetic attempts to coax them near enough to feed from his hand made them laugh. Although only the second day of February, it was nearly warm enough for spring so, instead of having to find a shelter to eat their picnic, they did the proper thing and found an ancient oak to sit beneath. Vernon had brought a groundsheet and spread it out, so Rose laid out the food. Then both of them spent more time finding and identifying insects than they did eating.

With hands almost touching, they lay on their backs and looked at the sky. One finger – Rose knew that if she extended one finger it would probably be enough to touch one of Vernon's. She wondered if he would try to hold her hand and what she'd do if he did. It wouldn't matter of course if he didn't try to hold her hand because they were becoming very good friends and a good friend is in many ways a lot better than a – how she hated the word – 'sweetheart'.

She came to with a start and realised she must momentarily have dozed off, then she lay some more, listening to Vernon's breathing and her own.

'Vernon,' she said.

'Yes?'

'Do you know much about spontaneous combustion?'

'In . . . what sense? Do you mean it literally or metaphorically?'

'How could it be . . . ?' But, of course, it could be metaphorical, and the very idea that he'd thought she might be talking about the two of them bursting into flames of – what – passion? . . . almost made her do it. 'No, I meant literally. Not people, of course, like in *Bleak House*. I mean paper and rags and things that just burst into flames.'

Vernon sat up. He'd taken off his glasses but put them on to speak. Rose was glad. There was something mole-like about him when he wasn't wearing his glasses.

'It's actually a very interesting topic from an entomological, or at least bacteriological, point of view. All living things obviously generate a certain amount of heat . . .'

And so they spoke of heat-generating bacteria, of the evaporative qualities of linseed oil and of the combustion temperatures of different materials until it was time to go home.

A deer came quite close, but they were too engrossed to notice.

CHAPTER THIRTY

c/o The Cross Keys Public House, Fetterick

Monday 3rd February, 1930

My dear cousin Arthur,

I cannot tell you how pleased we are to hear about Mila's recovery and trust that, by the time you receive this, she will be out of hospital, bursting with good health and back in her rightful place at hearth and home.

I am sad to report that we have had problems of a similar nature here in Fetterick over the past week. Poor Beryl came down with terrible stomach pains. The doctor was called, diagnosed appendicitis and shipped her straight off to hospital. Jack, as you can imagine, was worried sick. You will be glad to know, however, that the operation went well and when we went to see her, she was groggy and in a lot of pain but still managing to smile and make jokes. I am sure Jack will have his tango partner back in no time at all.

Your news about the butterfly has certainly lent a new urgency to our work here in Scotland. Upon receiving your letter my thoughts immediately ran to Mr Dugdale, the occultist and publisher at Aldwin House.

Now, I have an idea which I offer up for whatever it may be worth. You will probably dismiss this as very fanciful indeed, but I beg you to indulge me for a moment.

Edna Aziz must almost certainly have encountered Mr Dugdale during the buying and selling of the house. Well, what if she attended one of his 'Wednesday meetings' and as a result became caught up in his coven or sect or brotherhood or whatever they call these things? Now, I am not saying that her murder – and perhaps the cutting up – was part of some ritual sacrifice, because that would be assuming too much. On the other hand, it cannot be denied that these sorts of esoteric goings-on attract some strange people, with strange ideas.

I shall not go on. I am just stating a possibility and you must decide whether there could be any truth in it.

Anyway, feeling rather more like the detectives in the Sexton Blake mould than missionaries like Dr Livingstone, we decided to pay Mr Dugdale another call.

We found him in something of a state and very glad to see us.

When we asked him what was wrong, the first thing he said was, 'Did you know that Edna Aziz, the murdered woman found in the suitcase, used to live here?'

So, straight to the point without a single prompt.

We said that we had heard something to that effect.

He told us that at the last Wednesday meeting of his 'discussion group' the talk had turned to Edna Aziz and whether her troubled spirit was still a presence in the house. One woman in the group, a 'sensitive', which I think means a spiritualist or medium or some such, suggested they hold a 'seance' to try to contact the spirit. Lights were dimmed. Incense was lit. Hands were joined. But before things could get properly going, one of the company had a sneezing fit – the incense – which destroyed the 'sensitive's' composure, so the seance was abandoned.

Nothing of any significance happened, but later it appeared that the seance, though aborted, had had its effect: Edna's spirit had been unleashed.

Mr Dugdale took us into the kitchen. Mayhem. Cupboards had been emptied. Crockery smashed. Jam, flour and sugar spilt and smeared. It was the same in his study. Books and ornaments had been strewn across the floor.

It had happened in the night, while they slept. All three of them, Dugdale, Sophronia and Ottoline have bedrooms on the other side of the house and all are in the habit of taking sleeping draughts. No locks had been forced nor windows left open. I wondered whether it might have been an animal, although heaven only knows what kind of animal could cause a mess like that. It would have to have been the size of a deer and that still left the question of how it might have got in.

Mr Dugdale was sure it was the troubled spirit of Edna Aziz. He was very afraid, believing that, in some instances, spirits with unfinished business on earth can be so eager to find physical form that they take possession of a living human. The phrase 'possessed by demons', he said, is no figure of speech. He feared for his own soul and for the souls of Sophronia and Ottoline.

He said he wanted me to cast Edna's spirit out of the house. To conduct an 'exorcism'.

'And why do you think that I would be capable of such a thing?' I asked.

'Because you have been touched by angels,' he said, and he showed me a book that had the 'ritual of exorcism' and the words in it that I was supposed to say.

He said he'd already asked the priest at the Catholic church in Fort Blaine, and the ministers from the other denominations, too. They had all refused. I was his last hope.

I wondered whether the mayhem could be caused by Mr Dugdale himself, sleepwalking perhaps. Could the somnambulism be the result of a guilty conscience brought on by his having murdered poor Edna in some unholy ritual?

The matter clearly merited further investigation so I prevaricated about the exorcism and told him it might take a few days for me to prepare.

He respected that and gave us £5.

On the way back to the chapel, Norah pointed out that the wire mesh on the meat safe in the pantry could easily be pulled away and put back again without anybody being the wiser. It would give access to the house, far too small for an adult to climb through, but a skinny ten-year-old boy, like, for instance, Martin or Owen, the two scamps at the chapel, could do it without any effort at all.

After the meeting that evening, Mr Easy mentioned that he had seen Ben Murcheson crossing the Market Square in Fort Blaine. He stopped for a word and Ben told him he had been back for a couple of weeks, working on a roofing job in town, but the job had finished now, so he was looking for work and was thinking of going to Aberdeen. He was still off the drink.

Murcheson lives in a little terrace of cottages on Luggateside. So, the next day we knocked and he answered.

He is a compact man, not short of stature, but tight with muscle and sinew. He has a round head, piercing brown eyes, black, close cropped hair and the sort of chin that stays dark even after the closest shave. Norah said he looked like an Italian poisoner. I wondered whether he might be a descendant of those Spanish sailors who are said to have found their way to these coasts and to those of Ireland after the defeat of the Armada in 1588.

He listened politely, barely speaking himself, as we told him about our mission and our work at the Baptist chapel. He did not invite us in for a cup of tea, but neither did he seem in a hurry for us to leave. A calm, quiet, patient man.

We mentioned that we had heard that he used to be the gardener at Aldwin House. He looked sour about that and told us that the house had been sold up without a care for any of the people who worked there. He had lost his job, and so had the cook and the maids. The new owner did not want any of them. He had let the garden go to rack and ruin. 'Beautiful garden,' he said and then again, 'Beautiful garden.'

When we asked whether he might be willing to offer some help in our efforts at the chapel, he nodded and said, 'We shall have to see,' which I took as a polite way of saying no.

'There are deep subterranean rumblings there all right,' Norah said when we had got back to the main road into the village.

'What do you mean?'

'If Edna Aziz wasn't in love with him, she must have been blind and deaf.'

'You sound as if you are in love with him yourself.'

'One word of encouragement and I'd follow him to the ends of the earth.'

'Norah!' I was shocked.

I have honestly never heard her speak like this before. I worry that I may have been wrong about the innocence of the tango. It would not be the first time that my foolish naivety has made me blind to such matters.

The following day, just after we arrived to get the fires going. Ben Murcheson turned up driving a horse and cart piled with sacks and sacks of coal. He was covered in coal dust. 'I thought you might be running short,' he said.

It was true. We were. The pile that had seemed infinitely large when we began our mission to feed the five thousand was now a sorry little mound. He told me he had taken the coal – stolen I think would be more accurate – from the great mound at the old ironworks.

'They won't be needing it,' he said.

I offered to help him unload and tried one sack, but could barely lift it.

'You'll get your clothes filthy,' Ben said, and swung two sacks onto his back. He walked them down to the pile, emptied them, then went back for more.

I went inside and trimmed vegetables.

After a few minutes, I came out to fill one of the big pans and found Ben at the pump. He had finished unloading and was washing off the coal dust in the freezing water. He had removed his shirt.

I turned and saw May Balfour, the minister's sister, watching.

'Hello,' I said.

She started as if from a dream.

'Hello there,' she said.

'I hope the music and the singing does not bother you too much,' I said.

'It is no bother,' she said, and turned back to watch Ben button up his shirt.

As I went back into the chapel, I saw Norah's face at the window, but she quickly withdrew when she saw me looking.

Later that evening, as the five thousand were finishing their stew, Ben turned up again, this time carrying a four-pound tin of cocoa and a big bag of sugar in another huge pot. While everybody else danced the tango, he made cocoa for fifty people.

Norah thinks the suggestion that he may have murdered anybody is absurd, and even though her judgement seems to be clouded by worrying emotional turbulence, I can see what she means. He is strong enough to overpower a giant but carries himself with a gentle sort of precision. He is quiet and modest in speech, and his kindness seems to know no limits.

I can just hear your voice, cousin Arthur, saying, 'Ah, but then again many killers present themselves as kindly, gentle men,' and even, 'Perhaps it is all an act,' and I must defer to your superior knowledge of these things and admit that you could be right. But all the same I repeat that I am inclined to share Norah's view of the matter.

We asked our kind host Mr Chalmers why nothing was being done about the Abbotsbank people. I told him we knew about the requirement that they should be genuinely seeking work, but surely there was some basic assistance they could fall back on, provided, if not by the state, then by the parish or the local council?

Mr Chalmers seemed to know as little about the matter as we did but suggested that we ask at the council offices or, if we wanted to go right to the top, ask to see the Provost, Gordon Innes. Well, as you know, we had already encountered Gordon Innes at the choir concert in his role as headmaster of the boys' school and I am not ashamed to say I found him a forbidding character. Nevertheless, giving into cowardice would be to do a grave disservice to the starving of Abbotsbank, so, on the Friday afternoon, we decided to brave the lion's den and, in the name of our mission, knocked on Gordon Innes's door. He lives in a big stone house – possibly a grace and favour house for headmasters – in the posh part of Fort Blaine.

It was a fruitless visit, I am sorry to say. A maid answered the door. She told us that Mrs Innes was at the hospital where she volunteers two days a week as an almoner and Mr Innes was in Edinburgh. The children, one assumes, were at school. I asked when Mr Innes would be back, and she said – with a certain self-importance – that he had gone for the Board of Education meeting and would not return until Sunday morning. I asked if I could leave a message. Begrudgingly she said she supposed I could, so I took out my little notebook and pencil and, leaning on the door jamb, wrote to ask if Mr Innes could get in touch with a view to discussing the terrible plight of the people of Abbotsbank.

I must say I do not hold out much hope of receiving a reply.

My goodness I have written a lot. It is almost midnight and, as the French song says, '*Ma chandelle est morte*' and I can write no more.

I am ever yours faithfully in the joy of Jesus,
Alan

P.S. Margaret reports that the joint choir's visit to York Minster was very successful, and they came away with some sort of prize – not best overall, but commendable all the same.

The great fear on these sorts of trips is that one of the children will get lost. In this case, all the children came back safe and sound, but they lost one of the teachers. I think I may have mentioned Miss Shawcroft, the younger teacher who played the piano for the choir. I do not think that anyone is unduly worried. She is from that part of the world, anyway, so has probably just taken herself off to her mum's house.

'Do you know very much about sexual magnetism?' Skelton asked when he'd finished reading the letter.

Edgar was sitting at Skelton's desk, updating the appointments book. The ink was not flowing in his fountain pen. He shook it over the blotter.

'Not really,' he said. 'Why?'

'This chap Murcheson seems to have a lot of it.'

'Sexual magnetism?'

'Yes.'

'Do *you* know much about it?' Edgar asked.

'Not really. There was a chap at school called Appleton who I think may have possessed it. He put a girl in the family way and had to leave school to get married, which was generally considered a tragedy because he had an impressive aptitude for physical geography. He once made a relief map of the Mendips out of clay. Beautiful thing.'

Edgar licked the tip of his finger and wet the pen nib. Sometimes that got things going.

'And I was wondering,' Skelton continued, 'Edna Aziz, by all accounts, was a shy girl. It seems an odd match. The man dripping with sexual magnetism, the woman a keen mathematician.'

'Are you saying you can't drip with sexual magnetism if you're a mathematician?'

'I think I am, yes.'

Edgar shook his pen some more. When the ink emerged, it missed the blotter and made an unsightly mess on the appointments book.

CHAPTER THIRTY-ONE

An object lesson on the nature of sexual magnetism came the same afternoon at Kembles. Skelton was working his way through a plate of Russian pastries. Edgar took occasional nibbles from an oatcake.

'Looks very dry,' Skelton said.

'Oh, it is. So, you have to take very small bites and—' Edgar suddenly stiffened.

'What is it?'

'Don't turn around,' he whispered. 'Laurence Olivier and Jill Esmond.'

Skelton didn't need to turn round. In one of the mirrors, he could see a man with a large head, fleshy cheeks and a cleft chin sitting at a table near the centre of the room with a vivacious young woman, her face artistically divided by a long and elegant nose.

'Olivier was the chap I told you was so good in *Journey's End*,' Edgar said. 'Jill Esmond is his fiancée. They were both in *Bird in the Hand* a couple of years ago. I think that's where they met.'

Esmond was saying something and Olivier was leaning towards her, listening attentively. When he smiled, the fleshy cheeks formed deep parentheses around his mouth.

He was well-built, almost stocky, and inconsequentially dressed in an oatmeal tweed suit. But he glowed.

When Esmond finished her story, Olivier sat back in his chair and laughed, not too loud, not in an actorly look-at-me-I'm-laughing way, but all the same you had to watch. It was infectious. Skelton found himself wanting to laugh, too.

Olivier said something serious to Esmond. His eyes never left hers. It was as if he was taking part in a staring competition. Esmond couldn't sustain the attention and kept looking at this and fiddling with that.

Beneath the table Olivier took her hand. His voice was a low rumble.

Norman the proprietor came over and blushed and twisted and danced as Olivier ordered. When he'd gone, Olivier looked around to see who else was in.

He spotted Skelton and Edgar. He said something to Esmond, possibly, 'Those people over there keep looking at us.' Then he stood and came over. Skelton decided to say he was just looking at the back of his own head in the mirror.

'I do hope you don't mind my coming over like this, but I just said to my companion there, "Is that Mr Skelton?", and she said she thought it was, so if you're not Mr Skelton then please accept my most heartfelt apology, but if you are then

273

let me say how much I admire your work. Olivier, Laurence Olivier. Please don't disturb yourself.'

Skelton shook his hand awkwardly, without standing.

'Jill and I – that's my fiancée – we followed every moment of the Mary Dutton story last year with breathless excitement.'

'It's very nice of you to say so, Mr Olivier—'

'Laurence, please.'

'It's very nice of you to say so, Laurence, but I can really take very little credit for the happy outcome of Mrs Dutton's ordeal. This is my clerk, by the way, Edgar Hobbes.'

More handshaking.

'I saw you in *Journey's End* a year or so ago,' Edgar said. 'A triumph.'

'Oh, and then I shamed myself in *Beau Geste*,' Olivier said.

'I'm afraid I missed that.'

Olivier lifted his eyes to heaven and made a little gesture of supplication with his hands. 'The Lord be praised.' And he gave them the full-face smile. He began to withdraw. 'Again, please forgive my rather boorish intrusion. I really should be getting . . .'

He gestured to Esmond, who took out a compact and pantomimed that she was going to powder her nose.

'Cigarette?' Edgar asked, offering his Gold Flake.

Olivier seemed surprised but took one. 'Thank you so much. Did I read in the newspaper that you're working on the Wakefield horror?'

'Please, pull up a chair,' Skelton said.

'Oh, do you mind? I'm sure Jill's going to be an age.' Olivier seated himself at their table.

Skelton told him a little about the Aziz case. Olivier told

them about the time he'd recently spent in New York, when Jill was on Broadway, and his first, rather worrying, venture into film that would happen later in the year. Some remarks were addressed to Skelton, others to Edgar. When he turned from one to the other, the concentration was intense and the eyes never wavered. The voice sometimes rumbled, sometimes hardened, sometimes almost squeaked and the face expressed every thought and emotion beneath the words, so that no statement ever needed qualifying, no irony underlining or joke nailed home.

'Now, I wonder if I could impose a little more and take the liberty of asking some advice. You see, the contracts for these films I'm supposed to be doing are long and complicated and I do feel in grave need of legal guidance. I wouldn't expect you to bother with such an insignificant matter, obviously, but I wonder, do you know of anybody who might give the contracts a brief glance and tell me whether I'm being cheated?'

'I can recommend several good men,' Edgar said, and went on to do so. He wrote names and addresses on a page of his notebook, tore it out and passed it over to Olivier, who read it through, folded it and carefully placed it inside his notecase.

'I can't tell you how grateful I am. I know it's a terrible weakness, but I think all actors work better when they know the contract is above board and they are being paid fairly.'

'And lawyers are just the same, Mr Olivier,' Skelton said. And Olivier laughed in a way that suggested that Skelton was being absurdly generous to imply that his noble profession could be compared in any way to the grubby goings-on of theatricals.

Esmond returned to the table just as the waiters arrived with the food. Olivier apologised once again for his intrusion, thanked Edgar for the cigarette and the recommendations, and returned to his own table.

Skelton felt unfathomably light-headed. He noticed that his pulse had quickened, and his blood was beating against the skin of his face the way it does when you come in from the cold.

There was also, he noticed, a perceptible presence in the space that Olivier, a moment before, had occupied, as if he'd left part of himself behind.

He exchanged a glance with Edgar, who was visibly feeling the same, but, after a moment, managed to catch his breath enough to whisper, 'Sexual magnetism.'

'Isn't it essentially about possession?' Rose asked.

They had run into Rose on the way back to 8 Foxton Row and told her about their meeting with Olivier and Esmond – Rose hadn't heard of them either – and about sexual magnetism; although, in deference to Rose's age and sex, they used the phrase 'animal magnetism' instead, but she got the drift.

'In what way?' Skelton asked.

'It possibly develops as a result of childhood neglect. Some people crave love, affection and attention so vehemently that it becomes a single-minded mania that commands the way they move, speak, everything. It often becomes an obsessive need to possess. Essentially, it's a hunger – either conscious or unconscious – not just to be loved, but to be certain that you're loved, to know that you have captured the soul, or whatever you want to call it, of another person – or of all other people – and either temporarily or permanently you own it.'

'Is this Freud or somebody says this?' Edgar asked.

'There was a girl in my patrol in the Guides who was mad about films. She used to bring copies of *Picturegoer* and *Girls' Cinema* to camp and sit mooning over the film stars, and we discussed it a lot because her obsession seemed not quite right. One of the other girls had a brother who worked backstage at the Birmingham Rep and he'd told her about the way actors went on. The way they talked about "grabbing the audience" and "capturing the audience" and "having them in the palm of my hand". We talked about how strange it was to think about other people like that. As if you can own them. This girl's brother said they didn't just do it with audiences, they had to do it with everybody they met. They move and talk in certain ways and do certain facial expressions. Often, it's just a matter of talking to you, whoever you are, with this sort of intense concentration as if you were the most interesting, most important person in the world. Is that what Mr Olivier did?'

'Up to a point,' Skelton said, not wanting to acknowledge the extent to which Olivier had had him spellbound and excited.

'And of course, it's enthralling, compelling. In effect they make you fall in love with them, but there's no love on their part. Just the challenge of ownership. Once they know they own you, they move on to the next person.'

'Do you have experience of this, Rose?' Edgar asked, concerned.

'No. What makes you think that?'

'Nothing. Just—'

'I'm speaking objectively. From what I and others have observed.'

'Of course.'

'A lot of love talk that you read in books is all, "I want to possess you" and "You are mine". It's the same with songs. It's not at all healthy, is it?'

'It's no more than a turn of phrase, though, isn't it?' Skelton asked.

'Ah, but doesn't every turn of phrase conceal a truth about human nature?' Rose said.

'Does it?'

'In most instances, this need to possess is relatively harmless – as it is, I'm sure, in Mr Olivier's case – but sometimes it can lead to all kinds of horror. Well, we know about this, don't we, from the Mary Dutton case? Didn't her husband used to tie her to the bed and threaten her with a gun to make sure she couldn't run away? And his mother didn't love him, did she? So, there you have it. Perfect example. And Ben Murcheson's mother died when he was very young, didn't she?'

'And his father.'

'There you are, then. And, perhaps, this need to possess could have grown so strong in Ben Murcheson, the only way he could satisfy it – in the case of Edna Aziz at least – was to cut her up and put the bits in a suitcase.'

Skelton and Edgar looked at each other. Could that be it?

'You think that could actually happen?' Skelton asked.

'I'm sure it *has* happened no end of times,' Rose said.

'I don't think I can bring to mind—'

Edgar reminded him. 'The Bournemouth Trunk Murder, the Widnes Trunk Murder.'

'And there could be no end of other instances where the killer took more care hiding the suitcase, so it's never been found,' Rose said. 'Oh, and Ben Murcheson was twice apprehended for crimes of violence, after the war, by the way. I looked it up in the *Fort Blaine Weekly Chronicle*. And in one of the cases, he beat up a woman.'

Skelton tapped his knees with an inappropriate show of excitement. 'Did he, indeed?'

'I'll write it all up in a report when I get a moment and bring it round.'

'Thank you, Rose. That's excellent.'

Rose ran off to Hogg's Yard. She found herself running a lot these days.

'Do you think Vernon Goodyear has sexual magnetism?' Edgar asked, when she'd gone.

'If he thinks he's ever going to "possess" our Rose, he's in for a terrible disappointment.'

CHAPTER THIRTY-TWO

Mila continued to improve and increasingly found the injunction to stay in bed, to rest, to do nothing an imposition. She insisted she was now fully recovered and kept insisting until she actually got out of bed and had to sit down again suddenly.

'Of course I'm weak, I've been in bed for too long. How am I supposed to recover if they won't let me get up and move around? I can feel myself lying here getting weaker and weaker.'

She complained about the diet, too.

'They're not feeding me,' she told Skelton.

'I'm sure they are.'

'I can't live on nursery food.'

'It's an invalid diet.'

'How do they expect people to grow strong on rice pudding and semolina? And the endless gallons of clear soup and beef tea?'

'I think your digestion will still be very delicate,' Skelton said.

'I have the digestive capabilities of a wild pig or a – what are those animals that eat dead things?'

'Hyenas.'

'No, they laugh.'

'I think they eat dead things as well. Come to that we eat dead things, don't we?'

'Exactly. I need dead things to eat,' Mila said.

'They gave you chicken.'

'I want steak and kidney pudding with gravy and thick suet. I want . . . you could bring me a veal and ham pie.'

'I couldn't.'

'You could smuggle it in. I could eat it when they're not looking.'

'They're doctors and nurses. They know what's good for you. If they thought veal and ham pie was good for you, they'd let you have it.'

'It's also a matter of having the will to live.'

'What are you talking about?'

'Life without gravy is no life at all.'

'Beef tea is a bit like gravy.'

'And a butter knife is like a cutlass. Please.'

'What?'

'Bring me a veal and ham pie.'

'No.'

'You promised to love me in sickness and in health. Here I am in sickness and immediately you betray your promise.'

'Do you get custard?'

'Yes.'

'I don't know what you're complaining about, then,' Skelton said.

Every evening, he took her a great pile of books, newspapers and magazines. She read them voraciously and seemed to remember every word.

Then she wanted to talk about what she'd read, and Skelton wasn't sure whether picking over the political implications of the execution of Dost Mohammad in Persia or the repression of communist demonstrations in Hamburg was entirely commensurate with a trouble-free convalescence.

The night she started talking about income tax rates in Ceylon, he put his foot down.

'Can we talk about Primrose Moorfield?' he asked.

'The guinea pig?'

'Yes, I told you, Dr Spencer says we've got to get rid of it. Now, how am I supposed to do that without breaking Elizabeth's heart?'

'There is a school of thought that says that the whole point of giving pets to children is that the pets grow sick and die, and this inures the child to the setbacks and tragedies that life has in store for them.'

'So . . .'

'The sooner the guinea pig goes, the sooner she will learn one of life's great lessons. Hearts break. They are never mended. It's something you have to get used to.'

'It's making you ever so cheerful being in hospital, isn't it?'

'Put the guinea pig in a pie with suet crust and lots of gravy. Then bring it to me,' Mila said.

'I'm serious.'

'Take it back to the shop, get your money back.'

'I don't think there's much trade in second-hand guinea pigs. They're like rabbits. New ones are easy to come by.'

In the hospital foyer, on his way out, Skelton was overtaken by a man hopping along on crutches. After he'd passed, the man turned back and called.

'Mr Skelton?'

It was Jimmy Coyle, the left-handed riveter they'd run into in Whitley Bay.

'Jimmy, what are you doing in this part of the world?'

'I go where the work takes me, Mr Skelton.'

'What's happened to you?'

'Bit of an accident.' Jimmy's leg was in plaster. 'Fell off a lorry. What are you doing here?'

'I'm visiting my wife.'

'Oh dear.'

'No, she's well on the mend. They'll probably let her out tomorrow.'

'Well, that's good to hear. Been in the wars, has she?'

'She has indeed, Jimmy.'

Skelton motioned towards a couple of chairs.

'I won't sit down,' Jimmy said. 'Takes me a good half hour to stand up again. Ooh, while I think of it, Stanley Harrison at the Blamire.'

'Who's he?'

'The porter who was sending the postcards from the woman in the suitcase. I saw him just before I finished at Whitley Bay and he said he reckoned that was indeed Mrs Aziz in the suitcase, so he could kiss the second instalment of the four quid goodbye and it'd be all right if was to give you his name. Stanley Harrison at the Blamire Hotel, Whitley Bay.'

Skelton found a scrap of paper and a pencil and made a note.

'It's very good of you to remember, Jimmy. So, have you been working down this way?'

'Yeah, the Whitley Bay job finished a couple of weeks ago, so I signed up with the Royal Corps of Dregs – the Lynch Mob.'

'Yes, I remember you told me about it.'

'Working on the new bypass out at Twyford. They give us quarters in some old army place out there. Not too bad. And yesterday morning I was a bit late getting myself sorted and nearly missed the lorry when it came to pick us up. It was already halfway out the gate, and I ran after it, took a leap for the tailboard and wallop.' He indicated the leg.

'How long do they say you're going to be off work?' Skelton asked.

'Weeks. Maybe months.'

'Are they letting you stay on in the barracks?'

'For now, yes.'

'How d'you get there and back?'

'I can manage the buses and the walk if I take my time.'

Jimmy demonstrated his agility by walking with just one crutch, then the other, then doing a turn with no feet on the ground.

'Lynch's, is it?' Skelton asked.

'That's right.'

'I could get a friend of mine to write them a solicitor's letter, claiming the lorry should have stopped and asking for compensation.'

'I don't think navvying works like that.'

'Works like what?'

'Compensation. If you get hurt, it's always your fault,' Jimmy said.

'Not if a solicitor says it's not your fault and asks for £1,000.'

'That's just mad.'

'If he asks for a thousand, they'll almost certainly settle for a hundred just to make it go away.'

'And I'll never work for them again.'

'Do you want to?'

'I don't think I've got much choice in the matter.'

'How are you on wallpapering?'

'That's pretty much all I was doing in the end at the Royal.'

'Could you do it with a bad leg?'

Jimmy looked at the leg, then tried a couple of gestures with his hands, reaching up with the crutches still under his armpits. 'If I took my time. Not sure I could manage a ladder.'

'If you had somebody to help, you'd be all right, though, I bet. It's just the paper in my living room's in a shocking state. Pop round if you've got a minute. You'd be doing me and my missus a big favour.' He gave Jimmy his visiting card. 'We couldn't put you up, but Max at the pub nearby takes in boarders sometimes. And, of course, we'd cover your accommodation costs.' Skelton looked at his watch. 'Quarter to,' he said. 'Sometimes they bring a tea trolley round, but you can never be sure.'

Jimmy looked down the corridor; there was no sign of a trolley.

'I'd better be off, anyway. It's a bit of a walk from the bus stop to the barracks where they're putting us up and pitch-black if there isn't a moon. I'll have to go dead slow if I don't want to end up in a ditch.'

'On the road gangs, you never ran into a man called Ben Murcheson, did you?' asked Skelton. 'Scottish bloke.'

'Doesn't ring a bell. Not very likely, either. There's hundreds work on the roads. No end of Scotties.'

'Good-looking by all accounts. Makes the ladies swoon.'

'Now, that is unusual. Most of them have got faces like a jilted beetroot.'

'Doesn't drink. Or I don't think he does, anyway.'

'That does narrow it down. The only man I've ever come across who didn't drink was Murky McBean. Took the piss out of him rotten. He didn't seem to mind. Very quiet. Kept himself to himself.'

'Murky – Murcheson?' Skelton said.

'Could be. I don't think I ever knew his real name.'

'Was he good-looking?'

'Sallow. Looked more foreign than Scotch. I don't think I ever really spoke to him. Good worker. Somebody said he used to be a gardener on a big estate somewhere.'

'When was this?'

'When was he a gardener?'

'No, when were you working with him?'

'This would have been just last year, September time, building a road out to the new aerodrome at Chat Moss.'

'Don't think I know Chat Moss,' Skelton said.

'Lancashire. Just outside Manchester.'

CHAPTER THIRTY-THREE

'Aubrey thinks that with the Manchester connection we might have enough evidence for the case against Aziz to be abandoned and the police to reopen it with Ben Murcheson as chief suspect,' Edgar said.

'Does he really?' asked Skelton.

'He's made a very good submission to the DPP.'

'And I suppose Aubrey has dinner with the Director of Public Prosecutions on all the nights he's not dining with the Prince of Wales or His Holiness the Pope.'

Skelton was lying flat on the floor. The lack of sleep and constant toing and froing between London, Lambourn and Reading meant a chance to lie down, even if it was on the floor of his room at 8 Foxton Row, was too good to miss.

Edgar opened his notebook. 'I've made a list,' he said. 'Of

the various hypotheses that seem to have evolved. Do you want me to read it through?'

'As long as I don't have to get up.'

'Heathcliff Hypothesis number one. Ben Murcheson was in love with Edna Aziz from an early age and perhaps she was, for a time, in love with him. She, however, went off to university, met and married Dr Aziz. And Ben went off to war and took to drink. Then she turns up once again in Fort Blaine when her father dies. The romance is rekindled. They have many illicit trysts, the first weekend of every month – which we know from the postcards – who knows where? After a while, he grows more demanding, wants her to leave her husband. She refuses. In a fit of jealousy, he kills her, cuts her up and – double revenge – does his best to lay the blame on Aziz.'

'And puts her in a suitcase he bought specifically for this purpose in Manchester?'

'Exactly.'

'It brings us back to your original point, though, doesn't it?'

'Which original point?'

'Why does he get a suitcase that might be a tight fit rather than a trunk that could accommodate all the bits easily?' Skelton asked.

'Perhaps he wanted something he could carry easily on the train to wherever he cut her up.'

'He's a strong man. An empty trunk would be no weight at all.'

'Cumbersome, though.'

'The pathologist said that the way the body was dissected suggests it was done by somebody with experience at that sort of thing.'

'Perhaps Murcheson worked in an abattoir at some point. Or – who knows what he did in the war – he could have assisted a surgeon for a couple of emergency amputations at a dressing station.'

'Alan seems to think he went off quite frequently with the fishing fleet. I'm not sure that would be consistent with being available for a romantic tryst the first weekend of every month.'

'Which brings me to Heathcliff Hypothesis number two,' Edgar said. 'He loved her. She never loved him. She goes to university and marries Aziz. He goes to war, takes to drink. She returns for father's funeral. He's still in love with her. Then he finds out she has not just a husband but a lover, too. Outraged that she's taken a lover who isn't him, in a fit of jealous rage, he kills her and so on.'

'Who's the lover?' Skelton asked.

'I don't know. Possibly he killed the lover, too, but the body, which he put in another suitcase, hasn't been found yet.'

'You're saying he bought two suitcases in Manchester?'

'Or perhaps he already had a trunk.'

'Suitcase for the lady, trunk for the gent. Is there a Heathcliff Hypothesis number three?'

'No. Number three is the Secret Garden Hypothesis,' Edgar said.

Skelton didn't look hopeful. 'Go on.'

'Ben Murcheson loved the land.'

'Have you been reading Mary Webb?'

'She's a fine novelist.'

'You'll be calling him a "son of the soil" next.'

Edgar took a guilty look at his notes. Skelton suspected that 'son of the soil' was exactly what he was going to say next.

'He loved the garden. When her father died, she sold the house without a second thought for his feelings. So, he murdered her.'

'More than a year later?'

'These things fester.'

'And what about the lover?'

'That's the thing, you see, the lover is a complete irrelevance,' Edgar said.

'I can just about go with him getting angry about her selling the house and taking away his job, but not so angry as to put her in a suitcase. Is there a fourth hypothesis?'

'The Rose Critchlow Theory of Possession.'

'This is the "sexual magnetism is the expression of a need to possess that can, in extreme cases, lead to cutting people up and packing them in suitcases like spare shirts and shaving things"?'

'Exactly.'

'Do you think it's plausible?' Skelton asked.

'A jury might, if it was well presented.'

'The trouble is, as things stand, we're defending Aziz, not prosecuting Murcheson. Is there a way of suggesting that Aziz cannot have killed her because the murder has all the hallmarks of having been committed by somebody with a level of sexual magnetism that Aziz could never hope to possess?'

'Put like that . . .'

'Number five?'

'Nothing to do with Ben Murcheson at all.'

'Who, then?'

'Dugdale,' Edgar said.

'She was the victim of a devil-worshipping ritual killing?'

'It's happened.'

'Not since about 1673.'

'History has a circular tendency.'

'And how would we proceed with that one?'

'Perhaps Aubrey could suggest that the Scottish police should search Dugdale's house.'

'Even in the very unlikely event that the Scottish police would agree to such a thing they'd need a search warrant. So, they'd go to the magistrate – or whoever deals with such things in Scotland – and say, "We'd like to search the house of an ostensibly respectable publisher of school textbooks because he may have killed somebody in a satanic ritual." And the magistrate would say, "What evidence have you got?", and the police would say, "Mr Skelton's cousin, who talks a lot about Jesus and plays the banjo, thinks there might be something fishy about him."'

Edgar compressed his lips and looked down at his notes. 'Hypothesis number six.'

'Should we go for lunch, soon?' Skelton asked.

'I'm skipping lunch today. I ate rather too much at Maurice's last night.'

Maurice's was an intimate restaurant on Maddox Street. Skelton had never been there but from time to time mention of it cropped up in divorce cases.

'You went to Maurice's?'

'With Mrs Maynard.'

'Who . . . ?'

'She's a lady I met at the Egyptian legation.'

'You didn't mention her.'

'There are aspects of one's private life that should remain private.'

'Of course,' Skelton said.

Edgar took out a cigarette, then decided against it and returned it to the packet. Tobacco does help stop you feeling hungry, but overindulgence was making him hoarse. He wondered whether he should switch to Craven A, which had a cork tip and came with the promise 'Will not affect your throat'.

'So, you invited her for dinner?'

'If you must know, she invited me. At the Egyptian thing. I had drunk three passionfruit cocktails on an empty stomach and Mrs Maynard took advantage.'

'She . . . ?'

'No, nothing like that. We discovered that we had both seen *Romeo and Juliet* at the Old Vic last year and got engrossed in a discussion about John Gielgud's tendency to gabble his lines. And Mrs Maynard said she would like to continue our conversation over dinner at Maurice's and it would have seemed churlish to have refused.'

'Of course.'

'And besides, I wasn't sure whether there was any romantic intent on her part or whether she was just glad to have found somebody who shared her enthusiasm for Harcourt Williams.'

'Who's Harcourt Williams?'

'The new director at the Old Vic.'

'Right. And which was it, romance or Harcourt?'

'Over dinner she told me she's a naturist and an advocate of free love.'

'Oh Lord. Does she go to a camp?'

'What kind of camp?'

'They have camps.'

'Who do?'

'Naturists. Where they all walk around with nothing on. Clothes are forbidden,' Skelton said.

'Even when they're having their dinner?'

'I should imagine.'

'What do you tuck your napkin into?'

'I think napkins are forbidden as well.'

'Hot soup on your bare chest?'

'They'd take extra care.'

'What about pyjamas at bedtime?'

'I'm afraid I've never looked into the matter in detail. Did Mrs Maynard want you to take your clothes off?'

'She wanted to measure the plane of my moral evolution,' Edgar said.

'Your what?'

'My moral evolution.'

'What does that mean?'

'She said that most people have not evolved beyond a primitive understanding of morality, but there were those who had reached a higher plane.'

'And this is the plane where you practise free love and walk around with no clothes on.'

'Exactly.'

'And how exactly is your plane of moral evolution measured?' Skelton asked.

'I couldn't possibly tell you.'

'You could and you're going to.'

Edgar's voice dropped to a whisper. 'She said that if we went somewhere private where I could take my shirt and vest off, she would measure the distance between my nipples and my navel and use the proportions of the triangle thus constructed to calculate the level of moral evolution I've achieved.'

'And did you . . . ?'

'Don't be preposterous. I gulped down my coffee, tipped majestically, popped her in a taxi and ran all the way to Bond Street Tube station.'

'Less than ideal as a marriage prospect, then.'

Edgar pulled a face. 'Do you want to hear hypothesis number six?'

'Go on.'

'Jabari Turnbull and the Egyptian assassin.'

'Is that still in the running?'

'Could be.'

'On the basis of Dr Aziz's conjecture and something a gardening correspondent told you at a cocktail party?'

'A knowledge of gardening doesn't preclude insights into Egyptian politics,' Edgar said.

'Except Mr Turnbull's also dead and left no record of these insights.'

'Shall I move on to hypothesis number seven, then?'

'Yes, please.'

'We're barking up the wrong tree entirely. A Scottish butterfly indicates that her body was at some point in Scotland, and the whitefly possibly suggests that the body – or the suitcase – was, at some point, in a greenhouse or a house with houseplants. And we know that Ben Murcheson – and Mr Dugdale – both had a connection with Edna Goldie in Scotland, and both possibly have access to greenhouses. And, of course, Murcheson was near Manchester at around the time the suitcase was bought. Completely unrelated to any of this is the possibility that

Dr Aziz has been framed either by an Egyptian political faction or by his own family and that the true murderer is a professional assassin. But we have no actual proof of anything. And I can't help feeling we have all these pieces of the puzzle but we're trying to put it together in the dark. And it's missing the key piece.'

'No, we've got three or four different puzzles: *The Laughing Cavalier*, *Mona Lisa* and *The Hay Wain*, and all the pieces are jumbled up and they're all missing at least half the pieces.'

'We know nothing,' Edgar said. 'A Scottish lover could have killed her in Scotland. An English lover could have killed her in England then, for some reason, taken the body to Scotland in order to cut it up before returning it to Wakefield and dumping it in the quarry. Or the lover might have absolutely nothing to do with the murder. We don't even know for sure that there *was* a lover. Ben Murcheson, Dugdale, the Egyptian assassin could all be complete red herrings. All we've actually got is a butterfly, a whitefly and a suitcase shop in Manchester. Watertight prosecution case against two flies and a shop. The jury won't even have to leave the box.'

Skelton lay back and stared at the light fitting. It was very ugly. Edgar massaged his face from forehead to chin.

'The thing we have to remember, though,' Skelton said, 'is that he didn't do it.'

Edgar closed his notebook and screwed the cap on his fountain pen.

'Extradite,' he said.

Skelton stood, sat in one of the low chairs, filled his pipe, lit it and, when he was sure it was drawing well, said, 'What sort of age is Mrs Maynard?'

'Impossible to tell. Very solid. Like a tree. Could be anything between thirty-five and sixty. If you asked her, she'd no doubt claim thirty-five. You'd have to chop her in half and count the rings to learn the truth.'

Skelton didn't laugh or even smile. 'I've said it before and I'll say it again, even though it makes absolutely no sense at all,' he said, 'but it seems to me that, in this case, denying an innocent man the chance to prove his innocence would be a grave miscarriage of justice.'

'That's probably because you're at a much higher plane of moral evolution than I am.'

Skelton smiled. 'We'd have to get the tape measure out to make sure.'

CHAPTER THIRTY-FOUR

Mila was allowed out of hospital that afternoon. Before she left, the nurse had instructed Skelton in what she was and was not allowed to do and eat. Skelton wanted to say to her, 'You seem to be under the delusion that this woman will take notice of anything I say,' but instead listened carefully. He could, he knew, pass on these instructions to Mrs Bartram, who had ways of keeping Mila in line.

She was by no means well, and perhaps the thought of a relapse made her as afraid as it made him. On the way home, she submitted to sitting, half lying among the pillows and blankets he'd arranged in the back of the Bentley.

The children were ecstatic to have her home and she actually wept – a rare occurrence – to see them. She was delighted when Skelton allowed them to play quietly – *I said quietly* – in her bedroom. Elizabeth put on her tutu and danced for her. Not to be outdone, Lawrence went downstairs and played Bach's 'Prelude No. 1 in C Major' on the piano, and got nearly a third of the way through before the bad notes started to outnumber the good ones.

Mrs Bartram swore she'd keep her in bed even if ropes and straps were needed and, the result of reading the chapter on invalid diet in *The Home Doctor*, began to produce marvels involving strangely shredded beef, eggs and chicken, doused in cream sauces, followed by rice puddings, egg custards, semolina and blancmanges.

Nobody would wish further illness on their family, but when Skelton discovered that cold rice pudding was available every time he wandered into the kitchen, it was hard not to see pneumonia as a blessing.

On the Saturday, Skelton broached the guinea pig question. He had spent more time preparing his speech to Elizabeth than he'd ever spent on the summing-up at a murder trial.

'You know how Granddad's retired now,' he said. 'Well, that means he doesn't have to go to work any more, which is, sort of, a good thing, but he had a lot of friends at work and he misses them. So, you know what would be a really kind thing to do to help Granddad? I think he'd really like to look after Primrose Moorfield for a while. It would be company for him. It would also be a great kindness to Lawrence because of his—'

It wasn't going well. He'd lost Elizabeth's attention before he'd finished the first sentence. She had been interrupted in the middle of one of her incomprehensible games. This one involved making patterns on the floor with wool and jumping in them while muttering.

* * *

'What did she say?' Mila asked, when he brought her what she had taken to calling 'another bloody egg'.

'Broadly speaking she seemed glad to get shot of Primrose Moorfield, but played the distress well enough for me to promise her a pram.'

'A doll's pram? She already has a doll's pram.'

'She says she wants one like Princess Elizabeth's.'

'What does she know about Princess Elizabeth?'

'She sees the newspapers,' Skelton said.

'We should censor them before letting the children see them. Cut out anything to do with kings, queens or princesses.'

'And just leave the stuff about mucky vicars and scandalous divorces?'

'Precisely.'

'They're made in Leeds.'

'What are?'

'Silver Cross prams. The kind Princess Elizabeth had.'

'You've looked into this?'

'You can practically see the factory from our house. I'd imagine Mum or Dad'd know somebody who works there. Could probably knock up a dolly version out of offcuts or something.'

Mila looked at her egg with great sadness and said, 'You must do what you think best.'

The thought of driving to Leeds with a guinea pig on the back seat alarmed him. If it made a noise, he would be tempted to look round to check it was all right, plough into a lorry and die. He imagined the guinea pig, unhurt, scurrying from the wreckage to become dinner for a fox. If it didn't make a noise, he'd be tempted . . . same thing.

So, he went on the train with the cage on his lap from Lambourn to Paddington and the taxi to King's Cross. A porter put it into the guard's van of the Leeds train. It was out of his hands, then. If it escaped or died it would be the fault of the London and North Eastern Railway Company and would have nothing to do with him.

He'd told his parents they'd be doing him a great favour if they'd look after it for a while. His mum had reluctantly agreed as long as he was sure it wouldn't be a lot of trouble.

'Is that it?' she asked when she came to the door.

'Her name's Primrose Moorfield,' he said.

'Not if it's coming in here it's not.'

His dad was standing up.

'You all right, Ernie?' his mum said.

'Why wouldn't I be?'

'I'm so used to seeing you down there I'd forgot you had legs.'

Dad took the cage from Skelton and held it up against his face.

'What did you say its name was?' he asked.

'Primrose Moorfield.'

'Prinny, then.' He wrinkled his nose at the guinea pig and said, affectionately, 'Little bugger.'

'It can go out in the shed,' Mum said.

'In this bloody weather?' Dad said. 'It can stay here with me.'

'It'll smell.'

'The man in the pet shop told me it's a very clean animal,' Skelton said.

'All of them or just this one?'

'All of them.'

'There you are then,' his dad said.

300

Dad cleared the baccy, pipe, matches, Germolene and Zubes off his box and balanced the cage on the top.

'There's this as well, Dad, if you want it,' Skelton said. From his bag he brought out the crystal set kit. 'I got it for Lawrence for Christmas, only he hasn't seemed very interested, and I wondered whether you might like a go at it.'

Dad examined the box. 'What is it?'

'It's for making your own crystal set. Like a wireless.'

'We've got a wireless set,' Mum said.

'This is one you make, though.'

'Does it come with the doo-dahs over your ears?' Dad asked.

'The earphones? I think so, yes.'

Dad opened the box to look. 'I could put them on when Vera comes round.'

Vera was Mum's friend. She'd once had a septic whitlow and hadn't stopped talked about it since.

He didn't stay with his mum and dad. Preparing for Clifford Pitt's arson trial at the table where they had their tea wasn't practical. He got the five past five train and joined Edgar at the hotel in Durham.

The trial was a technical affair. That Clifford and his two friends had broken into the factory was beyond dispute. What was at issue was whether they had caused the fire and, if so, the extent to which it was done with malicious intent.

Skelton's star witness was Mr Hesketh, who'd been so helpful to Rose at the National Union of Printing, Bookbinding and Paper Workers. He testified that union representatives had submitted frequent reports about the mismanagement of the factory and the way in which waste was allowed to accumulate. This constituted a fire hazard, endangering the lives of union members. There had in fact been, he said, a small fire at the factory three years ago. The firm also had two other factories, in Halifax and Sunderland, where similar fires had occurred. Each time, the owners and management unjustly claimed that the carelessness of workers was to blame and, in some instances, had dismissed employees.

At this point in the trial, Skelton introduced, as evidence, a dustbin, borne by two ushers, which had been removed from the factory in Sunderland by the police at the request of Aubrey Duncan and the union. This caused a certain amount of amusement which the judge silenced and asked for Skelton's reassurance as to the relevance of its appearance. The bin was filled mostly with waste paper.

Skelton's next witness was a professor of chemistry from the University of Durham, who had conducted an investigation of the bin and found it to contain, as well as the paper, certain solvents and oils. He spoke of spontaneous combustion, of pyrophoricity and of hypergolic reactions. He explained the way in which the slow oxidation of hydrocarbons, and particularly unsaturated hydrocarbons, can gradually raise the temperature of the contents of such a bin until it ignites or even explodes, and how the heat generated by bacteria and moulds can speed up the process. Unventilated, overheated by the machinery and bone dry, the factory provided ideal conditions for spontaneous combustion.

As he spoke, Rose, sitting in the public gallery, nodded enthusiastically. The professor was practically reading from a script she had written. Meanwhile, the more cautious members of the jury cast wary glances at the bin.

When they adjourned for lunch, Stradbroke, the judge, asked a clerk, 'That thing isn't going to burst into flames, is it?'

The clerk, who believed spontaneous combustion to be something made up by Charles Dickens for one of his stories, assured him that it would not.

Various witnesses, including a fireman, were able to testify that the blaze Clifford stood accused of starting had not in fact got going until several hours after the boys had left the premises.

Throughout his cross-examinations, Skelton was aware that Phyllis Pitt was sitting up there in the public gallery, seething and critical. Only once did her impatience get the better of her. She rose to her feet and declared, in a voice that made hardened policemen quiver, 'This entire trial is an absolute farrago of lies and insinuations.' Ushers advanced. The judge called for silence and warned her that, if she interrupted again, she would be removed from the court.

Skelton prayed that she would interrupt again.

At the end of the first day, Edgar asked a passing usher whether there was a back way out. He and Skelton were led down a corridor to a service door from where, their hats pulled low and their scarves high, they made their escape. As they rounded the corner, they could see Phyllis standing on the courtroom steps, looking for them, still seething.

Back at the hotel, the porter said that there was a lady in the lounge, waiting to see them.

'It can't be,' Edgar said. 'Phyllis Pitt could not possibly have got here before us. Besides which, how could she have found out where we're staying?'

'Did the lady give a name?' Skelton asked.

The porter had made a note. 'Said her name was Miss Shawcroft.'

Skelton turned to Edgar. 'The vanishing music teacher.'

Edgar asked the porter to bring tea to the lounge.

Helen Shawcroft, tall, pale and frightened, stood at the mantelpiece. Thankfully the commercial travellers, one or two of whom could usually be found in the lounge, were celebrating something in the bar next door.

Introductions were made.

'I have some very important information for you, Mr Skelton,' she said, when they were all sat down. 'I didn't know whether to go to the police or not, but I read in the paper . . . it's about Dr Aziz. His trial is very soon, isn't it?'

'Yes, indeed,' Skelton said.

'And I thought I should tell you that I know he didn't do it. And I know who did do it. I teach music at Fort Blaine High School for Girls.'

She had a faint Yorkshire accent.

Edgar took out his notebook and pen.

Helen lowered her voice to a murmur. 'I have been – I'll put it straight because there's no point beating about the bush – I've been conducting an adulterous affair.'

She looked to see whether Skelton was shocked, surprised, outraged or what. He was making a huge effort to be nothing.

A handkerchief was screwed tight in her hand in case she felt the need to weep. She clenched it tighter. 'And I now believe that the man with whom I have been conducting this affair is in fact the murderer of Edna Aziz.'

Again, she looked up. Skelton remained impassive.

'Gordy and I—'

'Gordy?'

'Gordy. It's the name he likes me to use when we're together.'

'And his real name is?'

'Gordon.'

Skelton and Edgar exchanged a glance. This was indeed a turn-up.

'Gordon?'

'Gordon Innes, he's the Provost of Fort Blaine and the headmaster of the boys' high school.'

'And this is the man you've been having an affair with?'

'Yes.'

It took a moment for Skelton to rearrange his mental furniture.

'Miss Shawcroft,' he said, 'do you know a man by the name of Ben Murcheson?'

'No, I don't think so. Should I?'

'No.'

Edgar turned over a page in his notebook to start again.

'And what makes you think that Mr Innes killed Mrs Aziz?' Skelton asked.

'This,' Helen reached into her handbag and took out something wrapped in a scrap of tissue paper. She passed it to Skelton. He unfolded the tissue and found a wedding ring. 'There's an inscription on the inside,' she said.

Skelton pulled his glasses off and held them a little way from his eyes. Two letters: E. A. He passed the ring to Edgar.

'And why did you think E. A. might stand for Edna Aziz?' Skelton asked.

'I found it in a drawer at the cottage.'

'The cottage?'

'Yes, the cottage we used to go to at Graysmuir.'

'Perhaps you'd better start from the beginning.'

Helen nodded and picked a piece of cotton from her skirt.

'When did you first start seeing Mr Innes?'

'During the summer term, last year. I have a small flat a little further out of town than his house and sometimes in the mornings our paths would cross and we'd walk to school together. He was . . . he took an interest in . . . he was Provost and headmaster and . . . he seemed to take a great deal of interest in . . . things like my views on education, that sort of thing. He has a way of speaking to you . . . or a way of speaking to me anyway . . . that made me feel as if I was the only person that mattered in the world.'

Edgar took a note. Skelton leant across and saw that he'd written 'sexual magnetism'.

'When you see him around and talking in an assembly, or doing a speech as Provost,' Helen said, 'he has this very formal, very strict manner, but that, he said, was Gordon. Gordy has this . . . intelligence and warmth. He is a good bit older than me, of course. So, I never . . . suspected he was . . . he started encouraging activities between the two schools. We did *The Merchant of Venice* in the Great Hall at the boys' school with our girls taking the female roles. It was all very closely supervised, of course, so I spent a lot of time over there and Gordy seemed to know a great deal about verse speaking. And then . . .'

She held the handkerchief over her nose and pressed it hard to stop herself from crying.

'I'm sorry. Last July, it would have been, I was . . . it was a hot day and I was in the park, and I stupidly took off my shoes and stockings and went for a paddle in the little pond there. And I trod on some broken glass and had to go to the hospital to have stitches put in. And they were worried it might turn septic, so they kept me in for a couple of days. And that's when . . . he sent me flowers. And that's when I . . .'

She pressed with the handkerchief again.

'Then, when I came back to school . . . we were in the staff room after a choir rehearsal. Just the two of us. Everybody else had gone and we were discussing . . . I can't remember what we were discussing, but it was something quite absorbing and we'd sat down, and he was listening very closely to what I had to say. Then he began to speak and there was . . . he has a deep voice but very musical. And there was . . . I leant across and I kissed him.'

Helen pulled herself together and sat very upright as the porter brought in the tea tray. When she was sure he'd gone, she continued.

'We meet – met – I won't be going there again . . . he has a cottage, a tiny place at Graysmuir, a good way south of Fort Blaine,' Helen said. 'He took me there three or four times over the summer holidays, but could only manage a day here or a day there. Things got easier at the start of September.'

'Why was that?'

'First it was the Headmaster's Conference. Just a one-day thing, but he told his wife that it would take three, so he had one day at the conference in Manchester, then came up to the cottage in Graysmuir.'

'The conference was in Manchester?' asked Skelton.

'At the Manchester grammar school. Then, from the

start of October, it was the first weekend of every month. He would tell everybody that he was going to a Board of Education conference in Edinburgh that he said would take all day. He'd go up on the Friday evening and not return until the Sunday morning. Two nights to ourselves. I think there was a real conference, but he never went and as far as I know was never missed. On Fridays, I would claim to be going to see my mother and get the train into Edinburgh, then get the train out to Graysmuir. It's only fifteen, twenty minutes. Gordy would drive down in his car and meet me at Graysmuir Station and then we'd drive to the cottage, which is a bit of a way outside the village. Very remote. He said he wanted to run away with me, leave his wife and kids and go abroad. He talked about New York.'

'And was this something you wanted to do?'

'At first, yes. A big romantic adventure. You know. Swept off my feet, all that sort of thing.'

'Do you think he meant it?' Skelton asked.

'Very much so. All the time. It was me who had second thoughts. What would we do for money in New York for goodness' sake? And what about my mother? There's only me and my Auntie Tess and it's bad enough with me being in Scotland. We used to argue about it.'

Edgar poured the tea.

'Now,' Skelton said, when they'd settled, 'tell us about finding the ring.'

Helen nodded. 'I often suspected that I wasn't the first woman Gordy had taken to that cottage,' she said. 'Little things. When we first went there, he said he'd inherited the place from an uncle and hadn't been there for years, but you could tell that wasn't true. The place was dusty, but not damp as it would have been if the fire hadn't been lit recently. And he'd got clean sheets and blankets and pillows in the car and soap and towels. Remembered everything as if he'd done it a hundred times before. There was an English teacher at the school the year before who had left suddenly. I guessed it might be her. But never knew for sure. And anyway, it didn't matter because Gordy was quite vehement about me running away with him. He was set on it. But then, week before last, at the back of a drawer in the bedside cabinet at the cottage, I found the ring. Can I have a cigarette, please?'

Edgar obliged.

Helen held the cigarette awkwardly, like an amateur, and blew the smoke without inhaling.

'I only have the occasional one,' she said. 'I'm a thirty-three-year-old spinster still terrified my mother'll find out I smoke.'

'And what made you think E. A. could stand for Edna Aziz?' Skelton asked.

'I'd been reading about her on the train. And I knew she'd lived in Fort Blaine and went to the school and won the Adamson-Adie Scholarship. And . . .'

She carefully tapped the end of her cigarette over the ashtray to flick off the ash, even though there was no ash to flick.

'We had arguments about me running off with him. And once or twice I'd seen real anger in him. Once at the cottage, he'd brought brochures about liners. He was the headmaster; he was the Provost. He wasn't used to people defying him. I told him he was being silly. He started bellowing at me and I saw a terrible blind fury in him. I thought he might hit me.'

'Did he ever?'

'No. That time I think he would have, but I ran down the back of the cottage and hid in the woods for a bit. When I came back, he'd calmed down and put the brochures away. But when I found the ring, I knew straight away it could have been him. He could do that.'

'Did you ask him about the ring?' Skelton asked.

'Not while we were at the cottage. I was too frightened. But then, when we got back, the more I thought about it, the more I realised I was being silly. There was always something storybook about being in the cottage. Not real life. And this was just part of it. But back in real life, I was a teacher and he was headmaster at the school next door, and the very idea that he might have killed somebody seemed ridiculous. So, Friday before last, we were taking the choirs to York Minster for a competition – Gordy wasn't coming, just me and three of the other teachers, and the two choirs from the boys' and the girls' schools. In the mornings, Gordy and I had taken to walking to school a roundabout way, along the banks of the burn and then up a back road that brings you to the side gate of the boys' school. There's never anybody down by the burn, unless there's somebody fishing, so we always knew we'd be alone. I showed him the ring and asked him about it. He didn't even try making excuses. He didn't say, 'How could you think such a thing?' or 'It could have been in that drawer for a hundred years.' He just wanted the ring. He tried to snatch it from me. I don't think he was even angry. Just desperate. He wanted to grab the ring and throw it in the river, and probably wanted to throw me after it.'

'What did you do?'

'I ran. I was carrying my weekend bag for York, but even with that I could run much faster than him. I got to school, and everybody was getting ready to board the charabancs. He came to see us off, but of course there was nothing he could do because I had forty pupils and three other teachers with me. And in York, I was sharing a room with one of the other teachers and had people with me all the time, but all the same I was frightened he'd turn up and do something. And then, I didn't dare go back. So, on the Sunday, I got up before it was light and went to the station.'

'Where did you go?'

'I went to my mother's.'

'And where does she live?'

'Catterick.'

'In Yorkshire?'

'Where the racecourse is.'

'That's where you've come from now?' Skelton asked. 'From Catterick?'

She nodded. 'Like I said, I didn't think going to the police would do much good. I go in and say, "Edna Aziz's killer isn't her husband but the Provost of Fort Blaine," they'd think I was a madwoman. Then I read in the paper that you were going to be here in Durham.'

'And why wouldn't *I* think you were a madwoman?'

'I don't know. I just didn't know who else to tell. And I had to tell somebody because otherwise they're going to hang Dr Aziz and it'll all be my fault. *Do* you think I'm a madwoman?'

'No.' Skelton smiled, and scratched his chin, thoughtfully and turned to Edgar. 'Difficult to know how to proceed. We need to get in touch with Aubrey. See if you can get a call through.'

Edgar capped his fountain pen and left the room.

'Who's Aubrey?' Helen asked, worried that he was a doctor who would take her off to an institution and possibly tip Gordon Innes off as to her whereabouts.

'He's the solicitor on the case. Probably be able to offer a good deal more help than I can. Are you still afraid that Gordon Innes means to do you harm?'

Helen nodded.

'I'm sure Edgar will be able to find a hotel or somewhere you'll be safe.'

'I'd rather be with my mother. There's a train back just before seven.'

'Does Gordon Innes know where your mother lives?' Skelton asked.

'He knows it's in Yorkshire.'

'You feel safe from him there?'

'It's a very big county.'

'Does anybody else in Fort Blaine know your mother's address?'

'No.'

'They don't have it at the school?'

'No.'

'They didn't ask on any forms or anything for details of your next of kin?'

'I don't think there were any forms,' she said.

'Is your mother on the telephone?'

'No.'

'You'd better give me the address in case I need to get in touch.'

* * *

312

Skelton and Edgar put her in a taxi.

'Did you manage to get Aubrey?'

'The operator said to try again tomorrow morning.'

They busied themselves composing telegrams to Aubrey and Alan telling them they had a new suspect and an ironclad witness.

CHAPTER THIRTY-FIVE

The Times had once described Skelton as a 'master of forensic eloquence'. His summing-up in Durham was considered by many as his masterpiece, although others condemned it as a piece of meretricious exhibitionism.

Obviously, such things cannot be timed accurately. The dustbin had been chosen at random from many available at the Sunderland factory. The chemistry professor had examined its contents but disturbed them as little as possible. Hopes were raised when he reported the presence of boiled linseed oil, one of the more notorious agents of spontaneous combustion. Conditions were promising, too. The bin had been kept, along with the other evidence, in a dank basement at the police station where Rose, equipped with a hygrometer and a thermometer, knew that combustion was nigh on impossible. The courtroom, slightly overheated and dry as a bone, was a different matter. On the second day, though it was cold out, the sky was cloudless and the sun shone. The courtroom faced east to west and the high windows had a southerly aspect. Halfway through the morning she put a hand on some wood panelling that a sunbeam had found. It was gratifyingly warm. By lunchtime the sun had found the bin.

It happened a little late for perfection. Skelton had moved on in his summing-up from spontaneous combustion to the legal definitions of malicious intent. But it went well; not with a modest lick of flame but with an audible pop. There was no danger. Within what seemed like a couple of seconds, an usher appeared with a fire extinguisher and doused the flames.

Rose clapped her hands excitedly until silenced by a look from the judge. All barristers, she had been told, were essentially music hall turns who wanted a rabbit to pull out of a hat. The rabbit she and Vernon had provided went one better than just coming out of a hat. It burst into flames of its own accord. And the effect on the jury was magnificent.

After that it was downhill all the way. Clifford and his pals were acquitted on the charge of arson, although the charges for breaking into the factory still stood.

A cry rang out, 'You bastard!'

Skelton glanced up at the public gallery and saw Phyllis being restrained. What he, and the rest of the court, saw as his triumph, she saw as an abject failure. Although Clifford was not going to spend the rest of his life in gaol for arson, he was still going to be put away for three months and his university career was finished. Phyllis knew where the blame for his misfortune lay. Were it not for an usher and the policeman, she would have climbed over the rail of the public gallery and wrestled Skelton to the ground there and then.

He ran to the robing room, then joined Edgar. The two of them sneaked out of the back entrance, again. They had their bags with them so went straight to the station and caught the train to Leeds.

They stayed overnight at the Metropole Hotel, and Skelton went to see his mum and dad in the morning. Vera was there, in the kitchen with Mum, talking about her septic whitlow.

Prinny was in her cage on Dad's box, eating a carrot. Dad was at the kitchen table. He'd finished making the crystal set and was listening with the earphones on.

'You made that quick,' Skelton said. Dad took off the earphones.

'Eh?'

'I said, you made that quick. Was it hard?'

Dad looked down at the device. 'Few bits and bobs screwed down and joined up. Tuning coil, crystal detector, aerial, connectors for the wotsits.'

'When I had a quick look it all seemed very complicated.'

Dad gave him a disparaging look. 'I'm not a fool, son,' he said. 'I've got the Northern Wireless Orchestra here doing the "Dance of the Sugar Plum Fairy". You can have a listen if you like.'

Skelton listened. It was tinny but clear.

'You're getting a very good signal,' he said.

Dad pointed to the aerial wire he'd got snaking across the floor and out through a little hole he'd drilled through the window frame.

'Your mother's worried she'll trip over it and break her neck,' he said, and gave an evil smile. 'Chance'd be a fine thing.' He put the earphones back on and, speaking a little louder than was necessary, said, 'It's valves you need to make a proper one. Fellah at the shop told me you can pay five pound for the posh ones, but if you know what you're doing you can get 'em for six bob.' He removed the earphones to say, 'Bobby Stockdale says he can do you that pram, by the way, for little Lizzie. Make it the same shape and everything and he can slip one of the Silver Cross name plates into his haversack to stick on it. Might be able to get some of the actual paint as well, but I said as long as it's black and shiny she'll be happy. Said it'll be ready in a week or so.'

'I'll have to drive up to get it,' Skelton said.

Mum brought in the tea, then went back to Vera in the kitchen.

'You're doing the suitcase thing tomorrow?' his dad asked.

'I am.'

'Will he hang if he's found guilty?'

'Yes, he will.'

'Well, I hope he doesn't. Must be horrible when that happens.'

'It is, Dad. It's horrible.'

Dad sipped his tea. 'He had loudspeakers for thirty-nine shilling. But he said it's not worth it for a little crystal set. They've probably got a book at the library about how to make a proper wireless.'

'I didn't know you had a library ticket.'

'I've got four tickets,' he said. 'Two fiction and two non-fiction.'

'You're all set, then.'

* * *

317

Edgar joined him for lunch at the Metropole Hotel.

'You're wearing pumps,' Skelton said.

Edgar quickly sat and hid his feet, clad in black plimsolls, beneath the table.

'The pain grew so intense this morning that I really had no choice. It's very grand here, isn't it? I was worried I'd be refused entry on the grounds of being improperly dressed.'

'Do pumps count as improper?'

'I would have thought so.'

'You could claim they were a medical necessity.'

'I'll bear that in mind.'

'Any news from Aubrey?' Skelton asked.

'The Scottish police gave him a flat refusal. They will not initiate a possibly damaging investigation into the Provost of Fort Blaine on some baseless accusations levelled against him by a hysterical teacher.'

'That's what they say?'

'Yes.'

'And that's their final word?'

'Yes.'

'Could he speak to the DPP?'

'He said it won't make any difference.'

'So, I'm going into court tomorrow with—'

'Nothing,' Edgar said.

Skelton separated his sprouts into two neat piles, one either side of the meat. Edgar had already finished his plain grilled plaice with no vegetables.

'Have I been a bloody idiot?' Skelton asked.

Edgar didn't say anything.

'We should send a wire to Aubrey asking him to get on to the Egyptian embassy.'

'He already has. The great wheels of diplomacy have been set in motion.'

'I'll have a word with Aziz first thing in the morning and tell him we have no choice in the matter. Either before or after the trial, he's being deported to Egypt.'

Coffee came. Edgar took his black with no sugar. He lit a Craven A, took a couple of puffs, realised he needed a proper smoke, crushed it into the ashtray, took out another, tore off the cork tip, lit it and inhaled deeply.

'Now, if I could be spared for a few hours,' Edgar said, 'there is an exhibition of Cezanne's paintings at the Art Gallery here that I'm quite keen to catch a glimpse of. Do you like Cezanne?'

'They'd make lovely jigsaws.'

Edgar made his I-am-surrounded-by-Philistines face.

'I'm sorry, this is going to take some getting used to,' Skelton said. 'I'll retire to my room for a few hours' study. Shall we have dinner here?'

As they walked out of the restaurant, Edgar tried to think of something that might cheer his chief up.

'Oh, by the way, it's real,' he said.

'What is?'

'I was talking to Felstead and he said he once, in some emergency, had to go to Aubrey's house in the middle of the night and wake him up. He answered the door in his pyjamas, but the hair was all there, intact.'

'Really?' Skelton tried to raise a smile.

'So, if it's not a wig, it means he must be a secret drinker.'

'Must be.'

In his room, Skelton had barely got his pipe on the go when there was a knock at the door.

'Telephone call for Mr Skelton.'

There was a booth in the corner of the foyer where calls could be taken.

'Hello.' For a moment all Skelton could hear was crackle. Then Alan's voice.

'Hello? Arthur?'

'Hello.'

'Hello, Arthur. It's Alan, can you hear me?'

'Where are you?'

'I'm in the Cross Keys. I got your—Can you hear me?'

'Yes, I can hear you.'

'I got your telegram about poor Helen Shawcroft and Mr Innes. I thought you should know I was at the hospital visiting Beryl and she told me that Gordon Innes had been there with the police. Said he was investigating Helen's disappearance. Helen was a patient there last year and they have records of her next of kin in their files. He'll have her mother's address. You said she thought she'd be safe there, but I don't think that's the case any more.'

'When was this? When was Gordon there?'

'She said this morning, just before lunch.'

Skelton checked his watch. It was a quarter to four.

'How long would it take to get from Fort Blaine to Catterick?' he asked.

'I had a look at the map,' Alan said. 'I could not tell you what the roads would be like. A reckless driver in a very good car could possibly do it in three and half or four hours if he was really lucky, but I'd say five would be more realistic.'

'What about a train?'

'You'd have to look that up. And he'd have to go into Edinburgh and out again. And then, I'm not even sure if the—'

'I'm sorry, Alan. I have to ring off now.'

Skelton hung up and scanned the foyer hoping that Edgar would still be there. He wasn't, but he saw Rose, just arrived from Durham and talking to Felstead.

He rushed over to them. 'Gordon Innes, Provost of Fort Blaine, a town in Scotland, is the real killer of Edna Aziz,' he said.

'How can you . . . ?' Felstead asked.

'Be quiet and listen. He is very possibly on his way from Fort Blaine to Catterick, which is in Yorkshire, some way north of here, to kill a woman called Helen Shawcroft and her mother.'

Felstead said, 'But when you say . . .'

'Should we contact the police in Catterick?' Rose asked.

'I can't see they'd take much notice,' Skelton said.

Rose saw his point. Telling a desk sergeant that someone you think might be the suitcase murderer might be on his way to kill somebody at their mother's house would invite more than a degree of scepticism and would certainly fail to summon the sense of urgency required.

'All the same, it's worth a try,' Skelton continued. 'Felstead, can you try and contact the police? Get Aubrey on to it, too. See if Stanhope's have a man in the area. And tell Edgar what's happened. You might find him at the art gallery. Rose, I need to get there myself, warn her and take her to safety. See if you can hire a car or something. A fast one.'

'I can do better than that. Meet me at the front of the hotel in five minutes' time. And put on some warm clothes,' she said.

Skelton rushed back to his room to get Helen's mother's address and put on his overcoat, hat and scarf. By the time he got back down again, Rose was already waiting for him, sitting astride the saddle of a large and powerful-looking motorcycle.

'Where did you . . . ?'

'It's Clifford Pitt's. He asked me to look after it while he's in prison.'

'Do you know how to drive it?'

'I drove it all the way here from Durham just now and only had one really bad spill. You sit on the back. Give your hat to the chap there and put these on.' Rose handed him another pair of goggles while he gave his hat to the hotel doorman. He eyed the saddle suspiciously.

'What do I hold on to?' he asked.

'Me,' Rose said. 'And tight. It can go at seventy miles an hour. Catterick is just over sixty miles away. If we go top speed all the way, we could be there in well under an hour.'

'You're not really intending to go—'

'Hold on.' Rose pressed something, kicked something and turned something. Skelton felt himself slipping backwards, groped for something to hold on to but found only Rose. Throwing decorum to the wind he gripped hard around her waist and closed his eyes.

CHAPTER THIRTY-SIX

The cold was intense. Scarf and goggles kept the worst of the wind from his face, but his ears and the top of his head hurt. After five or ten miles his legs went beyond pain into numbness. This, he knew, meant he had lost them to frostbite.

Added to this was terror. On a long, straight stretch of wide, well-made, empty road running slightly downhill, Skelton had once seen the speedometer of his Bentley creep up almost to seventy miles per hour. It had been exhilarating. This thing tilted you over at impossible angles when you turned corners. It spat gravel up your trouser legs. And it did it in the dark. When Skelton dared to open his eyes, he saw Fuseli visions of trees and rocks, picked out in drunken perspective by the headlight. The noise was like God dropping an infinite number of saucepans from heaven to earth. It made you pine for the majesty of thunder.

Rose knew the way. Of course she did. Five minutes with a map and Rose would be able to take you straight to the green-eyed yellow idol to the north of Kathmandu or the lost kingdom of She-Who-Must-Be-Obeyed. In some places the road was barely tarmacked, and Rose had to slow to little above walking pace to navigate potholes that otherwise would have toppled them over and buckled the wheels.

At a little after six, Rose stopped in a street lit by a few dim gaslights. The silence when she switched off the engine made his head swim. They were both bone-sore and frozen.

Skelton sat on a wall until life came back to his legs.

'The house is at the end of this road,' Rose said. 'Legs warm up faster if you move them about.'

Skelton stretched his legs and flexed his knees. He discovered he could stand. His hip was in agony.

The house, when they reached it, was dark and silent.

'Should we knock on the door?' Skelton asked.

'Can we get round the back?'

Rose produced an electric torch from her satchel and switched it on, half shielding the beam with her hand. It revealed a gate at the side of the house. Skelton tested the catch. It was unlocked. The hinges squeaked, but less so if you lifted as you pushed.

A light from a back room flooded the lawn. Skelton put his finger to his lips, and they crouched, one either side of the window.

There was no sound. Skelton risked a peep. It was a dining room. The chairs and table had been pushed to one side and a tarpaulin laid on the floor. A tin bath stood in the middle of the tarpaulin. Somebody came into the room. Skelton ducked back down.

'There's—' he whispered. Rose wasn't there. He looked around and caught sight of her hiding in the shadow of a shrub. She had a telescope.

He crawled over to her.

'What can you see?'

'I don't understand,' she said, and passed him the telescope.

It took a moment to get the focus right. A woman had a case open on the dining-room table and was laying out knives and saws of one kind or another.

'Who the hell is that?' he asked.

'Doesn't look like a Gordon,' Rose said.

What was clear was that the woman was making preparations to cut somebody, probably Helen, into little bits.

Skelton told himself that there was no need to take action. Felstead would have got hold of the Catterick police and they'd be here in force at any moment, but he knew that was just a story he'd made up to justify his cowardice.

The woman left the room again. Skelton gave the telescope back to Rose, stood and tried the window. To his horror it opened. He climbed inside the room. At the exact same moment, the woman returned. They stared, each as shocked as the other.

'Who are you?' the woman asked.

'Arthur Skelton, very pleased to meet you.' Sometimes people find a polite approach disarming. 'I don't think I've had the honour of being introduced.'

The woman grabbed a thing with three snickering blades, all at least eight inches long and razor sharp. She lunged at Skelton. He sidestepped but wondered whether he should have bothered. He was no good at this sort of thing. Sooner or later, whatever he did, the woman would kill him and possibly it would be less painful if he were to let her get one big, fatal lunge in now rather than having to endure several little ones. Mila might find some comfort in knowing that he went quickly and wouldn't have suffered.

The woman picked up another implement, this one something you might use to quickly gouge a hole in a piece of hard bone, and, with knives in one hand and gouge in the other, lunged again. This time she tripped on the corner of the tarpaulin and had to recover her balance.

'Stay very still,' Rose said. Skelton hadn't noticed her come in through the window. She was holding a pistol. Like one of Tom Mix's six-shooters in a cowboy film, but thinner.

'Where did you get that?' Skelton asked.

It was having a wonderful effect on the mystery woman, who stood with her arms in the air, still holding her implements but as still as Rose had asked her to be.

'It was in the saddlebag of the motorcycle.'

'A pistol?'

Rose pointed the pistol at him to show that it was solid and real.

'Yes,' she said.

'Clifford Pitt had a pistol in his saddlebag? That's evidence,' Skelton said.

'Surely not in an arson case?'

'Does he have a certificate?'

'He's under 21.'

'There you are then.'

The woman was slowly bringing her arms down.

'I told you to keep very still,' Rose said, waggling the pistol in the threatening way she'd seen at the pictures.

The woman lunged; Rose pulled the trigger. Nothing

happened. The woman lashed out with her knife. Rose pulled back, but not soon enough to avoid a deep cut on her hand. She dropped the gun and it rolled across the floor.

The woman grabbed Skelton and held the knife to his throat.

'Get in the bath,' she said to Rose, indicating the tin bath she'd set up in the middle of the room. She had a Scottish accent. A possibility dawned.

'Are you *Mrs* Gordon Innes?' Skelton asked.

The woman repeated, 'Get in the bath.'

Rose, trying to staunch the bleeding, did as she was told.

Did the woman, Skelton wondered, hope to cut up two, and now possibly four, bodies without a trace of mess? Was that what the bath and tarpaulin were for? Did she hope, perhaps, that the police, when they finally broke into the house, would find no trace of anything and simply assume that Helen and her mother had gone for a long holiday in Bournemouth or Whitley Bay?

It occurred to him that he could foil that plan by forcing her to cut his throat right now. His blood would no doubt spray all over the room.

Another voice. 'Hold it right there.'

The woman turned, still clutching Skelton, until both were facing the newcomer.

It was Edgar. He was holding the gun. Skelton wondered how such a portly man had managed to climb through the window with such silent stealth, then noticed that he was not nearly as portly as he had been – strange how these things can creep up on you – and, of course, he was wearing plimsolls.

'Edgar, old chap,' Skelton said.

Rose got out of the bath and, holding her hand tight now to try and stop the bleeding, stood beside Edgar.

The woman was trying to calculate her next move.

'She knows the gun doesn't work,' Rose said.

'Doesn't it?' Edgar looked down and located the problem. 'No, you see, the safety catch was—' The gun went off. The woman screamed. Her grip on the three-bladed knife tightened just enough to slice through Skelton's earlobe before she dropped everything, clutched her leg, which had been shattered by the bullet just below the knee, and, still screaming in agony, fell.

After a few seconds, she stopped screaming and seemed to have fainted. Skelton felt his ear and examined the blood. There was a lot of it. Then he remembered Helen and her mother. Without a word, he left the room. Rose, still pouring blood from her hand, followed him.

'Where are you going?' Edgar asked, pointing the gun approximately at the unconscious woman's head. Nobody answered. 'I'll stay here, then, shall I? If she moves, I'll shoot her dead, I really will. Who is she by the way?'

Skelton and Rose found Helen and her mother bound and gagged in one of the bedrooms. Both were unharmed.

Skelton fiddled with the knots. 'I'm afraid we've made a terrible mess of your stair carpet,' he said.

The shot and the screams had been heard the length and breadth of the street. Two neighbours phoned the police and a few minutes later several constables arrived in cars and on bikes.

Meanwhile, Rose made good use of the training she'd been given for her Sick Nurse badge, took heed of the golden rule 'Stop the bleeding *first*' and advised Edgar, Helen and Helen's mother in the correct way to compress, disinfect and bandage. Helen confirmed that the mystery woman was indeed, as Skelton had guessed, Mrs Innes. Although Rose was well-versed in splinting up a broken bone, she knew nothing about bullet wounds or bones that had been shattered.

It took a while to convince the constables that the woman on the floor with the shattered leg was the bad person while the man who had shot her had saved the lives of many. The provenance of the gun proved a sticking point.

After another few minutes a more senior officer arrived on horseback. Thankfully he knew a good bit about the Aziz case, knew Skelton's reputation and had a decent ability to summarise key facts from a mass of circumstance.

Then an ambulance came. They admired Rose's first aid and took Mrs Innes away. Some more cars carried Skelton, Edgar and Rose to a hotel where the owner kindly produced cold beef and cocoa and brandy.

'Was that the first time you'd handled a firearm?' Skelton asked.

'Not by any means,' Edgar said, and gave them a seven-veils look.

Until the age of thirteen, Edgar had been a petty criminal, but didn't like to reveal the full extent of his villainy, probably because he knew that the listener's imagination would always make it a good bit more glamorous than it was. Guns would have been involved, though. They were ten a penny before the 1903 Pistols Act.

'But it was the first time I'd shot anybody,' he said. 'It is simultaneously horrifying and exhilarating, but I suspect my conscience is faking the horror because it knows it should be there. So, I'll settle for exhilarating.

I'm exhilarated. But I've barely touched on the full drama of the evening.'

'There's more?'

'Haven't you been curious about how I got here so quickly?' Edgar asked.

'I assumed you'd been clever with trains and taxis.'

'Pah!' he said. Then, 'So . . .' he paused until was sure he had their rapt attention, 'as you may remember, I particularly wanted to see an exhibition of Cezanne's paintings that happened to be at the Art Gallery in Leeds. I'd missed it in London. Do you like modern painting, Rose?'

'I don't think I really know very much about it.'

'Then I'll take you to some exhibitions. Anyway, on my way round the gallery, I encountered this lady who was walking around with some gentleman I took to be an official of some sort. She noticed my close examination of the brushwork and asked whether my name was H. E. Montague. I told her that it wasn't. She told me that Montague – he's apparently a journalist, critic, something, for the *Yorkshire Post* newspaper – was supposed to come. She asked me whether I liked the paintings and we fell into conversation. And it turned out that she *owned* them. And had kindly loaned them to various galleries in order that guttersnipes like me could enjoy them.'

An alarm bell began to ring in Skelton's head.

'Anyway, at that moment, Felstead found me and told me about your cousin's telephone call and your sudden departure for Catterick. I asked whether he'd looked into trains, and he said he had and told me he'd tried to hire a car. And then up spoke the lady and said, "I'm sorry for eavesdropping, but do I gather you need to get to Catterick in a hurry?"

'And I said, "Yes." And she said she could have me here in under an hour. So, I put myself in her hands. Outside she had – is there a very large motor car called a Hispano-Suiza?'

'There is,' Skelton said.

'Very long. Yellow.'

'Sometimes.'

'Well, she drove very fast in that car.'

'You get ill in cars,' Skelton said.

'Only closed ones. This was open.'

'Weren't you cold?'

'There were many rugs.'

'All the same,' Rose said. 'You can't have got here in under an hour.'

'No, the car was only the beginning of the journey. We drove to a field and in the field—'

'Was this woman's name Cissy Pemberton?' Skelton said.

'I was coming to that.'

'She's an old school friend of Mila's.'

'I know. She said as soon as your name was mentioned. Isn't that an extraordinary coincidence?'

'It is.'

'You haven't told me what was in the field,' Rose said. Her speech was slurring. Skelton wondered if she was drunk. She had allowed Edgar to put a tiny drop of brandy into her cocoa as a prophylactic against cold and shock.

'In the field . . .' Edgar said, again stretching the drama much tighter than patience would commonly allow, '. . . was an aeroplane.'

'You came here in an aeroplane?' Rose could barely say the word. She was definitely drunk.

'I was of course terrified. But knowing that one must

grasp any opportunity life has to offer, I conquered my fears and climbed into the . . . thing.'

'Cockpit,' Skelton offered.

'No, that's where the pilot goes.'

'Other chair,' Skelton said.

'Something like that. She gave instructions to a chap to have another motor car waiting for us at the other end and off we went. Up into the sky. Above the clouds.'

'Really?' Rose asked.

'Really.'

'In the dark?'

'In the dark and everything.'

'And were you terrified all the way?'

'Sick with terror.'

'Were you actually sick?' Skelton asked.

'I controlled my emetic tendencies.'

'Well done,' Skelton said.

Rose excused herself.

While she was away, Skelton swirled his brandy around the balloon and said, 'You're not thinking of marrying Cissy Pemberton, are you?'

'She's invited me to have dinner with her.'

'Where?'

'The Savoy.'

'Wonderful. When?'

'Saturday.'

'Marvellous.'

The manager of the hotel, who wanted to go to bed, popped his head around the door, saw that they were still there and, disappointed, went away again.

'Would it be wrong of me to want to marry her?' Edgar said.

'No. Not at all. No. I wish you all the best.'

He'd be too rich to want to work at 8 Foxton Row any more. And Mila would never speak to him. Still, Skelton wouldn't be the first person to lose a good friend to marriage.

Rose came back and the three of them fell into a contemplative silence.

'Today,' Edgar eventually said, 'I have flown with one lady in an aeroplane and shot another one in the leg. No end of larks.'

CHAPTER THIRTY-SEVEN

Moira Innes showed no remorse but rather gave every indication that anybody in her position would have done the same.

Gordon made his confession, too, and the whole story was pieced together.

There was a romance between the seventeen-year-old schoolgirl Edna Goldie and Gordon Innes, the young teacher at the boys' school. He had encouraged her to take the examination for the James Adamson-Adie Scholarship and argued against the naysayers.

Shortly after Edna had gone away to the university, Gordon had met Moira Traynor, daughter of Sir Redvers Traynor, the Provost of Fort Blaine and a man of great wealth and influence. Gordon was ambitious. Though Moira was a stiff, humourless woman, he considered her a prize worth pursuing.

How Edna had received news of his engagement we shall never know, and neither can we know whether her love for Aziz was well-founded or whether, heartbroken, she merely fell into the arms of the nearest man – who happened to be the Egyptian doctor who sat opposite her in the library.

Gordon saw action with the Scots Guards, returned a hero and, partly thanks to the position he held as Sir Redvers' son-in-law and partly as a result of so many other good men having lost their lives, he rose fast. When Sir Redvers died in 1922, Gordon, at the impossibly young age of forty, was elected Provost, and when, two years later, the headmaster of the boys' school retired, Gordon was given that post, too.

Edna, meanwhile, did not return to Fort Blaine for many years. Again, it's hard to say why. Did her parents disapprove of her marrying a foreigner, or was the prospect of running into Gordon Innes and his wife too upsetting?

But in 1928, when her father died, she had to return. There was a mother, a house and a business to deal with.

It was inevitable that she would encounter Gordon again. The pictures of the funeral were there in the *Fort Blaine Weekly Chronicle* for all to see – the two of them, side by side.

Gordon acquired the lease of the tiny cottage out at Graysmuir. On the first weekend of every month, he would drive there, and Edna, maintaining her pretence of visiting the aunt in Whitley Bay, would take the express to Edinburgh and then the local train out to Graysmuir.

But Gordon had his eye on Helen Shawcroft from the moment she came to teach at the girls' school. She was a good bit younger than Edna but had the same shy manner. He instituted a series of measures to encourage more joint projects between the two schools: music, school plays, chess tournaments, even carefully supervised social evenings. This of course gave him the pretext he needed to visit the sister school as often as he wanted and spend time with the young music teacher.

Though he was still seeing Edna on the first weekend of every month, during the school holidays, he found other opportunities to take Helen out to Graysmuir. His feelings shocked him. He was forty-six and reckoned, for the first time in his life, that he had found true love.

He was in what he told the police was a 'tizz'. Sometimes he planned simply to leave his wife and children and run off to start a new life with Helen. One day, in Manchester, he even bought a suitcase, then hid it in the shed when he got home before coming in through the front door.

But then, on sober reflection, he would realise what his achievements meant to him. He was Provost. He was headmaster. Could he live without honour, without influence, without prestige? Could he give all that up for love?

Giving up Edna was, of course, a much easier matter, or at least he thought it would be. In the event she took it very badly. She threatened to expose him, to tell his wife and the world of his adultery.

He assumed she was bluffing. She had as much to lose as he did. Both were guilty of adultery. She could not ruin his reputation without ruining her own. As wife of a respected doctor, she, too, had a position to maintain.

He misjudged her. A week later, Edna knocked on his door while he was at the school and spoke to his wife.

Moira already had her suspicions. She knew about the suitcase in the shed. The boastful, crowing way in which Edna confirmed her fear was unbearable. In her confession, she actually used the term 'red mist' and could not piece together what happened next. There was some sort of fight between the two women which spilled through the French windows and into the garden. The gardener had left a pruning hook on the little table where the children liked to take tea.

Moira dragged the body – as Vernon Goodyear had suspected when he discovered the whitefly – into the greenhouse. There was a tiled floor in there and a hose. Blood could be washed away. She knew what to do. She had been volunteering at the hospital since the early days of the war, first as a nurse, later as an almoner. She'd assisted at operations and amputations.

She loaded the suitcase into her car, drove it out to the moors and dropped it into a hole she found. She misjudged the hole's depth. Instead of the suitcase vanishing into the murk, a corner was still visible. By this time, it was too late to do anything about it. She had a long drive back and she had to be at home looking clean and unruffled when her husband and children returned from school.

She endured a week of sleepless nights waiting for the police to call. It wasn't a matter of conscience but of being caught. She had done everything in such a hurry. The case was visible. She might have left clues, footprints, fingerprints. In fact, she hadn't, but at some point, the caterpillar of a Northern brown argus butterfly had crawled into the suitcase and pupated.

A plan formed, but she knew she would need a long time to execute it. She stole Edna's excuse and claimed her Aunt May in Dundee had been taken sick and was asking for her. She would stay the night.

The hole took a bit of finding. She had taken with her a length of rope with a hook attached, used for towing, from the garage, snagged the suitcase and pulled it out of the hole. Then she drove to Wakefield. She had no particular grudge against Dr Aziz, she just needed to be certain that, if the body was found, there would be a suspect at hand, the investigation would be short and nothing would link the murder to Fort Blaine or even Scotland.

Gordon, meanwhile, had merely assumed that Edna had gone back to her husband and would bother him no longer. When he subsequently read of her murder in the newspaper, he had assumed, like the rest of the country, that it was the act of a jealous husband.

But Moira had been watching him closely. She already had suspicions that something else was going on. She saw the flowers he'd sent to Helen when she was in hospital with the bad foot. These suspicions were confirmed when Helen didn't return on the charabanc from York Minster and he flew into a panic. Helen's mum's address was easily obtained because she had had to give details of her next of kin when she'd been admitted to the hospital. Moira, the volunteer almoner, had access to all the files.

This time, wanting to do the job properly, she chose the tools she needed carefully from the sterilisation room.

EPILOGUE

July 1930

Skelton sipped his coffee on the hotel terrace. Mila walked up and down in her new polka dot beach pyjamas. Each of the legs had as much fabric as a Boy Scout's bell tent.

'It's not actually an audible flap,' Skelton said.

'I can feel the flapping, though,' Mila said. 'And the worry is that a gust of wind could blow me all the way to Le Havre.'

That morning, with the children, they had walked from one end of Les Planches to the other and marvelled at what the fashionable Parisians, *en vacances* in Deauville, were wearing these days. Then Dorothy had taken the children to the beach, and Mila, who had only brought her flying clothes and one or two other things with her, was persuaded by Skelton to do a little shopping.

'And besides, I look like a ladybird,' she said.

'Ladybirds are red with black spots.'

'Sometimes you get yellow ones.'

'A much less vivid yellow than that, though.'

'I think I'll go and change back into my flying trousers,' she said, and was gone before he could argue.

She was, her flying instructor had told her, a natural. Her sense of space, distance and speed was uncanny, and she quickly got the sense of how the 'crate' would react with each tiny movement of stick or rudder. By the end of June, she'd put in enough hours to get her 'A' licence, but by this time there was no longer any point in flying to Australia. Amy Johnson, a Yorkshire woman as Skelton liked to point out, had beaten her to it by a matter of weeks. So, she'd contented herself with a solo hop across the Channel and landed without mishap.

Skelton, with Dorothy and the children, had taken the boat train.

While Mila was changing, Skelton opened the letters that had arrived that morning and read through them.

Mila returned.

'Do they look silly without the boots?' she asked.

She pulled out the sides of the military breeches she wore in the cockpit. At the thighs they were wider than the beach pyjamas, but they hugged the calves like stockings. On her feet, she wore sandals.

'No more silly than half the stuff you see people wearing around town. You'll probably start a fashion.'

Mila caught the attention of a waiter and ordered more coffee.

'Who are your letters from?' she asked.

'One from Alan, one from Edgar and one from Mum.'

'What have they got to say?'

'Dad's got eight guinea pigs now and two of them are pregnant.'

'Are the babies called piglets?'

'Guinea piglets. I've no idea. He's thinking of showing them at some fancier's event in Sheffield. His Morse code is coming along well, and he says he's trying to get hold of something called a PM252 Super Power Output Triode. I don't suppose you've got one, have you?'

'Not on me, no.'

'Alan's gone to Liverpool. There's been an explosion in an oil-cake mill with great loss of life. He and Norah are bringing the joy of Jesus to the grieving and have learnt a new song called "I've Never Seen A Straight Banana".'

'Does the song mention Jesus?'

'He doesn't say. He's still in regular correspondence with Beryl in Fetterick. They're still feeding the five thousand at the Baptist chapel, but the new Proctor of Fort Blaine is a good bit more generous with poor relief.'

'And what has happened to the old Proctor?' Mila asked.

'Rumour has it that Gordy's gone to Australia, but nobody really knows.'

Moira Innes had been hanged in Edinburgh.

'It was glaringly obvious,' Mila said.

'What was?'

'That she was the killer. If you'd asked me, I would have told you.'

'Yes, but unfortunately you were unconscious in hospital at the time.'

Alan had never conducted Mr Dugdale's exorcism. Instead, he had told Mr Dugdale that the presence of a familiar soul in the house could do a lot to ease Edna's troubled spirit and suggested he should give Ben Murcheson his old job back as gardener and let him stay in the boathouse, just as he always had done. At the same time, Alan had had stern words with the two scamps, Martin and Owen, telling them to stay away from the house. And thus Edna's 'ghost' had disappeared.

Helen, as a self-confessed adulteress, could not have expected to keep her job as a teacher, but had returned to her mum and was giving piano lessons to the young musicians of Catterick.

'And what's Edgar got to say?' Mila asked.

'Ooh, lots of news there. He tells me that Vernon Goodyear – you remember him? The forensic entomologist.'

'The one Rose is in love with.'

'Nobody is supposed to know that.'

'Not even Rose or Vernon?'

'Especially not Rose or Vernon. Anyway, Vernon has accepted a post at a university in Germany. He'll be away for at least a year,' Skelton said.

'Is Rose heartbroken?'

'Edgar says she's putting on a brave face and has adopted a regime of exercises involving Indian clubs, which she practises with terrifying intensity. Oh, and d'you remember the ostrich feather case and the motor bandits and the wages snatch?'

'Vaguely.'

'You remember, in all three cases, there was a suspicion that a gang, or some criminal mastermind, was behind it all. A mysterious "Captain Musgrave" was mentioned.'

'Yes?'

'Phyllis Pitt,' Skelton said.

'The Women's Charity League lady? She's Captain Musgrave?'

'Described by Lumley of the Yard as "one of the great criminal minds of our age".'

'Good for her. Has she been arrested?'

'No. Clifford, the son, was released from Durham gaol in the middle of May and the pair of them absconded to Argentina. The infuriating thing was that Joe Soap was one of Phyllis's men, too.'

'Joe Soap?'

'You remember the bloodstained rug in Aziz's coal shed? He said a Joe Soap had called late at night with a badly cut hand?'

'Vaguely.'

'One of Captain Musgrave's gang. Phyllis knew all along that Aziz was telling the truth. If it had come to it, she could have saved him from the gallows.'

'Would she have?' Mila asked.

'What do you think? Clifford's sent Edgar a lovely letter, though, thanking him for all his help down the years. I thought I might drop him a line. Ask him to send Alan some tango records. What else . . . ?' Skelton looked through the letters. 'Doctor Aziz is back in Wakefield, happily welcomed by his old patients who never questioned his innocence for a moment. Aubrey Duncan has his scalp professionally massaged with bay rum twice a week and keeps the grey at bay by brushing it through with something called Brownatone. And Edgar's decided not to get married after all.'

'I never thought it was a wise venture.'

'No.'

'Was Cissy Pemberton ever a serious prospect?'

'They went for dinner. Once. She seemed keen, apparently. Played "footsie" under the table. Left him in agony. His sister talked some sense into him. She pointed out that while he adores his nieces and nephews, she is aware that his adoration tends to wane after two or three hours, which comes down to ten minutes if they're boisterous. She's also convinced him that wives are troublesome, expensive and difficult to dismiss if they fall short of expectations. She said that if he wants a home of his own, he should get an unfurnished flat and, instead of a wife, a suitable housekeeper. He's found a place in a mansion block in Belsize Park and a lady called Mrs Stewart who, he says, is a wizard with an electric iron. Spends all his time in Liberty's looking at furnishing fabrics.'

The coffee came. The two of them looked out at the sea and sipped for a moment in companionable silence.

'Am I troublesome and expensive?' Mila asked.

Skelton considered the question.

'You bought a bloody aeroplane,' he said.

Mila nodded. It was a fair point.

AUTHOR'S NOTE

Skelton's Guide to Domestic Poisons, the first Skelton book, was based, very loosely, on a real case. So is this one, except the connection between fact and fiction is even looser.

Buck Ruxton, known as 'the Savage Surgeon', was an Indian doctor, born in Mumbai (Bombay as it was then known) and practising in Lancaster. He was adored by his patients and generally well-respected in his community.

One night he flew into a jealous rage, killed his common law wife, Isabella, and his housemaid who'd witnessed the crime. Sometime later a woman in Dumfriesshire, Scotland found some human remains loosely wrapped in bedsheets and newspapers. The approximate time of death and the fact that the victims' bodies were transported to Scotland from elsewhere was established by a forensic entomologist who drew his conclusions from the pupae of blowflies. An essential clue was the realisation that the newspaper, the Sunday Graphic, in which the body parts were wrapped, was a special edition that could only be bought in the Lancaster area. Bloodstained carpets also played a part in the investigation (Ruxton claimed to have cut his hand on a tin of peaches).

Norman Birkett – the barrister on whom Skelton is, again, loosely based – defended Ruxton.

The main difference between the real case and the novel is that Birkett lost his case. Ruxton was hanged in 1936. Skelton has to win – of course he does, he's our hero, and, besides, Ruxton did it. Dr Aziz, although every scrap of evidence points to his guilt, is innocent.

It was, however, an early case in which forensic entomology played an important part. Again, significant details were changed. If Vernon had tried to lift a blowfly, gently and romantically from Rose's hair, it would immediately have buzzed off and they would have spent the rest of the scene chasing it around trying to swat it.

In early drafts of the novel, the local editions of a newspaper played a part, but after a while you find it hard to present such a discovery as a brilliant piece of detective work and start thinking that all the principles must have been slightly dim not to have spotted it from the word go.

On another matter. Many years ago, I found myself in a theatre bar during the interval. I can't remember the play nor the exact venue but suspect it may have been Wyndhams on the Charing Cross Road. Suddenly I was overwhelmed by a feeling so peculiar that I began to suspect that somebody had spiked my G&T. People were looking at me, or at least looking my way, maybe at something behind me. I turned around. An elderly, stocky gentleman was talking to some friends, or rather not talking, but listening intently to what the friends were saying. It took me a moment to recognise him. *Bloody hell*, I thought. *It's Laurence Olivier*. He was Sir Laurence Olivier by then, the most celebrated actor in Britain and possibly the world. The peculiar feeling was undoubtedly the result of his presence. And it had nothing to do with his being famous because it began before I knew he was there. He glowed – transcendentally or something. I watched him, like a rat entranced by a cobra. At one point he turned slightly, noticed my trance and gave me a brief smile. An obstruction rose from my viscera to my gorge. For a moment I was unable to breathe, but at least, I knew, if I died, I would die happy.

Afterwards I asked my friend Steve what that was all about.

'Sexual magnetism,' he said. 'North, South, male, female, straight or gay, it'll get you every time.'

If you've read this having read the rest of the book, thank you for reading it. If you're reading it before embarking on the story – enjoy!

ACKNOWLEDGEMENTS

This book was written during lockdown, which made me realise the huge debt of thanks I owe to that great institution, the British Library. My grief at being denied its inexhaustible supply of information (not to mention the ever-patient staff, the members' room, the shop, the chats with people you run into and the pencil sharpeners) was only partly assuaged by decent Wi-Fi. My search history would fill a couple of books, but diligent trawling did lead me to such delights as *Forensic Entomology of the Use of Insects in Death Investigations*, a learned work by Messrs Joseph, Mathew, Sathyan and Vargheese, and https://collins.co.uk/pages/historical-map-of-london which gave me a pre-war *A to Z of London*, indispensable for plotting Rose's routes around the capital. I can also recommend to anybody who's interested in . . . anything . . . the wonderful *Times* archive which

348

documents everything that happened – air crashes, Egyptian diplomatic incidents, ostrich feather thefts and the plague of Motor Bandits – between 1785 and 1985. And obviously my relationship with Wikipedia blossomed into a love affair.

Lockdown also encouraged me to augment my own library. To my trusty *Bradshaw's Railway Guide* and *Modern Home Doctor*, I added, thanks to Abe Books, a 1933 edition *Pear's Cyclopaedia* (which tells me that there are 20 quires in 1 ream and guinea pigs will 'clip the grass as close as a mowing machine') and various other works of reference. Ever so special thanks are owed to Bill Baker, an old school friend who provided me, from his own library, with some invaluable Ward Lock Guides, tram timetables and other goodies.

I'd also like to thank Robert Graves and Alan Hodge for their elegantly written, closely observed and often very funny *The Long Week-End – A Social History of Great Britain 1918–1939* (Hutchinson 1940) which has been a reliable bedtime read for the past thirty-five years.

Finally, the lack of the British Library caused me more than ever to seek information, help, advice, encouragement, criticism and strong drink from friends, neighbours, colleagues, relatives and socially distanced people at bus stops, including – with copious apologies to those I've missed out . . .

Angela Acheson Roberts, Andy Marshall, Michael Stafford, John Stafford, Susan Thompson, Brian Smith, Michael Moran, Stephanie Moran-Watson, David Prest, Alexei and Linda Sayle, Roberta and Nigel Planer, Bill and Laura Oddie, Charlie Dore, Tom Climpson, John Perry, Mick Conefrey, Ian Heywood, Mila Caley, Keith Erskine,

Martin Plimmer, Jane Stone, Malcolm Raeburn, Zoe Clough, Roger Darke, Majestic Wines, Georgia Stafford for being good at geography, Clemmie Kelly for her insights into family dynamics, Connie Stafford for her knowledge of Scotland and general wisdom, and Cosmo the Wonder Dog.

And, of course, Kelly Smith, Christina Storey, Lesley Crooks and Susie Dunlop at Allison and Busby, the best publishers in the world. And the nicest agents a chap could wish for, Carol Reyes and Warren Sherman.

Last but far from least comes Caroline, without whom nothing would be possible.

Any mistakes, by the way, are all my own work.

DAVID STAFFORD began his career in theatre. He has written countless dramas, comedies and documentaries including two TV films with Alexei Sayle, *Dread Poets Society* with Benjamin Zephaniah, and, with his wife, Caroline, a string of radio plays and comedies including *The Brothers*, *The Day the Planes Came* and *The Year They Invented Sex* as well as five biographies of musicians and showbusiness personalities. *Fings Ain't Wot They Use T'Be – The Life of Lionel Bart* was chosen as Radio 4 Book of the Week and made into a BBC Four TV documentary.

dcstafford.com   *@dstaffordwriter*